"Meeting like that. It *was* awkward, wasn't it?" Izzy asked in a quiet tone.

Chandler still didn't answer.

Please say yes. Please say yes. She did a mental eye roll. *Come on, Izzy. This was a colossal mistake.*

Chandler said nothing. She said nothing. And neither one of them moved.

Run, feet. Run!

But Izzy was a glutton for punishment, and she wanted to gauge Chandler's reaction.

But none came. He was as stoic as a professional poker player.

"I guess I'll be seeing you around the ranch. Hopefully not at school. Ha ha." *Izzy, how lame!*

"I make you nervous," Chandler blurted just as Izzy was prying her right foot from the asphalt.

She stomped her boot back in place. "No?" *No? She'd spoken the word as if it was a question.* Izzy made a sound of frustration low in her throat.

"I make you nervous," Chandler said again with more conviction, a jagged smile beginning to curl into his features.

Dear Reader,

Have you ever discovered a restaurant that was right around the corner but you never knew existed? And after this discovery, did you fall in love with it? That's what happens to ranch foreman Chandler Cochran. Except it isn't a restaurant. It's a woman he's known forever—Izzy Adams.

Izzy has just found her footing after her divorce. She's happy with her life. She's started a side hustle, decorating homes for the holidays, all in the hopes of giving her daughter a special Christmas gift. Who has time to love again? But when her daughter and Chandler's son get into trouble at school, she has to make time for Chandler. And given time, Izzy may just discover something special that was right there all along.

I hope you come to love the cowboys and cowgirls of The Cowboy Academy series as much as I do.

Happy reading!

Melinda

COWBOY SANTA

MELINDA CURTIS

HEARTWARMING

Harlequin®
HEARTWARMING™

ISBN-13: 978-1-335-05130-1

Cowboy Santa

Harlequin Enterprises ULC
22 Adelaide St. West, 41st Floor
Toronto, Ontario M5H 4E3, Canada
www.Harlequin.com

Printed in Lithuania

Recycling programs for this product may not exist in your area.

MIX
Paper | Supporting responsible forestry
FSC® C021394

Award-winning *USA TODAY* bestselling author **Melinda Curtis**, when not writing romance, can be found working on a fixer-upper she and her husband purchased in Oregon's Willamette Valley. Although this is the third home they've lived in and renovated (in three different states), it's not a job for the faint of heart. But it's been a good metaphor for book writing, as sometimes you have to tear things down to the bare bones to find the core beauty and potential. In between—and during—renovations, Melinda has written over forty books for Harlequin, including her Heartwarming book *Dandelion Wishes*, which is now a TV movie, *Love in Harmony Valley*, starring Amber Marshall.

Brenda Novak says *Season of Change* "found a place on my keeper shelf."

Books by Melinda Curtis

Harlequin Heartwarming

The Cowboy Academy

A Cowboy Worth Waiting For
A Cowboy's Fourth of July
A Cowboy Christmas Carol
A Cowboy for the Twins
The Rodeo Star's Reunion

The Blackwell Belles

A Cowboy Never Forgets

Visit the Author Profile page at Harlequin.com for more titles.

To my family, who always nod their heads when I talk about my book characters as if they are real.

CHAPTER ONE

THERE WAS NOTHING Chandler Cochran liked less than to be called into the principal's office.

Didn't matter that he was thirty-six. Didn't matter that Chandler had done nothing wrong or that his seven-year-old son had never been in trouble before, either. Chandler sat slumped in a chair in the lobby of the Clementine Elementary School office, knee bouncing, uncertain.

Just like the old days.

Chandler never knew what awaited him in the principal's office. A cop? A social worker? One of his parents? Whoever it was, it meant the same thing. Change. Uprooting. Uncertainty.

But that's not what's happening here.

Right.

Chandler stared at his hands while chattering kids came through the door and went back out again, while parents poked their heads in to wish the school secretaries merry Christmas, while holiday music played from a small speaker on the counter and gobs of tinsel shimmered on a small tree.

No one entered from the sheriff's office or county services.

History isn't repeating itself.

Sam was a good kid. Chandler was a good father and an upstanding citizen. He hadn't been called to the principal's office in decades.

But still, his knee bounced.

"What are you in here for, mister?" A stout lad of about seven or eight sat on Chandler's right. He pushed back the brim of his small, brown cowboy hat as he looked Chandler up and down. "I'm here because I wouldn't stop dancing during choir practice."

That gave Chandler pause. "I thought kids in choir did a little dancing nowadays."

The boy nodded, getting to his feet. "We were practicing our moves like this." He rocked his arms back and forth with a good bit of rhythm. "And then I did this…" He lifted his hands toward the ceiling and shimmied his entire body as if he was trying not to topple in the midst of an earthquake. "And then I was sent to the office." His arms fell to his sides, his shoulders slumped and he plunked back into his seat. "Our music teacher, Miz Cornwall, told me, *'Pete, you're too much. Go see Principal Crowder.'* So, here I am." Pete shrugged.

"Maybe you should try to tone it down," Chandler said carefully, not wanting to offend.

"Is it my fault that when I hear music I feel like dancin'?" Pete sighed, a dramatic, full-body action.

Chandler refrained from pointing out there was

music playing from a small speaker on the counter and Pete wasn't dancing to the "Carol of the Bells."

"I gotta do what I gotta do," Pete continued. "That's what my grandpa says. And it works for me."

And there it was. The reason for Pete's behavior. In Chandler's experience, there was always a cause kids acted out or behaved the way they did—divorce, a death in the family, a bad influence in school or at home. As a foster kid, Chandler had seen it all, not to mention been an example of that axiom himself, reacting negatively when the status quo was challenged.

Before Chandler could respond to Pete, the boy on his left poked Chandler's arm repeatedly. *Poke-poke-poke.*

"Are you here because you parked in the principal's parking spot?" Without waiting for an answer, the boy shook his head slowly. "You shouldn't do that. My ma did it once. Spent thirty minutes with the principal."

"That's not it, Matty. Look at how his knee is jumping up-and-down." Pete leaned around Chandler to look Matty in the eye. "I bet he's the one who jumped his place in the pickup line. You drove on the sidewalk, didn't you, mister?"

"No," Chandler blurted, shocked. The line moved slower than an old nag in the hot summer sun but he'd never do something like that.

Before Chandler could ask for more details,

the main office door swung open, and a reindeer pranced in—jingling all the way.

Oh, it wasn't a reindeer of the animal kingdom. It was a woman wearing brown cowboy boots, brown jeans, a brown sweater with Rudolph on the front—complete with blinking nose—and a headband with a large pair of brown antlers sprinkled with tiny, tinkling bells.

Antlers wobbling, Isobel Adams hustled into the school office like she was late delivering Chandler's feed order. Izzy was a wisp of a woman, short with white-blond hair and big blue eyes. She worked at Clementine Feed and was quiet, unassuming and efficient. So much so that Chandler never gave her more than a passing thought.

But today...

He'd never seen Izzy so bubbly. So...so *alive*.

Chandler couldn't take his eyes off her. She had a pair of tan leather gloves hanging from the back pocket of her jeans and red Christmas bulb earrings swinging from her ears. Her cheeks were flushed, and her blue eyes sparkled.

She reminds me of Mom, full of holiday spirit and not afraid to show it.

His foster mother, that is. Who knew how his biological mother felt about Christmas nowadays.

Reindeer Izzy trotted toward the row of chairs where Chandler waited, an out-of-character big smile gracing her fine features.

"Ho-ho-ho!" Izzy greeted the boys sitting with Chandler before seemingly registering there was

an adult in their midst. Her eyes widened. And then she removed her antlers and turned toward the office desk with much less joviality. "Hey, Ronnie. Am I late?"

"Nope." Ronnie, one of the school secretaries, grinned at her friend from the other side of the desk. She hadn't grinned at Chandler like that when he'd arrived and she was married to Wade, one of his foster brothers. "What's seven minutes when the principal is running behind?"

Chandler refrained from rolling his eyes. He'd already been waiting more than seven minutes to see Principal Crowder. As ranch foreman at the Done Roamin' Ranch, Chandler could pay several ranch bills online in seven minutes, plus return a phone call and adjust the work schedule.

"I bet she's the one who jumped the pickup line," Pete whispered, nodding toward Izzy.

Chandler shook his head. Rudolph channeling aside, Izzy was rule-abiding and reliable.

"I was stringing lights at April Forester's place," Izzy told Ronnie, rubbing the back of the hand that held the jingling antler headband. "Got stuck in her rosebush. Took some time to free myself and the lights."

Chandler took note of a long scratch on Izzy's hand and the thinness of the leather gloves in her back pocket. He managed forty cowboys at the Done Roamin' Ranch, give or take, and hundreds of heads of stock. If Izzy worked for him, he'd make sure she had a decent pair of leather gloves.

For whatever reason, it was easier thinking about Izzy and work than Izzy as the walking, talking embodiment of Santa's lead reindeer, perhaps because his foster mother was recovering from two intense rounds of chemotherapy this holiday season and, consequently, the Christmas spirit had been lacking at the Done Roamin' Ranch.

Yeah, that's it. The cause of Izzy's suddenly magnetic effect on me.

"How is the Christmas decorating business?" Ronnie was still making small talk with Izzy, unaware of Chandler's growing tension. "That's a cool side hustle, by the way."

"It's busy." Izzy reached over to the little Christmas tree in the corner and plucked off a paper star with a child's name and a toy request printed on it, sending a piece of tinsel drifting to the ground. She tucked the star gingerly in her front jeans pocket. Then she took two candy canes from a bowl on the counter and handed them to Pete and Matty without looking at Chandler. "I've found I have a knack for tangling strings of lights without meaning to. I'll either survive this gig victoriously with the best Christmas present for Della-Mae or Christmas will become my least favorite holiday." Izzy took a candy cane for herself, shifting from side to side while she unwrapped her sugary treat.

Reindeer Izzy was as fidgety as a bull in a rodeo chute waiting for the gate to open.

"How is Principal Crowder today?" Izzy asked.

"Ugh. Don't ask." Ronnie scrunched her nose.

"He's been swamped. Too many students have a case of holiday fever. Which reminds me… He needs to move things along." She walked away from the counter, knocked on the principal's closed door and then opened it a crack, saying something Chandler didn't catch.

Probably because Chandler wasn't happy to hear the principal was in a bad mood, his knee bounced more violently. He placed a hand on it.

Humming along to "Jingle Bells," Izzy turned toward the trio of chairs where Chandler was sitting, shaking those antler bells like a tambourine. "Pete, did you get into trouble for dancing in choir again?"

"Yup." The stout boy nodded glumly.

"Matty, did you get into trouble for sneaking candy during reading time again?" she asked the boy on the other side of Chandler.

"Yup," he echoed.

"And…" Izzy's gaze landed on Chandler with unexpected impact.

His heart pounded and his boot heel planted on the gray linoleum, as if his entire being needed to freeze and pay attention. To Izzy.

To Izzy?

Chandler couldn't believe it.

Izzy blinked, as if she, too, had felt something unusual in that moment.

"He's here cuz he parked in Principal Crowder's spot," Matty explained to Izzy.

Pete shook his head. "Nope. He cut in the pickup line."

"Chandler? Izzy?" Ronnie gestured them to come forward as a somber Vonda Jackson exited the principal's office and shepherded her little boy toward the exit. "Principal Crowder will see you now."

"Together?" Izzy looked as shocked as Chandler felt.

"IT'S BEEN A long day, so I'll get right to the point," Principal Crowder told Izzy and Chandler once they were seated across from him in his office. "It's got to stop."

Clueless as to what needed stopping, Izzy nodded anyway. She never wanted to be a bother. She slid a sidelong glance toward Chandler, who didn't look as if he knew what was going on, either. His eyes darted around the room and his knee bounced.

Izzy cleared her throat, wishing she hadn't taken the candy cane she now held awkwardly in one hand. "Can you…uh…be more specific?"

"Your kids, Della-Mae Adams and Sam Cochran, need to tone it down," Principal Crowder said crisply.

Mae, what have you done?

Izzy rarely used her daughter's full name, being more likely to call her Mae. Mae was a second grader and on the shy side, like her mother. Usually… Until recently anyway. Izzy was on a journey to be less of a wallflower.

The principal selected two file folders from the corner of his desk. "Samuel Cochran and Della-Mae Adams." He flipped open both files and laid them side by side, frowning while he studied the papers on top. He was approaching middle age and the eyes Izzy had previously considered kind seemed sharp and accusing today.

Ronnie did mention an outbreak of holiday fever.

And here Izzy had been under the assumption that Principal Crowder had called her in because he wanted to hire Izzy to decorate his house for Christmas. She'd left a flyer on his front door earlier in the week.

Izzy turned toward Chandler, meeting his gaze this time. His confused gaze. He'd looked at her like that in the lobby a few minutes earlier after she'd greeted the kids of some of her feed store regulars. He'd stared at her as if he'd never seen her before and didn't know what to make of her.

Well, she'd seen him before. And Izzy knew what she saw when she looked at Chandler Cochran. She saw an attractive cowboy a few years older than she was. A man with light brown hair, light brown eyes and a smile that rarely ventured past polite. He was tall and wiry, a man of few words, as if he'd learned long ago that speaking too many syllables would get him into trouble—a distinct possibility since he was a former foster cowboy raised on the Done Roamin' Ranch.

"Your kids have had quite a week." The principal's voice pierced Izzy's thoughts.

Years of working the checkout counter at Clementine Feed had Izzy facing uncertainty head-on with a neutral smile. "I'm afraid you'll have to be more specific."

"Yep," Chandler said in that deep voice of his as the first line of "White Christmas" drifted into the office from the radio on Ronnie's desk.

I bet Chandler has a lovely singing voice.

Izzy blinked, shifting in her seat, making her antlers jingle softly. *Where had that thought come from?*

She didn't have time to ponder.

Because Principal Crowder sighed the way Izzy did when needing to explain what she assumed was common knowledge. "Every day since the Thanksgiving break, one or both of your children have been sent to the office. *My* office."

Chandler rubbed his hands down the tops of his jean-clad thighs, halting that knee bounce. "This is the fifth day back from the long weekend. I haven't heard anything about this."

"Me, either." Izzy tossed her candy cane in the small trash can to the side of the principal's sturdy oak desk. This wasn't the time for sweet moments of holiday cheer.

Chandler leaned closer to the principal's desk. "It's my ex-wife's week with Sam. She's picked him up every day after school."

"Same as my ex-husband." And Izzy would bet anything her ex and her daughter had agreed that this would be *their little secret*. Mike always treated Mae more like a friend than a child he needed to discipline and set boundaries for.

Not that Mae had ever needed much discipline before.

"We sent notices through the school's electronic messaging system," Principal Crowder repeated in a tone that implied they should be up to speed. "All parents should have received them, regardless."

"I've never been able to log in to the new app," Izzy admitted sheepishly.

"Me, either," Chandler echoed. "I tried so many times that I was locked out. Same for my ex."

Izzy doubted Mike had even tried.

"That's what everyone has been saying." With what sounded like a growl of frustration, the principal scribbled a note on a notepad: *Norma, resend parents instructions for messaging system.*

"Principal Crowder..." Izzy used her most appeasing tone of voice. "What did our kids do?"

Setting his pen aside, the principal took a moment to glance at the handwritten forms in each child's folder. "On Monday, Della-Mae and Sam convinced everyone in the lunchroom to contribute their food for a Thanksgiving feast, buffet style."

"That sounds lovely." Izzy infused her words with positivity.

The principal winced. "Yes, well, it might have been if several kids with food allergies hadn't sampled items they shouldn't have. Parents were called and the nurse was busy all afternoon."

"Oh." Deflated, Izzy slunk down in her chair.

"That was Monday." Chandler nodded slowly, turning that cool brown gaze Izzy's way just as Bing

Crosby sang the closing notes of "White Christmas."

He should frown less and sing more.

Izzy wanted to roll her eyes or shake her head.

This is not the time for overactive imaginations.

"What about the rest of the week?" Chandler asked, shifting his gaze back to Principal Crowder.

"On Tuesday…" The principal flipped a page over in each file. "Their teacher—Mrs. Stodimeyer—had an…*incident*."

"Her water broke in the classroom." Izzy had heard about this through customers in the feed store. "She had a healthy baby boy at the hospital." Izzy made a mental note to add a baby item to Mrs. Stodimeyer's teacher gift this Christmas.

"She panicked when her water broke, hyperventilated and fainted," Principal Crowder clarified in that high-and-mighty voice of his. "And when she came to, Sam had put on the plastic gloves she kept in the first aid kit, sat next to her on the floor and was telling everyone that he knew what to do."

Izzy gasped, turning to stare at Chandler. "Sam knows how to deliver a baby?"

"He watched a cow deliver a calf last spring," Chandler said flatly. "You can't fault Sam for trying to help."

"Nor can I completely fault Della-Mae," Principal Crowder allowed. "She ran to the office to report the emergency. Although her exact words were, *'Sam's delivering Teacher's baby.'*"

"Makes a good story for the teachers lounge,"

Izzy said, trying to make light of the episode. "Anything else?"

That earned her a critical glance from Chandler, whose large hands still rested on his knees. "He's only on Tuesday."

"Right." Of course there was more. Five days, the principal had said.

Principal Crowder flipped more pages and bent over the next set of forms. "On Wednesday, during the Kazoo and Kitchen Pan Band practice, the substitute teacher had to escort two other students to the office for having a scuffle. While she was gone, Della-Mae and Sam organized the class into a marching band. They proceeded through school hallways, banging on pans, playing kazoos and disrupting classes."

"I got nothin'." Chandler glanced toward Izzy expectantly.

Oops. "I can give that context, I think. Last weekend, we watched the Thanksgiving Day Parade in town and then the one on TV in New York." On repeat. Izzy bit her lip. "Are you sure it was our kids who sent them marching?" Izzy was familiar with Sam since he'd been in Mae's class the past two years. But neither one seemed like the type to stir up trouble. In fact, they were opposites and Izzy couldn't imagine them working together at all.

"He's sure," Chandler said, not a bit defensively. In fact, Chandler sounded...like he wanted to move things along. "What about yesterday?"

The principal turned two more pages. "While

making cutout reindeer and sleighs to decorate the classroom windows, Sam encouraged everyone to draw anatomically correct reindeer. He was adamant about it, going so far as to sketch things on the classroom's whiteboard."

The antlers tinkled softly in Izzy's lap. She'd let Chandler handle this one.

"You can't fault Sam with that." Chandler cleared his throat, perhaps having second thoughts about voicing that statement. "He's a ranch kid. And we're a ranching community."

"And then today," Principal Crowder continued in a tone that indicated he did find fault with what Sam had done, "Della-Mae brought a rotten egg in for show-and-tell."

"No." Izzy shook her head. "I'm sure that's not true. We have chickens but I'd notice if she was saving a rotten egg."

But would Mike?

"It's a fact." Principal Crowder's gaze was unyielding. "Your daughter cracked the egg, intending to show the class that there was a chick inside. There wasn't, by the way. The contents were spoiled. We had to evacuate the classroom for an hour because the smell was unbearable."

Eew. Izzy nodded slowly, and in silence. This put a damper on her excitement over earning extra money for the holiday season. "What do you need us to do?"

"Have a talk with your children." Principal Crowder closed the files and placed them on a stack in his outbox. "Impress upon them the proper behavior at school. Praise them for their creativity, their understanding of the world and their leadership abilities. But caution them to think before they act. They've become as thick as thieves since the Thanksgiving break and..." He paused, as if reconsidering what he'd been about to say. "I was going to end this conversation with an option to move one of them to a different class—"

Chandler nodded.

"—but Mrs. Stodimeyer is one of our best disciplinarians," the principal finished.

"She's on maternity leave," Chandler said in a cool voice.

"Until mid-to-late January." The principal nodded. "During which time there are two weeks' vacation. I think it's better that the children remain where they are for the moment, if only because their actions were well-meaning. We wouldn't want to send the wrong message." He leaned forward, pointing at Izzy and Chandler in turn. "But in the meantime, you both need to learn how to log in to our online messaging system."

They both promised to do their best on that score.

CHAPTER TWO

CHANDLER HELD THE school office door open for Izzy.

Not because he wanted to work as a team to get their kids in line. No.

His brain was humming along the cause-and-effect highway. Why was Sam acting so out-of-character? Chandler kept coming back to the fact that Sam and Izzy's little girl hadn't been best buddies until they'd watched the Thanksgiving parade together last weekend.

Admittedly, Chandler didn't know Izzy's daughter that well, but she had to be the cause of all Sam's mischief.

"Well…" Izzy stepped past Chandler, stuck her antlers back on her head and looked at him without any of her previous holiday cheer, although Rudolph's nose was blinking on her sweater and had been the entire time they were on the hot seat with the principal. "We have some homework, don't we?"

Chandler made an unhappy noise and strode toward the school parking lot where he *had not* parked in the principal's space. The school grounds were nearly empty. The sun was low in the sky and the brisk wind was quickening, reminding Chandler that in his haste to get to school, he'd forgotten a jacket. His blue flannel shirt wasn't a thick enough layer.

"Hey." Izzy pranced next to him, trying to keep up on those short legs of hers. "What are we going to do about this?"

"Isn't it obvious? Keep our kids apart. It's what I do when livestock or cowhands cause trouble."

"You're… You're likening our children to livestock?" Izzy sounded flabbergasted.

Chandler nodded. "The same rules apply. Isolate. Retrain. Keep an eye on Della."

"It's Della-Mae or just Mae," Izzy muttered. "Her father insisted on naming her Della after his mother, despite the fact that it's what one of my best friends named her daughter. So, we compromised and added my mother's name, which is what I usually call her." Izzy caught hold of Chandler's arm. "Hang on. I've just realized what you're saying."

At her touch, Chandler came to a stop, facing Izzy, those big blue eyes, and that blinking reindeer nose.

"You think my daughter is to blame for all this?" Izzy sounded hurt and looked like an adorable, confused reindeer. "She didn't goad kids to draw the private parts on Rudolph or kneel down like a catcher in the big leagues and call, *'Batter up!'* when her teacher went into labor."

"You're missing the point." Chandler lowered his chin and the brim of his cowboy hat. "At the root of these events is a cause. There's a reason for an outcome. A reason a horse wants to kick up its heels. A reason a kid wants to do the same."

The confusion in Izzy's expression pinched and prickled until she was scowling at Chandler. "My daughter isn't a scapegrace. And neither is your son."

"A…a *what*?"

"A troublemaker." Izzy looked put out at having to explain. "I read historicals and sometimes a word from the past pops out when I'm upset. Like now. I'm upset at you for thinking the worst of Mae and Sam."

He'd expected Izzy to blame Sam. Her defense of both kids silenced Chandler. But only for a moment. Because kids just didn't go causing trouble without some scapegrace involved.

Scapegrace? Now she's got me doing it!

Chandler resumed his retreat to the parking lot. "Regardless of what the principal said, I think we should put in a request for separate classrooms on Monday. I hear Miss Cornwall is strict. She's also the music teacher. I think she can handle Della-Mae."

Izzy scoffed, trotted next to him, antlers tinkling. "I think we should consult with Mrs. Stodimeyer first, even if she is on maternity leave." *Jingle-jingle-jingle*.

Even though her idea had merit, Chandler resisted responding. He wanted what was best for Sam. And stability was the foundation of a solid upbringing. Stability. Predictability. And no scapegraces allowed.

"Hey…um…" Izzy cleared her throat. "Did you pick up a star from the tree in the office? I hear there are a lot of kids in need at school this year."

"You're changing the subject?" *Unbelievable.* Chandler walked faster. "We're in the middle of a crisis here."

"I'm offering you an olive branch. 'Tis the season, after all. And our kids are only seven, not seventeen. Now, I took a star and…" Izzy dug in her jeans pocket and then drew a sharp intake of breath. "Ouch. Darn rosebush." She held her scraped hand over Rudolph's blinking nose.

Chandler stopped and barely kept himself from reaching for her scraped hand.

He pressed his lips together, out of sorts over the situation, over Izzy trying to brush this problem off, but mostly over his reaction to Izzy, like she was part of his family circle and to be protected. "Were you even wearing your gloves earlier?"

"In the principal's office?" Izzy stared up at him with those innocent blue eyes, antlers floating over her white-blond hair, and reindeer nose blinking at him like a beacon trying to guide him home in a snowstorm.

"Not in the office." Chandler shook his head, trying to shake off the unwanted fascination with Izzy. "Were you wearing your gloves when you were installing lights at April's around her rose-bush?"

"Of course I was wearing my gloves." But Izzy didn't look Chandler in the eye when she spoke. "I know how to take care of myself."

Chandler frowned at the reindeer before him, not ready to take her at her word.

Something was happening here. Something more than Izzy's display of holiday cheer reminding him of holidays past with his Christmas-loving foster mother.

But Izzy's cell phone rang before he could puzzle the cause and effect.

And since Chandler was feeling out-of-sorts and off-kilter, he walked away.

"THIS IS FRANK HARRISON from the Done Roamin' Ranch." Chandler's foster father's voice came through Izzy's cell phone.

"Hey, Frank," Izzy said weakly, watching Chandler's tall, retreating back without having decided if he was an annoyance or a potential ally in this situation they'd found themselves in. There was something vulnerable in the way he looked at her that wouldn't allow her to classify him negatively. But still… She shivered. "If this is about an order, Frank, I can't help you. I'm not at the feed store right now." The store's biggest customers, like Frank and Chandler, had her cell phone number.

"Chandler handles most of our feed orders nowadays," Frank told her kindly. "I hear you're the one to talk to if you need help with Christmas decorating."

"That's right." Taking shelter from the strong Oklahoma wind at the corner of the last building next to the parking lot, Izzy stopped thinking about obstinate cowboys and children who tested limits and focused on Frank—a potential customer.

"You've probably heard that my wife's still recovering her strength after battling cancer most of the year," Frank continued in a voice thick with emotion. "Mary always goes all-out for the holiday—spreading cheer inside and out of every building. However, she's not up to decorating by herself this Christmas. And when I suggested the ranch hands do it, I had my butt chewed out. She wants a woman's touch. I'd dearly love it if you could see a way to fit us into your schedule."

Between working at the feed store, handling her existing holiday clients and being a mom, Izzy didn't have much time to spare for such a large job and said so.

Frank made a sympathetic noise. "You feel free to bring that little girl of yours along. I'm sure she's an angel. If you could see your way clear to doing some of the holiday baking, too, I'll make it worth your while."

Worth my while.

The image of the princess bed Izzy wanted to buy Della-Mae for Christmas came to mind. She'd been counting every penny from this extra work for the past two weeks and projecting her penny count for the next three. She was going to be short.

"The only way I can fit you in is to work on weekends. And maybe some nights." Izzy wanted to add, *"And not have Chandler and Sam around,"* but didn't. Instead, she said, "I don't want to intrude into your family time."

"When you're a rancher, you work 24/7. I have lots of time with family. Most of them work for me. You wouldn't be intruding," Frank reassured her.

Izzy thought Chandler would think differently.

"In fact, you'd be helping me keep Mary's spirits up," Frank said in that thick voice that gave away how important this was to him.

Having lost her mother to cancer, Izzy's heart broke for him. She relented and accepted the job.

The Done Roamin' Ranch was one of the largest spreads in the county. So what if Chandler worked there?

With any luck, Izzy and Chandler wouldn't cross paths.

CHAPTER THREE

A FEW MINUTES after leaving school, Chandler knocked on the door to his ex-wife's small house in Clementine, full of questions.

The sun was setting. Up-and-down the Craftsman-lined street, Christmas lights were flickering on.

Had Izzy put up any of those displays? Had she dressed in a holiday outfit while working? Had she worn her leather gloves?

"Not my bucking bulls," Chandler muttered to himself. "Not my rodeo."

Small feet pounded across the hardwood floor inside. The porch light flicked on. And then the front door swung open.

"Dad!" Sam leaped into Chandler's arms, all gangly arms and legs, and smelling of candy canes. "I made snowflakes today. Paper ones. Can we put them in my bedroom window at the ranch?"

"Yep." Chandler shifted Sam to one hip and entered the bungalow, closing the door behind him.

Stephanie's small house always made him feel too big. On a normal day, Chandler could barely walk around the coffee table to sit in the short couch or on the single chair. Now that there was a Christmas tree in the mix, it made him feel claustrophobic.

Stephanie was in the similarly cramped dining room on her cell phone, nodding and saying repeatedly, *"Yes."* She still wore her postal uniform and blue socks. Her long brown hair was held in two messy buns on top of her head.

No cowboy hat could fit over those hair buns.

I should have known before I married her that Steph wouldn't take to ranching.

His ex-wife was a town gal, through and through. But they'd been naive and believed that love could conquer their differences. He taught Steph the basics of riding. She introduced Chandler to fancy, overpriced restaurants. In the two-plus years since their divorce, she hadn't ridden a horse and he hadn't set foot in a white tablecloth restaurant.

Catching Chandler's eye, Steph held up a hand, indicating she was busy with her call.

"Hey, squirt." Whispering, Chandler lifted Sam's chin until he could see his son's expressive brown eyes beneath a thatch of unruly brown hair. "Did you spend time with Principal Crowder this week?"

"Yep." Sam nodded without a trace of guilt or remorse on his face. "Me and Della-Mae."

"What a coincidence." Still whispering, Chandler tried to make light of the situation. "Della-Mae's mom and me spent time with the principal today."

Sam grinned. "Did you have a good time?"

"With Principal Crowder?" Chandler chuckled, despite his frustration. "No. Did you?"

"Not exactly," Sam allowed, the beginnings of guardedness flattening his grin. "But sometimes you gotta do what you gotta do."

His son's words struck a familiar chord. "Have you been talking to Pete? The boy in the choir?" He'd said much the same phrase to Chandler earlier.

"I know Pete. Did you see Mom's Christmas decorations?" Sam changed subjects as adeptly as Izzy did.

"Yep. Seen 'em." Chandler nodded, considering how to turn the conversation back to Sam's school missteps.

"You haven't even looked at the decorations, Dad." Sam turned Chandler's head. "We gotta do our ranch house like this." Chandler lived alone in the foreman's house on the Done Roamin' Ranch except on weeks he had Sam. "Santa likes houses with decorations."

Chandler obediently looked around. He appreciated the Christmas spirit. Didn't mean he had to change things in his house to make room for it a few weeks every year.

Stephanie's Christmas tree stood in front of the plate glass window, glowing with colorful lights that reminded Chandler of Izzy again.

Nope, not going there.

Santa's sleigh and reindeer sat on a blanket of

white cotton on the coffee table. Rudolph and his blinking red nose were conspicuously absent.

Chandler pressed his lips together.

Two red stockings with white trim were hung from the small fireplace mantel, which had garlands and more twinkle lights on top. A fir wreath sat on the dining room table next to a box of pink and gold Christmas ornaments, a hot glue gun and a spool of shiny red ribbon.

Last year, when he'd seen his ex-wife's Christmas decorations, Chandler had felt empty inside. This year, he felt…nothing. At least, nothing to do with Stephanie. Izzy and her antlers were still on his mind.

Chandler shook his head, not wanting impressions of Izzy to linger. They were at cross-purposes at school. He wanted action and she wanted to wait and see.

Stephanie came to stand in the arch between the living and dining rooms, slowly lowering her cell phone and looking dazed. "I got it." She wandered over to the couch, sat without any grace and repeated in a shocked voice, "I got it."

"What?" Chandler experienced a nervous swirl in his stomach, one that reminded him he'd skipped lunch. He had a hunch that whatever Stephanie had to say might make him skip dinner, too.

He set his son down. "Hey, squirt. How about you pack up what you need for the weekend while I talk to your mom?" When Sam disappeared down the hallway, Chandler came to sit in a chair near his ex. "You got what?"

"An offer. Flight attendant training school." Stephanie stared at Chandler as if seeing him for the first time. "I thought they wouldn't take me because I'd needed three tries to correctly complete my application, but they did."

"Flight attendant training... Is this an online school of some kind?" Chandler couldn't imagine flight attendant training being available in Clementine any other way. And that meant... His stomach was swirling, and his knee had begun to bounce. "When does it start?"

"It's in-person training, Chandler. It means that the airline offered me a job." Stephanie began to smile, going so far as to laugh a little. But it was a stiff, uncomfortable laugh, as if she knew he wouldn't share her happiness. "It's my dream come true. They want me to attend paid training in Fort Worth in January. Sooner if I can swing it."

For the second time that day, Chandler was blindsided by the unexpected. "But Steph, you have a job. A great one." As a mail carrier, she had job security and good benefits, including health care for Sam. Chandler took hold of his knees to keep them still. "And...and Sam. You can't fly all over the world and pick him up from school during your week. Not when we'll be here. In Clementine."

Because that's where Chandler's life and family were. Dreams were important but so was the bottom line. And the bottom line was that their divorce and custody agreements had been based on them agreeing to make life-changing decisions together with Sam's well-being in mind. Yes, they'd amended the agreement, most recently to expand Chandler's weekend custody to full weeks twice a month. Was this why?

Silence stretched between them, broken only by the sound of Sam packing in his bedroom.

"Chandler, haven't you ever had to choose between responsibility and what your heart wants?" Stephanie closed her eyes, holding her cell phone over her heart. "It's not that easy to let go of a dream. They gave me a few days to think about their offer. Surely, we can work something out."

As far as Chandler was concerned, there was nothing to be negotiated. "What's to discuss? Taking Sam to Fort Worth?" He lowered his voice. "Not a chance, Steph. You don't have a support system in Texas to raise him right. Sam has to stay here. And he needs his mom." Chandler knew that was a cruel thing to say. But he also knew firsthand the gaping hole not having a mother put in a kid's heart.

Stephanie opened her eyes and stared at Chandler with the saddest expression he'd seen on her face since the day she'd told him she wanted a divorce. "I know the trade-offs I'd have to make. But it's *my* dream."

"And *our* son." Sam would be crushed if she left…if she chose her dream over raising him.

"Dad? Can we go swimming this weekend?" Sam shouted from his bedroom.

"We don't swim in December," Chandler called back, not taking his gaze from Stephanie, whose brows were drawing down determinedly.

"Darn it," Sam said. And then it sounded like a drawer was slid shut.

Chandler drew a deep breath, smelling fresh pine and seeing an abundance of Christmas, things that should have been calming. But the day continued to unravel, completely out of his control.

"You shouldn't do this, Steph." Unable to sit still, Chandler stood, moving toward the door, toward an exit and the last word.

He got so far as to gripping the doorknob. And then Chandler realized he couldn't leave. He had to wait for Sam. "Hurry up, squirt."

"Coming!" But it sounded like his son was rummaging through toys, a historically lengthy process.

"I don't work for you, Chandler." By the sound of the floorboards creaking, Stephanie got to her feet behind him. "You can't tell me what to do. And I... You know I've always wanted to see the world." Those last words were delivered as a plea for him to see her side of the situation.

Chandler could never understand choosing a life away from his child.

He turned to face her, this woman that he'd fallen in-and-out of love with. "Steph, you have to ask yourself if you want to see the world at the expense of not seeing your son. *Sam and I* aren't leaving Clementine. *Sam and I* aren't moving to Texas. At some point, you have to face the reality of the situation."

Stephanie shook her head, straightened her shoulders, looking determined. "Chandler... Can't you be happy for me? The airlines just called and... You know how much this means to me."

She's already made up her mind. She's already put herself and her dreams ahead of our son's well-being and happiness.

"Reconsider, Steph," Chandler pleaded, despite knowing his words were useless.

And that's why he didn't bring up the meeting with the principal. If Stephanie chose her career over raising their son, any discussion with her about Sam's behavior and subsequent parenting was a waste of breath.

"Mama!" Mae ran across the new car showroom floor toward Izzy, past a humongous Christmas tree, cowboy boots pounding on tile, frilly blue skirt swirling about the tights over her knees. Mae reached Izzy and wrapped her arms around Izzy's legs, staring up at her with happiness and adoration.

As if she hadn't gotten into trouble at school all week and had nothing to be repentant about.

Regardless, Izzy lifted Mae and held her close, breathing in her child's scent.

And if Izzy detected a lingering whiff of spoiled

eggs in Mae's white-blond hair, she'd chalk it up to the power of suggestion.

"I missed you, bug," Izzy whispered.

"I missed you, too, Mama."

Izzy set her daughter down, kneeled in front of her and smoothed the wrinkles from her dress. "Where's your dad?"

"He's been making money all day." Della rolled her eyes. "I've been playing in the parts department. Did you know they have Christmas lights for license plates? I'm going to ask Daddy to buy lights for yours, Mama."

"We've talked about this before. I don't want you to ask your father to buy me anything."

"Why not?" Mae's blue eyes widened. "He buys me everything."

"And he shouldn't, remember?" They'd had these discussions before. Mike's approach to parenting was to buy Mae things to make up for the time they spent apart. He could easily buy their daughter that princess bed, but Izzy was determined that she be the one to provide something Mae would enjoy for years. And Izzy had made a point to tell Mike that very thing. "Did Daddy pick you up from school today?"

Mae turned away with a murmured, "No."

This was a sticking point with Izzy and her ex. She didn't approve of his car dealership employees covering for him so often.

"Don't tell me he sent the service driver to get

you again?" That might explain why Izzy had been called to the principal's office.

"I like Turner." Mae rose up on her toes to peer into a sedan's window, breath fogging the glass. "He tells me stories about his search for a wife." She drew a heart in the fogged section of glass and dropped back on her boot heels. "Did you know that Miss Ronnie is trying to find him his one true love for Christmas?" In addition to working as a school secretary, Ronnie was a part-time match-maker. "Turner wants a woman who won't divorce him this time."

Everyone wants someone who won't divorce them.

"We'll talk about Turner and his love life later. I want to talk to your father before we leave." Izzy needed to find out if Mike had successfully logged in to the school's online messaging system and was up-to-date on their daughter's school high jinks.

"Mike is closing a sale with a customer," a cool brunette told Izzy, having somehow snuck up on them in her stilettos.

The woman—Reese per her name tag—wore a red cocktail dress, had applied makeup on the heavier side, and her hair... Not a strand was out of place. Izzy had never seen Reese before, but she knew the type—Mike's type.

With a polished smile and a flick of her wrist, Reese gestured toward the waiting area by the service desk. "We still have cookies at the coffee bar."

"No, thank you." Izzy opened the door to the

car Mae had been peeking into. "Since it's getting close to dinnertime, we'll wait in here, away from the cookies."

Reese appeared shocked that Izzy wouldn't do as she'd suggested.

Izzy didn't care. Reese was new. She'd learn. Izzy did what was best for Mae, even if it went against Mike's showroom rules.

"Get in, Della-Mae Adams." Izzy waited for her daughter to hop behind the wheel before walking around to the passenger side and opening the door. "We know the rules, Reese. We'll try not to smudge anything." And then Izzy sat in the passenger seat of the sedan and closed the door behind her.

Mae stared at Izzy warily. "Am I in trouble? You don't call me by my full name unless you're mad."

"Should I be mad?" Izzy realized the nose on Rudolph was blinking and reached inside her sweater to turn it off. She should have done so when she removed her antlers on the drive over. Or before being called into the principal's office...

Her self-image as a competent person took a hit. No wonder Chandler had treated her as if all the school shenanigans were Mae's fault and hers.

Still, Izzy was determined not to shirk her parental duties. She fixed her daughter with a firm stare. "What do you think? Would I be mad if I had a talk with Principal Crowder about you? Would I be upset if you and your father hadn't prepared me for it?"

"Oh." Her daughter faced forward and slumped low in the seat.

Guilty, as charged.

Mae traced the circle of the steering wheel with her fingers. "You don't sound like you and Principal Crowder got along."

"Should we have?" Izzy sighed wearily. "Does Daddy know you've been in trouble?"

"No." Mae tried to pull her long white-blond locks over her face.

"Of course not. He never checks his messages." Not from Izzy. And apparently, not from the school, either. "No wonder Sam's dad and I were taken by surprise."

"Oh." Mae perked up. "You met Sam's daddy?"

"Oh, I did." And Izzy let her tone imply what a disaster that had been.

"You didn't like him, either." Mae tried harder to disappear behind her curtain of hair.

"Was I supposed to?"

She shrugged.

"We're going to talk about your behavior at school, bug. We have the entire ride home to do so." Izzy brushed Mae's hair from her eyes. "Hiding won't get you out of an explanation."

Her ex-husband rapped on the driver's window nearest Mae, not smiling. Mike wore a classy-looking teal sweater that complemented his black hair and square jaw. He opened the door and gestured for them to get out. "What's the rule about *not* sitting in the merchandise, Della?" Despite his firm words, Mike switched tack when he turned back to an older woman flashing a smile worthy of all the sales awards he received every year. "I'll get this riffraff out of your car and have Turner take it around back to gas up."

"Riffraff." Izzy stood on the showroom floor muttering beneath a forced smile. "It's got comfortable seats, ma'am. I'm sure you'll enjoy it."

Mae stood next to Mike, beaming up at his customer like the well-trained sales accessory she and Izzy used to be. "Your car is pretty like my mama. Isn't Mama pretty, Daddy?"

"She can be." But Mike didn't look at Izzy. And he didn't sound sincere. He wasn't sincere about much more than the dealership's bottom line. He'd be no help disciplining their daughter.

Izzy decided then and there that she'd deal with this school issue by herself.

CHAPTER FOUR

"WHEN WAS THE last time we had a family meeting at breakfast?" Zane asked Chandler on Saturday morning, pouring a second cup of coffee from the pot before returning to his position at the pancake griddle. "Or on my day off."

"Why are you complaining? If you stop drinking coffee now, you could go back to bed when this meeting is over." Chandler used a fork to turn sizzling bacon in a large frying pan. "Unless Dad asks us to decorate the ranch for Mom for Christmas. Then you'll be busy all day."

"When can we decorate our house for Christmas?" Sam piped up from a chair at the kitchen table, feet swinging. He seemed so happy and carefree, unlike the boy who'd clammed up when Chandler had asked him point-blank about school mishaps last night.

"We can decorate after you give me answers regarding the trouble you've been causing," Chandler told his son.

Sam's feet stopped swinging. His bottom lip thrust out.

More cowboys filed into the kitchen in their stocking feet, having removed their boots and hung their hats in the mudroom. It wasn't the entire crew. A few were on vacation. Some had taken a trailer full of bucking bulls to the rodeo championship in Las Vegas. A handful of crew members had qualified to compete there. But all the men had spent the majority of their years in foster care at the Done Roamin' Ranch, a rodeo stock company and working ranch run by Frank and Mary Harrison, known fondly to the men as Mom and Dad. They may have been fosters but they were family. The men even called each other brother.

Wade entered the kitchen with his wife, Ronnie, the school secretary, and their daughter, Ginny, who was thirteen but determined to act like she was thirty and had already achieved the title of Rodeo Queen and Lawyer. She'd earned many nicknames from her Done Roamin' Ranch uncles, including "nosy gal" and "know-it-all."

But despite being precocious, Chandler couldn't remember Ginny ever acting up at school.

"Hey, Sammy." Ginny ruffled Sam's hair. "How was school this week? Things go the way you wanted?"

"No." Sam kept his head down, but Chandler caught a guilty expression. Was Ginny involved in this sudden wave of mischief making?

"You're burning the bacon." Zane hip-checked Chandler away from the frying pan and began removing the blackening bacon to a folded paper towel resting on a plate.

Ginny moved to the other side of the room as the kitchen filled up, chattering to cowboys about their horses as if she didn't have a guilty bone in her body.

Cowboys continued to enter. Soon every chair was taken. Soon every available cabinet and countertop leaned against. Male voices blurred and blended together while Chandler tried not to burn more bacon and Zane produced stacks of pancakes.

Dad entered the kitchen promptly at seven forty-five, the time he'd asked them all to assemble for a family meeting. After months helping Mom fight cancer, Dad was looking nearly as wan and worn out as his wife. His hair seemed whiter than ever. His face lined with concern. "Boys, I'll get right to the point so we can eat. As you know, your mother is in no shape to dig through boxes, climb up ladders to storage spaces or spend hours hanging ornaments, wreaths and lights around the ranch. But she refuses to let go of the Christmas decorating."

"Are we going rogue and doing it anyway?" Zane set two steaming plates of pancakes on the kitchen table.

"The thought crossed my mind." Dad leaned on the back of Sam's chair. "But then I remembered talking to someone at the Thanksgiving Day Parade in town. They'd hired a woman to help them decorate for the holidays."

Uh-oh.

Chandler crossed his arms over his chest, preparing an argument against hiring Izzy.

And then someone knocked on the front door.

"I'LL GIVE YOU THIS," Frank told Izzy while he waited for her and Mae to remove their cowboy boots in the foyer. He had white hair and was thinning in stature. The last year had taken its toll on him. "You sure do dress for the role."

"It's part of my service." Izzy stood, straightening her green sweater, which had green garland and red felt light bulbs sewn on it. Black jeans and a headband with a star floating above it completed her Christmas tree costume. "I bring holiday cheer from the moment I step on property."

"Me, too." Mae had gotten into the spirit as well with her red leggings beneath her red dress, and a Santa hat.

She was such a sweetheart. It was hard to reconcile Izzy's biddable little girl with her behavior at school last week.

"I'm grateful for your holiday enthusiasm." Frank patted Izzy's shoulder before indicating she should follow him. "The boys are in the kitchen."

"The boys…" *Chandler?* "You know, I work alone."

"Nonsense," Frank said, two steps ahead of her. "What's the point of having able bodies around if you don't put them to work?"

"Della-Mae!" Sam popped off his chair at the kitchen table the moment he saw Izzy's daughter.

He ran over and hugged her before turning to the room full of cowboys standing in their stocking feet and announcing, "Everybody, this is my best friend, Della-Mae." He dragged her back to the kitchen table, where they each half sat in his chair. "Ginny, look. It's Della-Mae."

"I see her." Ginny waved hello.

"And you all know Izzy," Frank completed the introductions, although none were needed.

Izzy knew all the cowboys by name through working at the feed store. Not that she wore costumes there, which she supposed was why she was receiving so many curious stares. She fought the urge to shrink behind Frank. When she'd decided on this path of being a holiday decorator, she'd committed herself to stepping out of her comfort zone 100 percent.

And so, Izzy held out her arms and said, "I guess you all have never seen a living Christmas tree before."

That earned her some chuckles and respite from the stares.

On the other side of the kitchen table, Chandler didn't laugh.

So much for the Done Roamin' Ranch being large enough that we wouldn't see each other.

"This is our Christmas decorator," Frank told the cowboys. "Give her a warm welcome."

There were mumbles of hey, good morning, and howdy.

For cowboys on a Saturday before breakfast,

a day most of them had off, that was practically an enthusiastic reception. Izzy should know. Most days, she worked the early shift at the feed store where cowboys picked up supplies with little more than grunts as greeting.

"Mom is going to direct Izzy regarding what she wants done," Frank went on. "And if Izzy needs any help finding decorations or putting things up per your mother's standards, I want you all to hop to it."

"I'm sure I'll be fine without an assist," Izzy assured them, although she said it mostly for Chandler's benefit. "I've got Mae to help me."

"And me!" Sam piped up, generating chuckles from the group.

Chandler turned his back on Izzy and busied himself flipping bacon.

"Grab yourself some food and coffee, Izzy," Frank instructed. "I'll go see if Mary's ready to come out to the living room and brief you." He left the kitchen.

And when he left, it was as if the tension in the room drained away. The men descended upon the bacon, pancakes and eggs. Their deep voices filled the room with welcome and warmth.

Ronnie came over to give Izzy a hug. She was a blast of strong color in her red velvet jeans, purple sweater, dark long hair and red lipstick. "You didn't tell me yesterday that Frank had hired you."

"He made me an offer after I stopped by the school."

A huffing noise came from the direction of Chandler's broad shoulders.

Ronnie linked her arm through Izzy's. "We're heading out soon to grab some things for Wade's trip to Vegas." Where he was competing in the bronc riding national championship the following weekend. "Otherwise, I'd stay and help."

"From the looks of things, I have all the help I need," Izzy assured her friend. "But any hints you can give me about pleasing Mary will be much appreciated before you leave."

Ronnie drew Izzy closer, lowering her voice. "That's easy. Mary covers every inch of the ranch in Christmas, including the bunkhouse and barn but especially this house. Just be glad you're charging by the hour."

Her husband, Wade, gestured toward the mudroom before touching his daughter Ginny's shoulder and nodding in the same direction.

"That's my cue to leave." Ronnie hugged Izzy again. "I know you're going to have a good time today. I'll call you later." And then she was gone.

Leaving Izzy to dive into the melee for food and coffee. Mae was eating a pancake. Izzy worked her way around the table, closer to the coffeepot and Chandler. She was too self-conscious to apologize for showing up on his turf unannounced when she knew she wasn't welcome. Thankfully, Chandler paid Izzy no mind as she poured herself a cup of black coffee and took a sip.

But she was unable to squelch her curiosity. "What did Sam tell you about school?"

Chandler's turned-up nose was answer enough. *Nothing.*

Izzy sipped her coffee again before admitting, "Mae wouldn't say anything, either."

Chandler grunted.

If Izzy didn't have so much experience helping cowboys at the feed store with everything from grain orders to selecting a pair of blue jeans, she might have been put off by his crusty demeanor.

"You're burning the bacon again." Zane crowded Chandler out of his way, taking over bacon duties and as a result…

Only Izzy's coffee mug came between her and Chandler's chest. Back to the wall, with the kitchen table and cabinets on either side of her, Izzy had no room to escape.

She stared up, up, up at Chandler, expecting a frown. Not seeing one.

Her pulse kicked up, sending her body on full alert: *Warning! Handsome cowboy within kissing distance!*

Izzy didn't date cowboys. She saw cowboys all day, every day at the feed store. She'd been working there since high school. On day one, Earl Lyon, the owner, had given Izzy a bit of advice to not date the customers in case things went sideways. And honestly, it had been easy to follow that suggestion. She wasn't much of a talker, and neither were they when they came in. By now, Izzy assumed she was immune to cowboys.

But here she was—pulse pounding, gaze softening—staring up at a hunk who didn't want her around. Or did he?

Izzy's ears buzzed with the rumble of masculine voices. It might have been her imagination, but Izzy thought she heard a female tone. An escape from temptation and embarrassment. Izzy latched on to it. "Excuse me, Chandler. I hear Mary and Frank in the other room. Time to go to work."

Thankfully, she hadn't misheard. Frank and Mary were in the living room.

Mary sat lengthwise on the couch beneath a red-and-white Christmas blanket with Frank standing nearby. Mary wore a gray sweatshirt with a smiling elf on the front and a red knit cap with a cheery white pom-pom. Her cheeks were thin and her complexion sallow. But her eyes... Her eyes still had the same zest for life they always had whether she was hosting a community Fourth of July picnic or helping to organize the annual Santapalooza Christmas Day horseback parade.

"Izzy." Mary held out a frail hand toward Izzy. Her grip was surprisingly strong as she drew her to sit at the end of the couch by her legs. "Thank you for coming. Now she's here, Frank, you can shoo. I love you but I don't need you hovering."

Frank leaned over to kiss his wife's cheek before leaving them.

"I know I look like a dead fish on ice at the supermarket," Mary said in that frank way of hers, ignoring Izzy's protests. "But I'm over the worst. My hair's starting to grow back, and I've still got all my teeth. It's my stamina that's gone missing. Set me back emotionally, too. And seeing Frank worry…" Mary blinked teary eyes. "But you're here now. Everything is looking up. Including Christmas. I know my boys are all well-meaning, but their idea of decorating is putting up a tree, tossing some plain baubles on it and then forgetting to turn on the lights."

Izzy smiled because Mary had been a vital part of Clementine's community for as long as she could remember. And the contradiction between the strength and humor in her voice and the visual frailty of her body was simultaneously alarming and heartwarming. Unlike Izzy's mother, this was a woman who had defied the odds against cancer.

Izzy knew then and there that she wasn't going to charge the Harrisons for every hour she spent making Mary's Christmas perfect. That would be her gift.

Having a better idea now of what was needed, Izzy smiled more easily. "Mary, where do you want me to start?"

CHAPTER FIVE

"Dad, can we have a dog?"

"Nope." Chandler was up to his elbows in soapy water when his son's question came out of left field nearly an hour after Izzy's arrival. He handed Della-Mae a breakfast plate to dry, studying her little face, looking for any trace of mystery. "Do you have a dog, Della-Mae?"

"No, sir." The little girl was soft-spoken, well-mannered and dainty. She was dressed like one of Santa's elves, cute as a button, the opposite of a troublemaker stereotype. Certainly not a scapegrace.

But Chandler hadn't been born yesterday. Appearances could be deceiving.

"Why can't we have a dog?" Sam stood on a stepping stool on the other side of his little friend, the upper cupboard open above him. When Della-Mae handed Sam a plate, he rose up on his toes to put it on the stack in the cupboard. "You said you like dogs, Dad."

"I do, squirt." Chandler handed another plate to Izzy's little girl. "We used to have ranch dogs, but they got old and crossed the rainbow bridge."

"Which is why we need a puppy!" Sam cried, full of his usual exuberance.

Della-Mae giggled.

"What's so funny?" Chandler swiped another plate clean in the sudsy water.

"You aren't like Sam." She beamed at Chandler, looking angelic with those big blue eyes and white-blond hair. "He's loud and a talker. And you're not."

"Plus, he's taller than me and doesn't like dogs." Sam sounded very disappointed.

"I like dogs," Chandler said.

"Not enough to have one," Sam countered, full of sass and vinegar.

Chandler's father laughed. He was sitting at the kitchen table drinking his coffee, having left Mom and Izzy alone to discuss decorating strategy. After breakfast, he'd sent Zane and Dylan to select three Christmas trees of various sizes from a local lot.

Della-Mae smiled at Chandler as if she had a stake in this conversation. "My uncle Earl says that every cowboy needs a horse and a dog." She handed Sam a dry plate.

"That's a law in Oklahoma. Isn't it, Dad?" Sam stood on his toes to put the plate away.

"Nope." Chandler handed Della-Mae another wet plate. "Your pony isn't much larger than a dog, Sam. Maybe that checks both boxes."

"It's not the same," Sam lamented. "A pony isn't a horse or a dog. Besides, I'm too big for Baby Bear."

Chandler knew his boy was getting to the age

where he could handle a horse of his own but something inside him continued to whisper, *"Not yet."*

"Did you have a horse and a dog when you were a kid, Dad?" Sam asked.

"Nope." Unbidden, the sound of his biological father's drunken voice filled Chandler's head along with the image of the empty hook in the hallway where his biological mother's coat had always hung. He stiffened, unsettled by the memories of unpredictability and loss. Chandler drew a calming breath, tucking the past back where it belonged. "My reals, my real parents I mean, weren't the type of people to have pets." They couldn't afford them and didn't have room in their hearts for more than themselves.

"So…" Sam frowned. "Are we like them?"

"No!" Chandler blurted. "I'm not…" A man with a hair-trigger temper or a woman who disappeared without Chandler when her husband wouldn't sober up. "I'm not like them. And you aren't like them, either."

Della-Mae regarded Chandler with wide blue eyes, so like Izzy's. And then she did the darndest thing. She reached up and patted his arm consolingly. "It's okay, Mr. Cochran."

Chandler imagined he heard the jingling of bells, imagined that he felt the warmth and promise of happy Christmases. And all because of the touch of a little girl.

Of Izzy's little girl.

"I'm glad we're not like your first parents." Sam

grinned, yanking a plate from Della-Mae's other hand. "That means there's a horse *and* a puppy in my future."

Behind Chandler, Dad laughed again. "He's got you there, son."

"I told my dad I wanted a puppy for Christmas," Della-Mae said in a soft, wistful voice. "He told me no. My mom doesn't want a dog, either. She says we aren't home enough so it wouldn't be fair to the dog."

"Wise woman," Chandler mumbled, wishing he'd used that excuse earlier.

"But we spend a lot of time at the feed store," Della-Mae continued. "And Uncle Earl said I could bring a dog there if I had one."

Earl wasn't the girl's uncle by blood but Chandler supposed that Izzy had been working there long enough to be considered family by the old man, who had none of his own.

"Wouldn't it be great if we got puppies from the same litter?" Sam danced on the step stool. "They'd be brother and sister. Can we, Dad?"

"Nope." But it was as if Sam and Della-Mae didn't hear him.

"What kind of dog do you want, Sam?" Izzy's daughter smiled dreamily. "I want a dog that goes with me everywhere. Sits in my lap while I watch TV. Sleeps in my bed with me at night. Goes outside to play with me."

"That sounds like a Labrador, doesn't it, Dad?"

Sam gripped the counter and jumped up-and-down on the step stool some more.

Chandler took in those hard-smiling young faces with suspicion. "This sounds like a setup. Did you two work this out ahead of time?"

Instead of answering, Della-Mae reached into the soapy water and took out a plate to dry.

Sam wasn't as good at hiding his emotions. His cheeks were flushing red. *"Dad,"* he said in a tone of voice that translated to, *"Don't ruin this for me, Dad. I want a puppy."*

"I wonder if Mary would benefit from having a puppy around," Dad mused from the table behind them.

"Grandma Mary would love it." Sam pounced, grinning again. "I'd share a puppy with her."

"She might need something a little less energetic than a Labrador," Dad continued in a distant voice.

Chandler turned to face his foster father. "Might be she could have one of those barn kittens instead. They're small and cuddly."

"Oh…kitties," Della-Mae cooed as if this was something she hadn't considered.

"No kittens, Della-Mae," Sam said firmly. "They scratch."

Scratches. That made Chandler think of Izzy and the way she'd trotted into the school office yesterday with that gouge on her hand.

"I'd veto kittens, too." Dad frowned. "The last time we had one in the house, it kept climbing into the Christmas tree and trying to leap out on unsuspecting passersby…mainly, me." He rubbed his arm as if remembering past hurts.

"We were talking about dogs, everybody," Sam gently chided. "Dogs."

"My uncle Earl has a puppy board. He says I should wish for one for Christmas." Della-Mae looked wistful.

"There will be no animals given as presents for Christmas this year," Chandler said firmly. He had enough to contend with already what with running the ranch, watching out for his foster parents and worrying about his ex-wife's misplaced priorities. The last thing he needed was puppies. Or a woman. "No animals," Chandler repeated. "Especially not for kids who won't talk about misbehaving in school."

Sam's lip jutted out. "We could talk about it if you agree to a puppy."

"Ah, so you do admit to making mischief in school?" *Finally.*

Della-Mae ducked her head.

But Sam. He looked Chandler right in the eye and told him exactly how he felt with one put-upon word. *"Dad."*

"THE BOXES IN the attic were exactly where you said they'd be, Mary." Izzy set a large plastic tub on the carpet next to the coffee table, the last of that lot stored in the attic. She'd spent the past few minutes ferrying dusty storage boxes marked *Christ-*

mas and *Holidays* from the unfinished attic to the living room.

"Christmas!" Sam ran in from the kitchen and opened the nearest cardboard box. "Come on, Della-Mae. We have to help Grandma Mary decorate." He began tossing out the contents—glittery gold garland, colorful beaded garland, fake fir tree garland—quickly making a garland mound around his feet.

"Hold your horses, Sam." Izzy waylaid Mae before she could open another box and do the same. "We have a plan."

Sam stared at Izzy, the spitting image of his father with those brown eyes, soft brown hair and stubborn chin. "But we want to help." And then he pouted, something his father would never do.

Mary and Izzy chuckled.

"And help you will," Izzy said as Chandler and Frank entered the room.

Chandler looked at the pile of garland at his son's feet and sighed, much the same reaction as Izzy had when a notoriously difficult customer entered Clementine Feed. He spared Izzy a guarded glance.

What is going on behind those brown eyes of yours?

Izzy didn't have time to wonder. Kids were waiting. She lifted the lid from a large plastic tub labeled *Christmas Village*. "Sam and Mae, I want you to arrange Mary's Christmas village on the coffee table."

The two kids lunged at the tub while Frank picked his way around it to sit in a recliner near Mary.

"Hang on. The Christmas village doesn't go on the coffee table." Chandler eased the children out of reach of the tub's treasures. "The Christmas village is always set up on the bookshelf behind the couch."

Izzy laid a hand on Chandler's arm, surprised at the hard length of muscle beneath her fingers, stunned that Chandler didn't immediately frown and pull away. "Mary thought the village would be easier for her to enjoy if it was on the coffee table this year." Izzy glanced at her client, waiting for confirmation. It was possible that Mary would back off from the idea.

"It was my idea, Chandler." Mary nodded. "Not to mention that I can watch the children play with it here." She gestured toward the wooden coffee table.

"Really?" Chandler sounded more hurt than sarcastic. "You never let us boys play with it. Or anything in this room."

"That's because you can't allow a houseful of rambunctious teenage boys access to fragile things." Mary smiled, softening her words. "There was always a game of catch with whatever wasn't nailed down, a fight with my best couch pillows or target practice with crumpled wrapping paper. Not to mention, noogies and pokes and jokes that had your energy levels supercharging your growing bodies until you tripped over your own feet. It's amazing to me that I have any nice things left. And now that you're all grown, I'd like to appreciate them and allow a precious few…" Mary gestured to Sam and Della-Mae. "…to enjoy them, too."

"Whatever you want, Mary," Frank said with a nod.

"Whatever you want, Mom," Chandler echoed, although he stared down at Izzy when he spoke.

And oddly, Izzy could imagine that obstinate cowboy saying those words to her in answer to whatever request she made of him.

What do you want for dinner, Chandler?

Whatever you want.

What do you want to do on New Year's Eve, Chandler?

Whatever you want.

Can you kiss me a little bit longer, Chandler?

Whatever you want.

Chandler's glance shifted to his arm…

To my hand on his arm!

Izzy withdrew her hand as if she'd been burned, managing to inch away from Chandler and her unexpected and mesmerizing attraction.

The room was silent. More than one pair of eyes was turned her way.

Izzy needed to say something about…something. But what?

Her mind raced about nonsensically.

And then her gaze lit upon the Christmas village. *Ah, yes.* "You kids can arrange the village any way you want, as long as you don't break anything."

"We won't!" her helpers cried, leaping into action.

Chandler stared at Izzy in silence, looking like there was a lot going on in that handsome head of his. But he merely drew a deep breath and said, "I guess it's finally time to drag the outdoor lights from storage in the garage and check that they're working. You want to help me, Dad?"

"Yep." Frank got to his feet.

Together, the two cowboys headed toward the kitchen and the mudroom, presumably where they'd left their boots, jackets and cowboy hats.

Izzy opened another box of Mary's decorations and began poking through the contents.

Meanwhile, the kids had already struck gold.

"Look! Here's a horse." Mae held up a small figurine—a horse pulling a sleigh with a couple sitting close together, bundled up in coats and hats.

"And a dog!" Sam's excitement made his grandmother laugh. He held the figure toward her with a big smile and a charmer's look in his eyes. "You want a puppy for Christmas, don't you, Grandma?"

Oh, he's going to be a heartbreaker.

Izzy returned her attention to the box before her. She unwrapped a small, chipped Christmas mug, a pair of cracked snowmen salt and pepper shakers and two pieces of a small crystal bowl, barely big enough to hold enough mints to satisfy all Mary's cowboys on Christmas Eve.

Izzy dug deeper.

"A puppy, Sam? I hadn't thought about asking for an animal for Christmas." Mary tsked, but she was smiling at her grandson. "Puppies are a lot of hard work and I'm afraid that I've been creating more work for family lately. I won't be asking Santa for a puppy this year. But perhaps you can get me another dog for my Christmas village. That would be fun."

"How about a horse?" Sam switched tactics, smile just as bright. "Wouldn't it be great to have a new horse for Christmas?"

"I have a horse." Mary's gaze looked wistful. "I haven't ridden Taffy in months."

"But you will. You always ride in the Santapalooza, Grandma." Sam spoke confidently, apparently unaware of Mary's frailty.

Izzy set aside a small ceramic Christmas tree since some of the bulbs were broken. The box was fast becoming a bust, mostly a testament to things broken but perhaps too precious to be discarded.

"We might need to get you on a wagon for this year's Santapalooza, Mary," Frank called from the mudroom. "Wouldn't want you to fall off Taffy."

"I've never fallen off a horse!" Mary called back with some of that spunk that had been in her eyes earlier. She gestured toward Sam and Mae, and the houses they were arranging on the coffee table. "You two are my witnesses. Mark my words. I've been through a lot, but I'm not going to start falling off horses now."

The kids dutifully nodded.

Sensing a fight brewing, Izzy jumped in. "Maybe you could ride in a wagon, Mary. I've seen some fancy ones in the Santapalooza parade over the years." And wished she could have ridden in some.

"Pish," Mary muttered.

"Posh," Frank replied in a louder voice. "That's a great idea, Izzy. My Mary will ride in a wagon on Christmas Day." He walked across the kitchen wearing his boots, pausing in the doorway in between the two rooms to waggle a finger at his wife. "Doc said to take it easy until your strength fully returned, remember?"

"How can I forget when you continuously remind me?" Mary huffed. "And how does Doc measure my strength? He asks me, that's how."

"You're still sleeping most of the day, darlin'," Frank said in a placating voice, plopping his wide white cowboy hat on his head. "A wagon will be safer."

"A wagon?" Mary's eyes narrowed. "Don't embarrass me. I can ride. It's not like I plan to gallop through the streets of Clementine wearing my Mrs. Claus costume."

Izzy interrupted, hoping to restore the festive atmosphere. "Look at these great candle lights." She held up a pair of vintage candlesticks with light bulb flames that had been at the bottom of the box she'd been rummaging through. "Do you want me to put these in the living room windows?"

Chandler appeared behind his foster father. "Mom always puts those in the bedroom windows that face the ranch yard."

"*Always*... I'm not as predictable as all that." Mary drew herself up on the couch, in full-on contrary mode, mood at odds with that cheery elf on the front of her sweatshirt. "*I* think they'd look great in the living room windows, Izzy. And I'll be asking Doc Nabidian if I can ride in the Santapalooza this year, Frank. No wagons for me."

"And I'll be right there with you when you ask Doc," Frank told her, as if this wasn't the first time they'd quarreled about the doctor approval. "Just so we're on the same page. In the meantime, since you're turning up your nose at a wagon, I'll call around to see if anyone has a carriage we can borrow, something magical and romantic."

"We don't have a horse trained to pull a buggy," Mary protested, eyes filling with tears. "I know you're watching out for me. But you'll just create more work for everyone. I've already spent most of the year being a bother."

"This is an adorable snow globe. And it has a music box." Izzy was still trying to play peacemaker via distraction. She wound up the snow globe she'd found in another box. It began to play "Silent Night." "I wanted one of these on my nightstand when I was a kid. I thought it would help me fall asleep." The Christmas after her mother died.

"We always put that on the mantel." Chandler

hadn't budged from his position behind Frank. His sense of repetition hadn't budged, either.

Always-always-always.

"I think I want that snow globe next to my bed this year," Mary said in her ornery tone of voice.

"But you never put it there." Chandler frowned. "In fact, every year, you tell us we can't open our stockings until the music box winds down to the last note. It's part of our holiday tradition."

"Are you going to argue with me?" Mary stared from Frank to Chandler. If her eyebrows had grown back, she might have raised them, daring those men to contradict her wishes.

"Nope. Doc said not to upset you." Frank turned on his heel and started walking. "Let's go check those lights, Chandler."

"Yep." Chandler stuck a straw cowboy hat on his head and followed his dad from the room.

The kids were quietly unpacking the Christmas village. Mary sniffed. And Izzy silently debated the importance of ranch traditions versus Mary's need for independence.

When the men had left and the back door had closed behind them, Izzy perched on the chair next to the couch and said to Mary, "I think I should put your decorations where they usually go. Just to keep the peace all around."

"Sam, can you and Della-Mae go get me a glass of water, please?" Mary waited until the kids had scampered into the kitchen. "Izzy, I believe change is good. And most of my family don't mind it. Now

Chandler… He doesn't appreciate change or unpredictability. You have to give him a good reason to accept change. And if this is my last Christmas…" Mary choked up.

Izzy took Mary's hands and gave them a little shake. "It won't be."

"But if it is… If the cancer comes back…" Tears filled Mary's eyes once more. "I don't want my boys to make this house a shrine to me. Always putting things where I did."

"You should do whatever makes you happy, Mary," Izzy said softly. "*I'll* do whatever makes you happy."

"Work with me, Izzy." Mary's voice was gruff. "My boys…even my Frank…look big and strong on the outside but underneath, they have soft centers. Mostly because they come from homes that were broken somehow."

Having grown up in Clementine, this wasn't news to Izzy. Anyone from the Done Roamin' Ranch was known to come from a less-than-perfect beginning. But she hadn't thought of Chandler in that light before.

"How was Chandler's…" Izzy shook her head. "I shouldn't ask about what circumstances he comes from."

"You should. You should ask him," Mary contradicted her. "As I understand it, yours and Chandler's children are in cahoots at school. Can't work as a team if you don't understand one another."

Speaking of… Sam and Mae were talking quietly in the kitchen. Were they plotting more mischief? Chandler might suspect them of it. But Izzy couldn't quite sell herself on the idea.

"I can tell you this. Chandler never knew what to expect from his parents," Mary continued in a low voice, drawing Izzy's attention back to her. "As a result, he sticks to schedules, watches out for others and avoids surprises as much as he can."

That explained why he'd been cranky at school yesterday, having been as blindsided by the reason for the meeting with the principal as she was. But... "No surprises? Not even at Christmas?"

Mary smiled gently. "Maybe at Christmas."

Izzy's phone dinged with a message from another client, a reminder that she had work to do. And there was an important issue at hand. "Still... I should put things where you've put them in the past." Izzy frowned at the collection of small houses the kids had left on the coffee table. "Including this village."

"I'll say it again. I want you to put things where it makes me happy." Mary took hold of Izzy's hand and gave it a determined squeeze. "Even if it's in a new place."

"But... What about Chandler?"

"Change may be difficult but it's the best way to move forward when you're stuck, like my Chandler."

Mary's smile fell away. "His house here on the ranch hasn't been decorated for Christmas since his divorce."

"Not even for Sam?"

"Not even for Sam." Mary tsked. "Sad, isn't it?"

Izzy nodded. "We should do something about that." She stared out the window thinking about Chandler alone without any decorations. And then, she felt Mary's eyes on her and added, "For Sam, of course."

Mary beamed at Izzy. "I knew you were the right person for the job."

CHAPTER SIX

"YOUNG SAM HAS a good idea." Dad handed Chandler a bulb to replace one that wasn't working. "He needs a puppy."

Kneeling on the concrete floor, Chandler's attention in the large, chilly garage was divided between the lit string of lights in front of him, the changing state of Christmas and an unwanted fascination with Izzy's holiday exuberance. She'd touched him in the living room—just her hand on his bicep—and he'd been rendered speechless. Why? He couldn't work it out.

But at his father's comment, Chandler came completely back to the present. "A puppy? With me running stock to rodeos most of the year, I'm home less than you are nowadays. Not to mention Sam spends half his time at Stephanie's."

Although Sam would be at the ranch full-time if Stephanie moved to Texas.

"A puppy might give Sam something to think about other than mischief at school." Dad rummaged in a box for another replacement bulb while two ranch hands lifted weights at the opposite cor-

ner of the garage. "Besides, there's always someone around here to take care of a dog, including
your mother."

"Then it wouldn't be Sam's dog." Chandler fit
the new bulb in place and held out his hand for another. "It would be Mom's dog. Might as well get
her one for Christmas."

"Pfft." Dad pooh-poohed that idea. "Your mother
and I have been talking about you. You're the one
who needs a dog or a woman to make you smile
again. Maybe both."

"A dog or a woman?" Chandler stood and stepped
over one strand of lights to the next, moving to
kneel by another bulb that wasn't working. There
seemed to be a lot more burnt-out bulbs than usual
this year. "Don't tell me you and Mom hired Ronnie to find me a match."

"Not yet. But we could…" Dad teased. He followed Chandler, handing him another replacement
bulb when needed. "You're in a rut since the divorce. You work. You take care of Sam. You don't
go into town with the rest of the boys to grab a
beer on Saturday nights. You don't date. And—"

"I'm too old to date." Too set in his ways.

"Too old?" Dad checked his phone, and then
tsked. "Last I checked, you were thirty-six."

"Going on thirty-seven," Chandler pointed out,
sliding a bulb into a socket. It beamed cheerfully.

Dad made another disapproving noise. His wide
white cowboy hat brim hid his expression from
Chandler. "Is this how you see your life playing

out? Single, running the ranch, raising Sam? Seems like you're missing out on more, including companionship. *Especially* companionship."

"Finally, your reason for saying I need a dog or a woman is clarified. Let me reassure you. I'm not lonely." How could he be when he was surrounded by family and an all-encompassing job?

"But are you living a satisfying life? As I recall, you used to dream about traveling the world."

"That was Stephanie's dream. Mine was to restore old cars." The bumper of the 1967 Mustang Chandler was working on caught his eye. He hadn't had much spare time to work on it lately. In fact, he couldn't remember the last time he'd tinkered underneath the hood. Two years ago? Three? It couldn't have been before Sam was born…could it?

Chandler frowned, gaze following the rest of the twisted strand of green wires, looking for more unlit bulbs. Was Dad right?

The jingle of Izzy's antlers echoed in the corner of Chandler's mind, enticing him to come out and play.

Nope.

Chandler firmly rejected the idea. He didn't feel as if anything was missing from his life.

He pulled the last few feet of lights closer and then removed another burnt-out bulb, pushing thoughts of Izzy and loneliness from his mind.

Dad handed Chandler another bulb. "My point is that there are places to go. There are people to meet. There's love and curiosity and limits to be explored. Son, there's more to life than working."

"Says the man who bounces in and out of retirement." Chandler got to his feet too quickly, sending blood rushing in all the wrong directions.

"How are the lights?" Izzy walked up the driveway.

And it must have been the sudden hit of vertigo because Chandler wanted to reach out and hold on to her in the hopes that she could steady him.

Nonsense.

"Five strings of lights are good to go." Dad returned the box of spare bulbs to the now-empty plastic tub marked *Christmas Lights.* "Since you're here, I'm going to head inside to watch over Mary and the kids. Think about what I said, son."

Think about dating Izzy, Chandler thought he meant.

Chandler scoffed. Dad didn't realize that Izzy was wrong for him. She'd been surprising him from the moment he'd seen her wearing those antlers yesterday. She wasn't the Izzy he was used to. Not to mention, she was at least five years younger than he was, maybe more. That was practically a generation gap. Sort of.

And Chandler was beginning to show some wear and tear. He'd started going gray last summer, everything from his whiskers to a sprinkling of hair on his head. If Izzy had noticed—*and who's to say she hadn't?*—she probably thought Chandler was ancient. Curmudgeonly, even, given his comments about decorations being put up where they always belonged.

Izzy scuffed the sole of her boot on the concrete, looking uncomfortable. "Sorry to interrupt your conversation, Chandler. But I want to apologize. I'm sorry about making new suggestions inside the house. I understand how change can be unsettling to some people."

"Yes… Uh… Thanks." Her apology was unexpected. Had Mom said something? Or was Izzy attuned to his upset? "I guess you know I'm a same-old, same-old type of guy." Emphasis on *old* and *same*.

"Normally, that's how folks describe me," Izzy said.

Chandler laughed a little, shaking his head.

Izzy's brows lowered. "Don't laugh. I know what folks in town think of me. I'm milk toast—"

There she went with another term he wasn't familiar with.

"—easily overlooked and boring. And you—"

"Not so fast." For some reason, he couldn't let Izzy describe herself that way. He pointed at her face. "You're head gear isn't easily overlooked. And if milk toast means you're boring, that sweater is anything but. Any woman who wears those outfits without shrinking when a group of cowboys look at her twice does so because she has character and Christmas means something to her." Chandler paused, in awe of his speech. And regretting it, too.

"Notice that everything in your argument relies

on what I've been wearing the past two days." Her expression conveyed disappointment. "Admit it. Before yesterday, you would have said I was milk toast, forgettable and boring."

"I never would have said milk toast," Chandler tried to tease, although his words felt as if they landed wrong. "And you had my respect before yesterday. I can't say the same about everyone I deal with."

Izzy bit her lip.

Chandler was digging a hole. And he cared that he was floundering, so much so that he kept talking. "But do you know what? When I saw you yesterday, I didn't think *this can't be Izzy*. Which means I must have seen you as something more before I ever spotted those antlers of yours." He was surprised to realize that was true.

A smile took shape on Izzy's face, chipping away at Chandler's regrets. "Do you really think…" She shifted her weight, trailing off.

"Go on," Chandler urged.

"Do you really see me that way?" Her fingers twined together at her waist, an indication of unease.

Chandler wanted to take those hands in his and reassure her somehow. But he stayed where he was, hands holding a string of lights. "Yep."

Izzy turned, staring at the main ranch house. She was silent for a good while, and Chandler was okay with that, not wanting to ramble on and make a fool of himself more than he already had.

When Izzy faced Chandler once more, her smile was warm. "When I think back on my childhood, I was more like Sam than Mae. Outgoing, carefree, exuberant. But then Mom got sick, and I didn't know how to handle my emotions or everyone telling me how sorry they were. I couldn't find the words and my dad… Well, he was no help in the emotion department." Izzy sighed. "And after my mom died, I gave up trying, other than with my friends. It was as if I found a shell, closed it up with me inside and then I called it home."

Chandler nodded, more because Izzy seemed to want some kind of acknowledgment from him than because he remembered her as she described herself before her mother died.

"And then Mike came along, and, for a while, I felt different. No shell needed." Her gaze seemed more intense when she looked at Chandler. "But then things fell apart, and the shell returned."

Ah, this… This he understood. This he felt to his very bones. "Divorce."

Izzy nodded. "And then this year, two weeks before Thanksgiving, Mae was offered a role in the Christmas pageant. Mrs. Stodimeyer called to tell me about it and that Mae turned it down. When I asked Mae why, she told me that she couldn't imagine getting up on stage, because she couldn't imagine *me* getting up on stage." Izzy plucked at the green garland on her sweater, cheeks reddening. "And that made me realize I needed to be a better role model for my daughter, even if I need to pry myself out of my shell."

Chandler's interest was piqued. "You think it'll get more comfortable as time goes on?"

"I hope so." She chuckled wryly. "Look at me. Do I look comfortable to you?"

Chandler was looking. And what he saw wasn't a woman who was easily overlooked or stuck in a shell. In her own succinct way, she'd told him something personal. Her confession touched him. In foster care, they stressed that you had to keep moving forward, that you shouldn't let the past anchor you in place. He'd forgotten that. Chandler realized he'd been anchored in the ranch foreman's house. And to this ranch. His foster parents had noticed. And Sam... His son wanted something different from him. Perhaps he hadn't noticed Chandler's anchor. But he would when he got older. If Chandler didn't change.

"Chandler?" Izzy's soft voice brought him back to the present. "Earth to Chandler."

He grunted, carefully returning to the task of coiling lights. But coiling didn't require looking. And Chandler's gaze drifted until it landed on Izzy once more. The morning sunshine reflected off her hair, making everything around her look brighter, more optimistic, more...achievable.

Like the man at her side could do anything he set his mind to.

Chandler bumped the brim of his cowboy hat back. He wasn't usually poetic. And that was disconcerting, too. As if his anchor couldn't find purchase. Chandler risked another look at Izzy.

Her unusual hair color accented her pretty face the way silver tinsel did on the branches of a green Christmas tree. Christmas signified family. And family meant you had someone to reach out when you raised your anchor and drifted off course.

Chandler settled his cowboy hat more firmly on his head. "I'm listening to you." With caution.

"I was wondering…" Izzy began with a tentative note in her voice. "While I'm working around here, I could help you with your decorations."

Chandler's shoulders cramped. "Why?"

"Because I could use the work." She laughed self-consciously. "And because Sam seems to love Christmas so much."

Guilt speared toward Chandler's heart, hardening his voice. "Not everyone celebrates the holidays the same way."

"I know."

"I know you know," Chandler snapped. But guilt was building inside Chandler like a charging bull picking up steam, and he was having trouble diffusing it. "I admit. I don't sing Christmas carols with Sam just because. And I don't rearrange my furniture and put up a tree that's just gonna die in a few weeks and leave needles in my carpet for months. And I'm sure that's not you. I'm sure you sing carols and string popcorn with Della-Mae. You probably have Christmas kitchen towels, Christmas guest soaps and Christmas knickknacks out all over the house, just like my mom does. But that doesn't mean I don't have the Christmas spirit."

"I can check all those boxes," Izzy said, sounding like Izzy from Clementine Feed, not Reindeer Izzy.

Retreating to her shell.

Chandler didn't want to be the cause of that. "I was out of line. Feel free to walk away and ignore me." But selfishly, he hoped she wouldn't.

"Gosh, you're a miserabilist." Izzy tsked. "Sorry. I meant a guy who seems happy to be doom and gloom. Can you tell me why?"

"Why?" Why wasn't she demanding an apology?

"Yes, why no holiday decorations in your house? A lot of my clients are elderly who've had setbacks," Izzy explained. "They haven't had any Christmas cheer because their health hasn't been good, or their spouse has died. But you…" Her blue gaze was no longer naive. It was piercing, searching to understand Chandler. "You say you have Christmas cheer but not at your house. Enlighten me."

It's none of your business.

Except…a part of Chandler wished that it was.

"Are you still in the divorce funk?" she asked, still looking at him closely. "That's real, you know. It's like whatever your spouse did in the relationship is off-limits. The first year I was single again, I didn't take care of my SUV. No oil changes. No new air filter. I didn't even check the pressure in my tires. And it wasn't until I turned on the engine and it shook so much that it practically hopped out of my driveway that I put on my big-girl jeans and took it in for service."

"Divorce funk…" Chandler had never heard of such a thing. And didn't think it applied to him.

"If Stephanie is anything like Mary, that might be why you can't put up Christmas decorations." Izzy gave him a brisk nod. "Just food for thought."

"Thank you, Dr. Adams. Do I put a nickel in a jar for your diagnosis?" Chandler found his footing. "I suppose whatever reason is behind my lack of a Christmas tree makes me the Grinch."

"It makes you something," Izzy allowed, not looking at all put off. She had thick skin beneath that Christmas star on her head. "But it's not for me to judge. I could help you decorate, though. If you're too busy."

"Thanks, but your services aren't needed at this time." The last thing he needed was this woman in his personal space.

"No worries," Izzy continued, sounding as if she found this exchange awkward, too. "I have no problem putting the lights up where they've always been outside for Mary. If you give me a brief rundown as to where they go, I'll get right on that."

Chandler handed her the coil of lights. "I'll give you a hand." And then he began to coil the next string.

"No. I'm sure you have other things to do."

Her gaze might have drifted toward the neglected Mustang.

Or maybe that was an impression created by that conversation with Dad.

"And besides, Sam is here. You need to spend time with him," Izzy barreled on, not looking Chandler in the eye. The garland on her green sweater shimmered in the sunlight. "I'll have Mae help me outside. Mary's making a list for me to do inside while supervising the kids in their effort to make cookies."

"It's too soon to bake holiday cookies," Chandler said without thinking. "I mean… Mom bakes the week before Christmas."

Izzy nodded slowly, curious gaze tempting him to move closer and share why same-old, same-old was so important to him.

He fought the impulse, wondering how Izzy kept circling around and circumventing his defenses. "Didn't we agree our kids shouldn't spend time together?"

Izzy huffed, putting a hand on one slender hip. "Oh, give it up. They're great friends."

"Yes. They're such good friends that they'd both like a puppy for Christmas." Despite everything—Sam's acting up at school, Mom's slow recovery, Stephanie considering taking a new job, Izzy being…not the Izzy he was used to—Chandler smiled. Because it was funny. "Not only that. Sam and Della-Mae suggested getting puppies from the same litter. If that isn't trouble, I don't know what is."

"Ha! Those two." Dropping her hand from her hip, Izzy shook her head, smiling a little and sending that star balanced over her head swaying. "But that doesn't mean they can't be friends."

Or that we can't be…

Chandler didn't finish that sentence. He was unable to take his eyes off her. His chest felt tight with an unidentified emotion but his mind… His mind counseled him to abort this fascination before it was too late for his heart. It was just that Chandler couldn't seem to act completely on that idea. "There's no telling what mischief they'll be cooking up next," he managed to say because she was waiting for him to say something.

"Hopefully that mischief today is just overly frosted sugar cookies." Izzy tugged down her Christmas tree sweater. "Let's make a pact. No puppies and no classroom changes."

"No puppies." Chandler wasn't willing to commit to the other, despite getting to know Della-Mae better this morning. He took a trick from Izzy's playbook and changed the subject. "What got you into the Christmas decorating business?"

Her cell phone buzzed. She ignored it. "I want to buy Della-Mae a canopy bed. Her father spoils her all the time while I'm just trying to make the most out of the few dollars that are left after paying our bills every month. And this bed…"

"You used to dream of one as a kid?" he guessed. She seemed the type.

Izzy nodded. "I'll probably bring it home and Mae won't care for it at all, in which case, I'll be sleeping in it." She grinned. "Imagine that. A thirty-year-old sleeping on a canopied four-poster twin bed."

He had a sudden image of Izzy's head resting on a frilly pink pillow, a smile gracing those lips as she looked at him, and all that lustrous hair spilled out behind her. He removed his hat and ran his hand through his graying hair. Maybe if she noticed their age difference, she wouldn't smile at him like that.

"Did you have a dream when you were a kid?" Izzy asked.

"Yep." That was easy. Chandler put his hat back on his head and glanced around.

There was the arena where he'd learned to ride a horse. And the pasture where he and his brothers played musical chairs, except using horses, not chairs. There was the bunkhouse where he'd spent many a hot summer night in his youth talking to other foster boys about girls and baseball and rodeo. And that was the thing about growing up and living on the Done Roamin' Ranch. There was family everywhere. Chandler was rarely alone unless he was inside the foreman's house that was his and his alone. And if he was always willing to pick up someone's shift or walk the outbuildings before he went to bed at night when Sam was with Stephanie, that didn't make him a workaholic. His emotional well-being relied upon him keeping the ranch running smoothly, working how it was supposed to, being how it was supposed to be—a thriving family operation for generations to come.

"This ranch was my dream. Still is." Chandler cleared his throat, transferring a coil of lights to Izzy's other arm. "Not this ranch exactly. But a place I could call home with a family who cared about my well-being and happiness."

Izzy nodded. "Home and family. You put me to shame." She gave a wry laugh. "You probably think I should quit on the idea of the princess bed and get Mae something more practical, like a pair of new cowboy boots."

It was Chandler's turn to laugh. "I'm always up for a new pair of boots, but… She doesn't own a pony, much less a horse, does she?"

"She gets invitations to ride with the children of my friends. Like Ginny." Izzy gave him a searching look.

"What's wrong?" Chandler rubbed his chin with the back of his hand. "Do I have tinsel or glitter on me?"

"No." She shook her head slowly, eyes narrowed not in scorn but in thought as she seemed to consider him. "You didn't agree to my pact about not changing the kids' classrooms."

"No." And he wasn't going to, either.

THERE WAS SOMETHING about Chandler that struck Izzy on different levels, from attraction to annoyance.

Oh, Izzy had to hand it to him. Chandler disguised his need for continuity of decoration placement beneath a thick veneer of helpfulness. Not that he fooled Izzy.

"No-no, Izzy. I'll go up the ladder." Chandler didn't give Izzy time to argue. "I know where the hooks are for the lights under the eaves. It'll save you time."

He was helpful, the way gentlemen were supposed to be.

Izzy was used to coworkers at the feed store assuming she could heft her weight in grain, dog food, hay, two-by-fours or fencing supplies. No one treated her with this much consideration at work. And it was…charming.

"Just hand me the coil of lights," Chandler told her quickly, although…not unkindly.

True to form, she'd already tangled one strand and he hadn't teased her about it.

He was nice. She'd known that for years.

What she hadn't known was his dream. Dreams told Izzy a lot about a person. Mike had told her he wanted stability that financial success would bring, having come from a family that struggled to put food on the table. But he'd never admitted he also wanted power and status.

Chandler's dreams involved intangibles, like the love of family and security. Izzy wanted much the same, but she also wanted to give her daughter the childhood dream she'd never had. It made her feel shallow.

No wonder Chandler kept looking at Izzy as if she was speaking a foreign language and he didn't know if he should pull out his guidebook to translate or not.

"What are the tires doing over there?" Izzy asked, steadying the ladder for Chandler as he climbed down after the last strand was hung on the main house.

Tires of various sizes were stacked on the side of the garage.

"We keep them there until Mom complains about them, and then we haul them to the tire recycle place."

"It would be fun to paint them white—fun for the kids, I mean—and then we can stack them from largest to smallest like a snowman." Izzy warmed to the idea. "A little black paint for coal faces. A few sticks for arms and…" She faltered when she got to hats because Chandler had reached the ground and was frowning. "Are you telling me that you want everything in its usual place *and* nothing new?"

"That's me. Same-old, same-old."

"Old?" Instead of moving aside to give Chandler space, Izzy stayed put. Because for some reason, while he was charming, he also annoyed her with his stubbornness. "You aren't old. And you prob-

ably weren't chanting this same-same-same man-
tra when you were a kid."

"No." Him and that frown. It didn't impact her
the way he probably thought it did.

Izzy didn't back down. "Better watch out, Chandler, or that frown crease in your forehead will become permanent." Without thinking, she pressed
her thumb to his forehead.

Yikes! What am I doing?

"Sorry." She yanked her hand back. "That was
inappropriate."

"Let's get going on the trees." The way he *didn't*
react, as if her touch hadn't fazed him, had her
stepping back and feeling rejected as he turned and
strode toward the biggest tree in the yard. "We always start the lights at the bottom of the tree trunk.
Then around and around we go. And finally, the
lights always continue in a circular pattern through
the branches. Always."

Always? The man is like a brick wall.

"Hanging them with a swoop from one branch
to another is quicker," Izzy said patiently, waving to Mae, who stood inside the kitchen window,
smiling face streaked with flour. "And the garland
swag is just as pretty as a circular pattern."

"But it's not the same." Chandler rested one hand
on the trunk and stared up into its branches.

It's not the same.

Standing a few feet away from him, Izzy stared
up at the heavens, gritting her teeth. She bent to
retrieve the pole she used to lift light strands and

planted one end in the ground, standing on the grass like Poseidon and his trident. Except all her mythical power was being drained by Chandler and his need to avoid change.

She sighed, gaze dropping to her feet where she'd somehow managed to work her own brand of magic. "Oops, I tangled another strand of lights."

"On purpose?" Chandler looked from the tangled heap of lights at her feet to Izzy.

"No." *Maybe.*

Thankfully, Zane drove into the ranch yard before Chandler could challenge Izzy on that score.

Zane honked the horn, waving to them. He parked and hopped out, waving some more. "Hey, Izzy. I've got three Christmas trees for you!" Lickety-split, he and Dylan lifted them out of his truck bed, leaning them against the tailgate. "Where do you want them, Izzy?"

She opened her mouth to answer and—

Chandler butted in. "The tallest one always goes on the front porch. And the small one in the bunkhouse house. And—"

"Mary said she wanted Papa Bear's tree inside this year," Izzy cut Chandler off, using the Goldilocks reference so he wouldn't take offense. At Chandler's wrinkled brow, she added, "Mary said she wanted the biggest tree you could find so when she napped on the couch, she could wake up and that's all she'd see."

"That's not what we usually do." Chandler sounded uncertain.

"But that's what Mary wants this year," Izzy said firmly, despite feeling guilty over upsetting Chandler's apple cart. "Just a little change isn't so bad...is it?"

Chandler didn't answer, but his gaze was fixed on Izzy. Or maybe the star on her headband was off-kilter.

She fiddled with the placement of her headband.

"Change is fine by me." Zane pounded the trunk of the medium-sized tree on the ground without it shedding too many needles. "Where does Mama Bear's tree go?"

"On the porch outside Mary's bedroom window." Izzy ignored Chandler's weary sigh. "That leaves Baby Bear's tree in the bunkhouse. But before you put these trees up, can you tell me..." Izzy smiled at the cowboys the way she smiled at customers down at the feed store—*nonthreateningly*—right before she asked them if they wanted their order delivered for an additional fee. "Can you tell me what you look forward to at Christmas here on the ranch?"

"Why?" Chandler took a step back, as if she'd crossed a sensitive boundary. "Why would you ask that?"

"Because..." Izzy hung on to her smile. "...if there's something that is super-duper important to you at the holidays, I want to try and honor that for you." Even if Mary was intent upon shaking things up.

The three cowboys exchanged glances that

didn't include Izzy—*fair enough*—and seemed to communicate with a language of their own, accented by the barest of shrugs, the slightest of nose scrunches, the nearly imperceptible shifting of weight.

"Mom makes sure there's Christmas everywhere. The beautiful part of Christmas, you know." Zane's nose wrinkled as he hurried to explain. "Before I came here, Christmas was something I admired from afar." He rubbed his nose, as if uncomfortable admitting that much. "At my house, we didn't have any Christmas. None. No tree. No stockings. No Santa."

Izzy's heart broke a little.

"Yeah." Dylan took up where Zane left off, shrugging. "There was Christmas at school but none at home. And what Mom does for us during the holidays…" He paused, blinking watery eyes, clearly moved. "She makes Christmas special *and* for us."

"Right down to the packages she puts so much care into wrapping," Chandler added in a low voice Izzy almost didn't catch. He was rocking slowly, side to side, as if he held a child in need of soothing.

"And the variety of cookies she bakes from scratch…" Zane had a faraway look in his eyes. "Makes Christmas last practically 'til New Year's."

"Sugar-glazed ham, homemade biscuits and sweet potatoes dripping with marshmallows." Dylan rubbed his flat stomach. "I'd never been so full before."

"She makes us sing carols before we eat Christmas dinner," Chandler murmured, almost smiling. "Taught me all the words."

Izzy was touched. Mary was right. These big strong men had soft centers.

They deserved the finest of Christmases, too. Even the annoying ones.

CHAPTER SEVEN

"DAD!" SAM CRIED, standing on a chair at the kitchen counter when Chandler and Izzy had finished the outside lights on the house and yard. Sam had white frosting on his cheek and flour on his nose. "We made cookies!"

"I can see that." Chandler looked at the formerly clean counter, which was blanketed with cooling racks and sugar cookies of various shapes covered with layers of brightly colored frosting and several different kinds of sprinkles.

Mom would freak if she saw this.

It was all Chandler could do not to start cleaning right away.

"We're good at making cookies, too." Della-Mae stood on a chair next to Sam. She swirled her finger in a bowl of green frosting and then stuck her finger in her mouth. She had green frosting streaks in her white-blond hair and flour on her cheek. "Do you want one?"

"Try my Santa, Dad." Sam held out a cookie with a blob of red frosting. White sprinkles fell from it to the kitchen floor.

If we had a dog, it would lick those sprinkles right up.

Chandler accepted his son's work, took a bite, heard Izzy's footsteps and turned, inexplicably wanting to watch her enter the room. She'd been surprising him all afternoon with her honesty, while he… He'd avoided opening himself to her.

Because I'm past the age of head-spinning romance.

And yet…as he looked at Izzy… He regretted holding back. Izzy made him want to be a young buck, open to love and adventure, able to let others take on responsibilities he'd been bearing without complaint.

"Are you kids in here alone?" Izzy padded in, having shed her boots and star headband. Her cheeks were pink from the cold air outside and her white-blond hair was mussed.

Chandler could imagine his hand doing the mussing.

Stop it.

"We've only been alone a minute, Mama." Della-Mae offered her mother what might have been a Christmas tree cookie. It was triangular shaped and frosted with green.

"Where's Grandpa Frank?" Chandler glanced around, taking another bite of his cookie.

"He's putting Grandma in bed for a nap." Sam nibbled on another red-frosted cookie. Blue sprinkles tumbled to his feet on the chair. He watched them fall, laughing. "There's Christmas every-where, Dad."

"Yep." Chandler didn't dare say more to ruin the children's holiday spirit. They meant well, but... Mom kept the kitchen spotless, tidying up as she worked.

There were several bowls filled with frosting of different colors on the counter. A big bowl sat in the sink with the remains of what looked like dough. Flour was everywhere. On the kitchen table. On the floor. The counters looked like the kids had been finger painting with frosting. And sprinkles...

They probably made a rainbow coating on the bottom of his white socks.

"I know what you're thinking, Chandler." Smiling, Izzy breezed past Chandler as if she faced chaos in the kitchen every day. "You're thinking the kitchen never looks like this when your mom bakes."

"Yep." He sighed, feeling staid and predictable. "And I'm thinking that we don't bake this early in December."

"Why not?" Sam wiped his red frosting-coated fingers on his T-shirt. "These cookies are so good."

"Grandma Mary boxes up her cookies to give as gifts the week before Christmas." Chandler popped the rest of his cookie in his mouth, which might not have been the best idea given the ratio of frosting to cookie. For a few seconds, it felt as if he'd taken a huge bite of peanut butter. But he managed not to choke when he swallowed. "Time to wash up, starting with you two."

"Aw," Della-Mae and Sam chorused. But both dutifully held out their hands for Chandler to wipe the frosting off.

"And then we've got to clean the kitchen," Chandler told them.

"Aw," Della-Mae and Sam chorused again, showing him their best pouts.

"Yep." Chandler moved on to wiping their faces and hair.

Izzy tsked. "Kids, we've got to hurry on the cleanup if you want to help decorate three Christmas trees."

"What?" Della-Mae's mouth dropped open. She stared up at Chandler while he tried to remove a blob of green frosting from her hair. "Three trees?"

"Yes, ma'am." She was a cute little thing. Possibly an incredible mastermind but cute nonetheless.

"And each tree is going to receive a different decoration treatment." Izzy turned on the faucet and began to fill the largest of the bowls before darting around the room and collecting all the dirty dishes. "Mary wants the tree on the front porch decorated with Sam's toys. She mentioned he has a big collection of superhero action figures."

"And villains." Sam growled, making imaginary claws with his fingers.

"How did the Christmas village turn out?" Chandler gave up on cleaning the children and went to get a broom.

"So cool." Sam hopped from the chair to the floor, landing with a thud. "Tomorrow, I'm going to move the people in a circle around the church to sing carols." He took a running start and then slid in his stocking feet, crashing into the pantry cupboard across the room.

"Sam," Chandler warned.

"Ah. It was just one time, Dad." Sam proceeded to sock-skate around the kitchen, no doubt energized by all that sugar.

"The village is so pretty." Della-Mae gingerly climbed down from her chair. She was delicate in everything she did.

Chandler could see Izzy's daughter being overjoyed at the prospect of a princess bed. Now Sam… Sam would love bunk beds, especially the kind with a play cabin as the top bunk and perhaps a beanbag to leap into.

Della-Mae dragged her chair back to the table. "I wish we had a village like that, Mama."

Izzy frowned at the dirty bowls in the sink, perhaps chastising herself for not being able to grant all her daughter's wishes.

"I'm sure you'll get something just as beautiful this Christmas," Chandler told her, catching Izzy's eye and giving her a reassuring head nod.

The front door banged open. The kitchen occupants all stopped what they were doing to listen.

"Easy now." That was Zane's voice, coming from the living room.

"I'm not the one who smashed the Christmas

tree into the door like a bull intent upon tossing a crash barrel," Dylan snapped with very little good cheer.

There were sounds of boots shuffling across hardwood, as if the tree they carried was heavy.

Izzy turned off the water and applied a sponge to the bowls while Chandler swept around her.

"Della-Mae, the tree is here." Sam ran into the living room, footfalls heavy for such a small tyke. "Come on!"

Della-Mae skipped after him, feet barely making a sound.

The two kids were such opposites. Why were they friends? Chandler shook his head, unable to answer his own question.

Sounds of tree branches scraping across walls reached Chandler. He resisted the urge to go out there and take charge.

Because I'm finally alone with Izzy.

Chandler rubbed his forehead.

That's not it at all.

"This tree is too tall," Dylan said from the living room.

"I told you we needed to trim the bottom before bringing it in," Zane replied, not without some agitation. "Now we've got to take it back outside."

"We'll help," Sam piped up. "Me and Della-Mae."

"You know the rule, Sam," Zane said firmly. "You can't leave the porch if you don't have your boots on."

"Then we won't leave the porch," Sam countered.

"Never-ever," Mae seconded.

Boots scuffled back across the hardwoods. And then the front door closed.

"Those two. What a pair, right?" Chandler moved chairs out of the way so he could sweep beneath the table. "And I mean Zane and Dylan, not our kids."

"Sure you did," Izzy teased. "Don't you want to help with the tree? How will you know if they put it where it belongs?"

"I deserve that, I suppose." Chandler swept sprinkles into a dustpan. Once disposed of, he searched a top cupboard for cookie tins to store all those cookies.

"By the way, Chandler, Christmas doesn't come with a rule book." Izzy had her head bent while she did the dishes. "And sometimes there's an advantage to the surprise and delight in something new, like my Christmas costumes or Mary changing things up. I know my outfits don't bring you joy, but my clients seem appreciative."

"Who said I don't appreciate you and your holiday cheer?" Chandler teased.

"What?" She glanced at him. "I don't believe that. If that was true, why haven't I seen you wear a holiday sweater? I can't even recall you ever dressing up in costume, even for Halloween."

"My work doesn't leave me time for…"

"Personal expression? A bit of whimsy?" she guessed when he faltered.

"Are cowboys known for their whimsy? I think not." Chandler opened several tins and when Izzy didn't answer him, he added, "I told you I'm old and set in my ways."

"Does it matter what I think?" Izzy plunged her hands in the water and scrubbed vigorously, seemingly unaware that Chandler was hanging on to her every word. "And you're not old. Earl is old." Her employer at Clementine Feed.

"I have gray hair. I'm old. And stuck, like you said." And if that didn't destroy the attraction between them, Chandler didn't know what would.

"I have gray hair. And I'm not old. And look how I'm stepping outside my comfort zone." She turned to face him, resting a soapy hand on her hip. "You aren't old, either."

"You don't have gray hair," he said, countering her challenge. Chandler started loading cookies into the tins, starting at the other end of the counter and working his way toward the sink. His pulse picked up the closer he got to her. And his lips… His lips were smiling as if…as if… Chandler stopped trying to think and just let himself feel. And what he felt was a welling sense of excitement. He came to a stop next to Izzy. "Show me your roots."

"No." She laughed. "Trust me. I have grays." Izzy didn't back down. Her hand still rested on her hip. She didn't back away. Her stocking feet stayed in front of the sink. But her smile faded, and her gaze became wary. "I'm lucky. They're translucent so they blend with my hair color."

He was tall enough to see the top of her head,

even if she tilted her face up to look him in the eye. He saw no grays.

"I think I got my first gray hair when my mom died," she admitted softly, working hard to hold on to her smile. Failing. Her hand dropped to her side. "And I got another when my dad left town with her nurse," she said, just as softly.

More than anything, Chandler wanted to take that hand.

Chandler remembered those events vaguely. They'd happened at a distance from his side of Clementine. At the time, he'd considered each of those separate events sad. And Chandler must have made a mental note about her father skipping town because in this moment, standing before her, he could remember thinking back then, *"She knows how I feel."*

"My mom left when I was twelve." Chandler ran his hand through his hair. "But I didn't start going gray till this past year."

"Must mean you're tougher than me." Izzy's smile was more solid now, not so wobbly. "I found more grays when I was trying to decide whether or not to divorce Mike. Little did I know that while I was weighing the pros and cons, he was drawing up divorce papers."

"Jerk," Chandler blurted, earning a smile from Izzy.

"Well, he draws up paperwork for a living at that fancy car dealership in Friar's Creek." Izzy bobbed her head from side to side, as if trying to make light of what Chandler knew firsthand had to have been a gut-wrenching time for her. "It was all very businesslike."

"Can't say the same," Chandler admitted gruffly. "I fought hard for my marriage but…" He shrugged. "Turns out what I really wanted to fight for was Sam and his well-being." Still did.

"That's wise."

"Since I only reached that conclusion this past year, that's probably why I got these gray hairs." He tried to make light of it.

They stared at each other. Not smiling like they were falling in love. Not drowning in the depths of each other's warm gaze. Not even staring with yearning to explore the feel of each other's lips. Because despite being at odds over their children's behavior and his need for decorative status quo, they had a lot in common. And the acknowledgment of it was a bit mind-bending.

This wasn't Izzy, the quiet, polite woman from the feed store with little personality he never thought twice about.

This was Izzy, a soft-spoken, resilient woman with layers of character and more courage than he had.

Chandler didn't think he'd look at another ugly Christmas sweater without thinking of her.

Made him wonder what Izzy thought of him beyond not old but set in his ways.

"I'm just going to say this out loud." Izzy tucked a lock of white-blond hair behind her ear. "It's weird to be talking to you about gray hair and divorce. Especially when we didn't talk about much before yesterday besides feed orders and the weather."

He nodded. She was right. "Mom always says the best conversations happen in the kitchen." He moved to Izzy's side, picking up a dish towel. "You wash. I'll dry."

And they did just that for a few minutes in companionable silence.

Children's laughter drifted in from outside.

"We can't separate those two," Izzy said softly.

"Cold day today." Chandler changed the subject because he believed they could divide the pair and be better for it. Izzy may confound him but of this, he was certain. "And it'll be nippy Monday morning when I pick up my feed order."

Scoffing, Izzy shook her head.

The front door banged open again, bringing the sound of voices and branches dragging across hard surfaces.

Izzy extended her arm to put a bowl on the drying rack just as Chandler reached to take it above the sink. Wires crossed, their forearms brushed together, and they both jolted apart, staring at each other warily as if unsure what could or should happen next.

In that moment, Chandler realized that his father was right. He was living a closed-off life.

How else could he explain that one random touch from Izzy and he was consumed with the desire to kiss her? And from what he saw in her eyes, Izzy must have felt the same. Why not kiss her? In fact, Chandler was already acting on that impulse. He was slowly leaning forward, bending down, reaching for her...

"Chandler, can you give us a hand?" Zane called.

Chandler lurched upright.

"Dad?" Sam shouted.

Izzy blinked up at him and took a step back.

"I should...um...go see what they need." Chandler backed away from what would most certainly be a mistake—getting closer to Izzy and her tempting lips.

He dealt with her at the feed store. He dealt with her in the principal's office. For the good of the Done Roamin' Ranch's business, for Sam's well-being and his own peace of mind, Chandler had to keep Izzy in the place he'd discovered her years ago—the barely friend zone.

"CAREFUL," IZZY MUMBLED to herself after Chandler left the kitchen, speed washing the remaining bowls and utensils. *"This isn't wise."*

She wasn't supposed to find they had things in common, things that made Chandler more appealing to her, things that made her want to share things about herself she didn't usually or ask things about a man that were personal.

She wasn't supposed to find Chandler magnetically attractive, stocking feet, gray hair, same-old, same-old and all.

She wasn't supposed to be this curious as to how Chandler's lips would feel pressed on hers.

Izzy liked her life the way it was…present dilemma with Mae's behavior excepted. She made decisions about her life with hers and her daughter's best interests at heart. And Chandler did the same. She knew that the way she knew that only hot water could melt that thick red frosting from the surface of that plastic mixing bowl. She and Chandler were too much alike—wounded by what should have been love, lost when their mothers disappeared from their lives, juggling single parenthood, gray hairs and how to keep their kids in line.

And yet, despite those similarities, they were too different from each other to work as more than friendly acquaintances. Chandler was grounded and predictable, as resistant to change as gray hair was to hair color. She'd seen the way he looked at her holiday cheer outfits. She'd never seen him wear anything holiday-related. Not Christmas. Not Halloween. And not so much as a T-shirt to support a sports team or indicate where he'd gone on his last vacation.

Does he even take vacations?

Izzy doubted it.

No. They weren't suited at all.

So why was she listening to Chandler's deep voice and wondering what he'd sound like during the singing portion of church service? Or singing Christmas carols around the house?

Him? Sing around the house? She chuckled.

Without realizing it, Izzy had washed every bowl, every spoon and spatula, every cookie sheet.

She took a wet rag to the counters and table.

She wasn't interested in male companionship and kisses. She'd had romance, a dream wedding, and then spent too many years putting herself last. In her experience, that's what relationships and being a mother were all about. Take away a husband, and she had more time for Mae and for herself, for reading and girlfriends and a quiet moment with a cup of coffee or a glass of wine.

I don't miss the warm parts.

Holding hands, walking arm-in-arm, whispered endearments and exchanging tender kisses.

No. They came at a cost. The risk that the warmth wouldn't last. The risk that being part of a couple would undercut her self-worth and confidence.

Izzy turned, taking a good look at the kitchen. It was a large, open space with cupboards around three walls and a humongous table in the middle, one that could easily seat twelve, more in a pinch. There was a large bulletin board on the wall in one corner. It was covered with photographs of teenage cowboys, many Izzy recognized, having grown up in Clementine. More recent photographs were from weddings. There had been quite a few Done Roamin' Ranch cowboys married recently. But that wasn't the impression that would last in Izzy's head about the ranch kitchen. This was a room built for family. For lasting family that withstood the test of time. And family was what Chandler valued most.

"I understand," she murmured, thinking of Mary and what she'd said about Chandler and her boys.

Chandler valued the permanence the Harrisons had created on the Done Roamin' Ranch. The traditions. The bonds he'd formed...bonds that wouldn't be broken through divorce or parents abandoning him.

"Are you okay in here?" The cowboy she'd been thinking about poked his handsome head in the kitchen.

"Yes. Is the tree ready for me to decorate?" Izzy hung the wet rag she'd used over the faucet and would have hurried out of the kitchen if not for Chandler's hand held up in the universal sign for stop.

He smiled like a kid bursting to reveal a surprise. "We already decorated the tree. You'd be amazed at what three cowboys and two kids can do when they work together. But I thought you'd want to give it a once-over before Mom comes out." Still smiling, he returned to the living room.

Leaving Izzy in a brain fog that slipped past her defenses as easily as mist drifted over pasture fences.

Chandler is nice.

Chandler is attractive.

Chandler is probably a good kisser.

An ache filled Izzy's chest, bringing with it an acknowledgment.

I miss the warm parts.

Holding hands, walking arm-in-arm, whispered endearments and exchanging tender kisses.

Oh, this is bad.

But it wasn't bad enough.

Izzy also wanted the warmth that rare smile of Chandler's promised. She felt like she knew every single cowboy in the county and suddenly, out of the blue… *No other cowboy will do.*

She needed a few minutes to rid herself of that notion. She went to the mudroom and retrieved her headband with the gold star on top, reminding herself that she liked her life. She was finally at a place where she liked herself, too.

Why muck it up by falling in love?

CHAPTER EIGHT

"I LIKE HER." Zane pushed back his chair after dinner that night.

"Your new mare?" Chandler asked, swiping his biscuit through the remains of his white gravy.

"My mare?" Zane grinned. "Gee, Chandler. I know you can't think of anything except running this ranch, but seriously? I'm talking about Izzy."

Chandler lost his hold on his biscuit. It dropped on his plate, an action that might have ignited a firestorm of teasing had more ranch hands been at dinner. Luckily, it was just a handful of cowboys, plus Sam, Mom and Dad.

"You know, Izzy? Our Christmas lady." Dylan nodded his agreement with Zane, gathering his dinnerware. "All these years of seeing her at the feed store… Who knew she had such a cool personality?"

"Right?" Zane got to his feet, setting his utensils on his empty plate. "She's all business at the feed store. So quiet."

"Never letting on she had something interesting to say. Kind of like you, Chandler." Dylan nodded again. "Might just ask her to dance tonight at the Buckboard if she's there."

Chandler felt an unwelcome stirring of jealousy and two pairs of eyes upon him—Mom's and Dad's.

Mom had her chin resting on her hand. "Imagine that. A woman with hidden depths."

"Might be a relationship worth exploring," Dad said, gaze drifting around the room.

"Or a fun dance partner." Mom bid Zane and Dylan farewell. "I like Izzy and little Della-Mae, don't you, Sam?"

Chandler's son nodded enthusiastically. "Della-Mae is my best friend. She has such good ideas."

Jealousy was elbowed aside by curiosity. Chandler leaned closer to his son. "What are some of her ideas?"

"She said cookies shaped like stockings don't always have to be red and white." Sam fidgeted in his chair, chewing a bite of steak. "I frosted one blue. She made one yellow."

That wasn't the idea Chandler had been hoping to hear. He'd wanted Sam to tell him little Della-Mae had been the mastermind behind the Thanksgiving buffet and the impromptu musical parade.

"Della-Mae gets her creativity from her mother." Dad rubbed a hand back-and-forth across Mom's shoulders. "You need to eat more, Mary."

Mom pushed her plate away with a hand so thin her tendons were visible. "I'm not hungry."

"That's cuz you ate a cookie before dinner." Sam

was fully turned around now, spine to the table. "Can I have your biscuit?"

Mom laid the biscuit Dad had carefully buttered earlier on Sam's plate.

"Thanks." Sam ran his hands across the chair back. "I like biscuits almost as much as I like cookies."

"Me, too," Mom said, despite not touching hers.

"Table manners, Sam." Chandler used his hand to guide Sam to a normal sitting position. "What other ideas has Della-Mae had?" He really wanted ammunition against his unwanted feelings toward Izzy.

Sam reached for his biscuit and tore off a piece. "She said a dog would run next to a horse and sleigh, not be running through our Christmas village all alone. Because if you have a horse, you need a dog." Wonder of wonders, Sam wiped his mouth with a paper napkin. "And um... Oh, yeah. She said my superhero action figures fighting villains in the porch tree would make Grandma Mary smile."

"That they did," Mom said wearily. She'd been up and about longer than usual today.

Through the window, Chandler saw Zane and Dylan go inside the bunkhouse. In no time, they'd be leaving for town.

For the Buckboard. For Izzy.

"And what about at school?" Chandler continued his gentle interrogation. "Does Della-Mae have good ideas at school?"

"She always raises her hand in math." Sam stuffed too much biscuit in his mouth, pausing to chew, swallow, then drink milk before continuing. "And she shushes me when we have reading time."

"Sounds like your best friend does have some fine ideas." Dad nodded at Sam, and then turned his attention to Chandler. "Are you headed into town tonight?"

"Nope. Got Sam." And boy, was Chandler grateful for that. The last thing he needed to do was go into town and get caught mooning over Izzy while she danced with Zane and Dylan, especially since she was coming back to the ranch after work next week.

"We can watch Sam," Mom offered. "It's been a long time since we've seen some of his action heroes on TV. And since they're in my Christmas tree, I should get a refresher course."

"Sounds like a plan," Dad said.

"Yay!" Sam cried, running over to hug Mom.

"Yay," Chandler echoed, not nearly enthused.

"How did it go today at the ranch?" Ronnie asked Izzy that night at the Buckboard. "The outside lights looked pretty when I left for town tonight." She and her husband, Wade, lived in the original farmhouse next to Frank and Mary's house at the Done Roamin' Ranch. "Not to mention the porch Christmas tree was cheery."

Allison, Jo and Ronnie all looked toward Izzy expectantly. Allison was humming to the music.

Never as demonstrative, Jo was bobbing her head slightly in time to the beat. And Ronnie... Well, Ronnie was leaning forward on her elbows, ready to hear every word that dropped from Izzy's lips.

Ronnie has a nose for attraction.

And Izzy had to be careful that her friend didn't sniff out the conflicting feelings Chandler had created in Izzy today.

The four friends had just finished nearly an hour of line dancing at the Buckboard and were receiving a round of drinks from their waitress.

"You can thank Chandler for those outside lights tonight, Ronnie." Izzy quickly explained how Sam's dad was a bit of a control freak when it came to holiday decorating, ignoring the way painting Chandler in an unflattering light felt like a lie. "To be fair, Chandler, some cowboys and our kids decorated three Christmas trees." And under Mary's direction, Izzy had redecorated two.

"Sounds like Chandler ruffled your feathers." Ronnie looked disappointed. "Is this because of your kids and their mischief?"

When Izzy didn't immediately respond, Allison stopped humming to the music being played by the DJ. "Is Mae in trouble?"

Izzy quickly explained about the mishaps at school, some of which made her friends laugh.

"They're good kids," Ronnie added when Izzy was through, which was a nice affirmation given she was one of the school secretaries.

"Thanks." Izzy smiled with pride. "They both

helped put up decorations today. And they baked cookies. Mae was still talking about everything we did when I dropped her off for a slumber party earlier."

"I love the lights at the Done Roamin' Ranch," Allison said, staring off in the distance as if seeing them in her mind's eye. "Dix brought me there for Christmas dinner last year. Seeing them made me feel so happy."

"Me, too," Jo chimed in, tipping her wide white cowboy hat back. "I saw them on New Year's Eve when Ryan brought me and the boys over. I wish the Done Roamin' Ranch was closer to town or the main road. Mary always goes to so much trouble. It seems a shame more people can't enjoy her display."

"What if Frank and Mary opened the ranch to visitors?" Ronnie sat up. "We've all been concerned that she isolated herself for the most part during treatment. And now, she's taking a long time to get her strength back." She waved her hand. "Mary goes to church on Sunday, but it exhausts her. And I've had her friends mention to me that they hesitate to call or visit because they don't know how she's feeling. But this…" Ronnie frowned. "It would be a traffic nightmare, like the ranch's Fourth of July celebration. The ranch yard turns into a big parking lot. And it takes forever to get out when it's over." Ronnie shook her head. "Oh, it's a bad idea. Forget I said anything."

"Are you talking about scheduling visits to see

the lights?" Izzy sipped her beer. "Or creating some kind of circular drive-through like the church's nativity scene?"

"A turnabout is brilliant, Izzy." Ronnie's eyes sparkled. "Mary could be bundled up near where cars drive past. Brief well-wishes might do her good."

"Well, you get right on that, Ronnie," Izzy said flatly. "You know, if I suggest it, Chandler will shoot it down as something they *never* do."

"I'll plant the seeds with Mary and Frank." Ronnie spoke with authority, as if the roundabout Christmas Tree Lane idea was a done deal. "And then you'll work with Chandler to rearrange the ranch yard."

"As if." Izzy rolled her eyes and reached for her beer.

Zane appeared at their table, looking handsome in his dark blue shirt and fancy gray cowboy hat. "Ladies, I'm looking for a dance partner." And he was looking at Izzy, the only single woman in the booth.

"Me?" Izzy squeaked, nearly choking on her beer. "I mean, me?" she said in a deeper voice, cheeks heating as she set her beer on the table without spilling.

"Yes, you." Zane extended his hand.

Ronnie, Allison and Jo stared at Izzy with raised brows.

Izzy wanted to refuse. She shouldn't be dancing with Zane for the same reasons she shouldn't be kissing Chandler...not that any kisses had yet to occur. But still...

Beyond Zane, movement at the bar caught Izzy's eye. Chandler? When had he arrived? Regardless, he'd swung around on his barstool and was staring at her with an inscrutable look.

It's not like he's asking.

Izzy took Zane's hand, swinging her legs out with ladylike grace since she wore a silver sweater dress and her best dancing boots.

On the dance floor, Zane swept Izzy into his arms and led her in a skilled two-step. He was a strong and masterful dancer. He was handsome, with prominent cheekbones and thick, dark hair that was probably silky to the touch. But there was no tingle of attraction, no longing to inch closer or stare deeply into his eyes and try to make a soulful connection.

After a few songs, Zane escorted Izzy back to the booth and thanked her. "See you at the ranch."

And then he was gone, leaving Izzy under the scrutiny of her friends.

"Well?" Ronnie asked while Izzy sipped her beer.

Izzy shrugged. "He's a good dancer."

Ronnie leaned forward, slapping her palms on the table. "He's an excellent dancer, a real looker and a hard worker. I can't tell you how many of my matchmaking clients want to date him. He's a catch. Are you honestly telling me you felt nothing?"

"Yep." Izzy channeled Chandler's monosyllabic response.

Ronnie collapsed back in her seat with a very Ronnie-like flounce. "Girl, we need to have a conversation."

"Leave her be, Ronnie." Jo raised her beer glass to clink against Izzy's. "Even I can see there was no spark."

"Izzy." Dylan appeared at their booth. He wore a burgundy shirt with leather yoke accents and a brown felt cowboy hat. He smiled at Izzy as if she was part of his inner circle. "You up for another bit of dancing?"

"Of course she is," Ronnie said before Izzy could politely say she'd rather visit with her friends. It was, after all, girls' night out. "Tell him, Izzy."

Chandler turned her way at the bar again and Izzy felt a flare of annoyance.

Why is my dancing any of his business?

"Of course I'm up for more dancing." Izzy put her hand in Dylan's, casting a dark look at Ronnie over her shoulder as Dylan led her away. She'd much rather send Chandler a dark look but he'd already turned to say something to Chet, the handlebar-mustached bartender.

Dylan wasn't as good of a dancer as Zane. He covered too much ground, leading them quickly around and around the dance floor. But he sang along with the chorus of every song and made small talk during the verses, which was endearing. All in all, dancing with Dylan hadn't been horrible. But again, Izzy felt nothing more than the fun of the dance.

When Dylan returned Izzy to her booth, she was breathless.

"Well?" Ronnie peered at her. "Your cheeks are flushed."

"Do not matchmake," Izzy warned.

"She's sweaty, not glowing," Allison noted.

"Yep." Izzy sipped her now-warm beer. *Ugh.* She pushed it away, tugging the high neck of her silver sweater dress, trying to cool off. "I need to get going. I have a long day tomorrow and a long week ahead of me." Izzy gathered her phone in its wallet and her keys. She'd given up on purses years ago.

"Are you running away before someone else asks you to dance?" Jo asked slyly.

"She is," Allison confirmed.

"No." Izzy made a face.

Ronnie simply frowned at Izzy.

"Okay, I *am* running away." Izzy got to her feet and slid her arms into her coat. "But I also need to rest and recharge. Working two jobs is exhausting." With a wave, Izzy headed toward the door.

Only to draw up short when Chandler stepped in her path, coming off that barstool with a panther-like grace when to her he was generally more like a giraffe, given the significant differences in their height.

"Hey," he said, smiling, his jacket slung over his shoulder.

"Hey." Izzy jingled her keys in her coat pocket. "I was just heading out. I'm spent."

"Right. Me, too." Chandler stretched those long

legs and beat Izzy to the front door, sliding into his jacket with panache, as if he dressed on the run all the time. "I'll walk you out."

The cold winter air flowed over Izzy and she had the strongest urge to run past Chandler and disappear into the night. But her knees were weak and with her luck, she'd trip over the pointed tips of her best boots.

They walked into the chill.

Izzy shivered, despite her thick wool coat, and nearly stumbled.

"Careful." Chandler's hand came to rest on her hip.

There was no way she could feel the warmth of his hand through a sweater dress and a wool coat. But she did. And, unlike with Zane or Dylan, a spark lit within her, urging her to move closer, to stare up at him, to part her lips.

Instead, Izzy walked faster. Not that she could run away from Chandler's touch. He kept pace with her. As if he could take whatever she threw at him.

But could she take whatever he threw at her?

Izzy ground to a halt. Uncertain…about too many things. The giddiness of attraction wasn't supposed to strike single moms who were happy being single.

"What? What's wrong?" Chandler stopped, hand still on her hip. "This isn't your SUV."

"Chandler…" Izzy faced him, turning the long way around so that Chandler had to either drop his hand or draw her into the circle of his arms.

And wouldn't you know it? She ended up with his arms around her.

"Chandler…" she repeated, breathless and heated and hesitant.

"Izzy?"

"I…" Izzy didn't trust herself to be this close to him. She didn't trust herself to look into those brown eyes or place her palms on his chest. But somehow… She had inched closer. She was looking into his eyes. She had placed her palms on his firm chest. "I…"

And suddenly, Chandler was kissing her. He was drawing her closer, practically lifting her off the ground and into his embrace. And Izzy… She was hot and cold and lost in a moment she hadn't seen coming and didn't want to end. Because his kiss promised joined hands and whispered endearments and private jokes and weekend afternoons spent entwined on the couch watching rodeo.

And then…

As quickly as the kiss began, it was over.

Izzy's feet landed on the ground with a spine-jolting thud, as if Chandler had suddenly come to his senses just when she was giving up on hanging on to hers.

"There… That's done…" Chandler didn't move. He just let the words hang between them as if reporting a chore had been completed.

Izzy stared at Chandler with the distinct impression that he was withdrawing and building up his defenses so that fabulous kiss might never happen again.

That fabulous kiss…

That too-addictive kiss…

Already, she was open to him giving her another. But then his words came back to her.

There… That's done…

Those were the words of a man who had a unique slant on *always*. As in: *I always think one kiss is enough to test an attraction and put an end to it.*

Whereas Izzy…

Izzy *always* considered a doozy of a kiss as an avenue to a different kind of always.

I always kiss you without holding back.

We always kiss goodbye, even if you're only going to the grocery store.

Those weren't sentiments it seemed Chandler had in mind after that kiss. Which meant…

He had regrets.

"Oh no." Izzy covered her mouth with one hand, buying time as she formulated a fib. Because she could see the future at the feed store with Chandler and his regrets making things awkward year-after-year, just the way Earl had predicted. "I'm sorry. *I* shouldn't have kissed you like that."

"You?" Chandler frowned.

"How awkward when we're stuck in this situation at school," Izzy rushed on, dropping her hand. "And then there's me working at the ranch and you coming into the feed store. I must have had too much to drink. In fact, I'm just going to walk home.

Alone." Which would have been great if her boots had started moving away. But they stayed rooted where she was just in case she'd read the situation wrong.

No-no-no. I didn't read him wrong.

Even if he wasn't moving. Even if he wasn't voicing an opinion. And that was because...

"It *was* awkward, wasn't it?" she asked in a quiet tone she associated with the last six months of her marriage. And if that wasn't bad enough, Chandler still didn't answer.

Please say yes. Please say yes.

She did a mental eye roll.

Come on, Izzy. This was a colossal mistake.

Chandler said nothing. She said nothing. And neither one of them moved.

Run, feet. Run!

But Izzy was a glutton for punishment, and she wanted to gauge Chandler's reaction to her excuses, that kiss, *them.*

But none came. He was as stoic as a professional poker player.

"I guess I'll be seeing you around the ranch. Hopefully not at school. Ha ha." *Izzy, how lame!*

"I make you nervous," Chandler blurted just as Izzy was prying her right foot from the asphalt.

She stomped her boot back in place. "No?" *No?* She'd spoken the word as if it was a question. Izzy made a sound of frustration low in her throat.

"I make you nervous," Chandler said again with

more conviction, a jagged smile beginning to curl into his features.

"No!" Izzy said in a stronger voice. "Let's just forget this ever happened and go on with our lives. You can be old and predictable. I can continue prying myself out of my shell. But we'll do it separately. Isn't that what you wanted?"

Chandler's mouth worked as if he was considering and rejecting several different words.

They stared at each other in silence until laughter from inside the Buckboard drifted to them.

And then Izzy ran away, leaving her vehicle and Chandler behind her.

CHAPTER NINE

"DAD!" SAM LANDED on top of Chandler. It was Sunday morning. "Wake up."

"Oof." It took Chandler a moment to fill his lungs with air, to wrap his arms around his growing boy, to find the clock on his nightstand.

Eight o'clock. He should have been up two hours ago.

Sam rolled off Chandler, brown hair sticking up in every direction. "You never sleep in, Dad. Can we have French toast for breakfast?"

"Yep." Chandler sat up, ruing that kiss with Izzy but unable to stop thinking about it.

Was it foolish to regret something so soul-shakingly intense? *Nope. Nada.* Not even if that kiss had ignited a feeling deep inside him that said, *"You're my person, my future, my everything."* Chandler had felt that before with Stephanie. He refused to believe it a second time.

Sam is my everything. My family is my everything.

Regardless of how he'd felt, Izzy had taken the blame. And then she'd been the smart one and run away.

After which, Chandler had driven home and spent too many sleepless hours wondering what had possessed him to walk her out of the bar in the first place or put a hand on her waist in the second place or gather her close and kiss her in the third place.

It made no sense. She'd looked like she'd enjoyed dancing with Zane and Dylan. And he'd...

I was jealous.

Chandler hadn't felt jealous in years. It made no sense. He'd known Izzy for years. Overlooked her for years. And then in a span of less than forty-eight hours, she'd spoken to something inside him that had lain dormant since Stephanie broke his heart.

He should avoid Izzy. At school... In town... At the ranch...

Chandler rubbed his forehead. Ignoring her would be impossible. Smart, but impossible.

And yet, Chandler wanted to see her again. Not to hold her close and kiss her, but to look into her eyes and see what had caused this inexplicable wanting inside him.

"Dad, did you hear me?" Sam bounced at the foot of the bed.

"Nope. Say again." Chandler rolled out of bed, brain kicking into gear. He had to check on stock and get ready for church.

"If we had a puppy, we'd both be up early." Sam leaped toward Chandler, who caught him midair and swung him to the floor. "Dogs are like roosters. *Bark-a-doodle-doo!*"

"I don't need a puppy to wake me up. I have you." Chandler opened his closet. But instead of seeing his options to choose for church, he saw Izzy's face after he'd kissed her. There was that brief moment when she'd looked entirely...blissful. *"Crud."*

"What's wrong, Dad?"

Besides Izzy disrupting his every waking moment? "We're going to be late for church. Go shower and get dressed."

Instead of moving, Sam's jaw dropped. "But what about French toast?"

Chandler did a quick calculation. "Breakfast. No shower. Let's move it, cowboy."

And surprisingly, his son did.

"CAN I PUT a pair of bunnies on Christmas layaway?"

"Nope." Izzy was cranky Sunday morning. And Evie Grace wasn't one of her favorite people on the best of days.

"It says you have layaway." Evie pointed to a sign behind Izzy. Her nails were painted red and white like candy canes. Her blond hair was up in a full ponytail tied with a sparkly ribbon that looked like tinsel. She wore skinny jeans and a navy sweater that had a line of dancing elves along the hem and cuffs.

In Izzy's opinion, Evie was the epitome of holiday cuteness and although she hadn't been at the Buckboard, Evie should have been the object of Chandler's kiss last night.

Ugh. Just the thought of Chandler kissing another woman annoyed Izzy on too many levels to track. Add that to Evie's unnecessary request about layaway... And wow. Izzy's annoyance increased exponentially. "Evie, the small print says your purchase needs to be fifty dollars or more. Two baby bunnies aren't going to cost you more than twenty."

Evie huffed. "I suppose I'm going to need a cage. How much is that?"

"A small cage will get you up to forty," Izzy said evenly, and not without some satisfaction. Last year, Evie had tried to win the baking contest at the county fair by buying up all the peaches in the area so no one else could make peach anything, including Allison. A girl had to stick by their friends.

"And with bunny food it will be...?" Evie pouted and waited as if that got her what she wanted, usually.

Izzy did a quick calculation. "A large bag should get you to around sixty." Ten dollars over the minimum for layaway.

Evie rolled her eyes. "I don't want to spend sixty dollars on my nephew for Christmas."

"The bunnies are for Pete?" Izzy liked the boy. His exuberant dancing in the school choir was contagious, always bringing a smile to her face. Pete and his granddad came in most Sundays after church to buy dog treats for his aging Saint Bernard, during which time Pete talked nonstop.

"Don't you have discount rabbits?" Evie was nothing if not a cheapskate when it came to spending on someone else. Another reason not to like her.

"Only the stuffed rabbits are discounted. Buy two, get one free." Izzy could have left it at that. But it was the Christmas season and Evie was shopping for Pete, after all. "Do you know what he'd really like, Evie? Pete would love one of those big dog toys we have in the pet aisle for your dad's dog, Thurman."

"Double bonus. Dad and Pete." Evie dashed toward the pet aisle to the closing chords of "Grandma Got Run Over by a Reindeer."

"Merry Christmas," Izzy mumbled. She glanced around the store to see where she was needed.

Since Clementine was so small, the feed store stocked a wide variety of goods. On weekdays the store was filled with ranchers needing feed and building supplies. Afternoons and evenings brought parents swinging by for an item or two as they ran other errands. Saturdays and Sundays were for families and shoppers who had a need for something they couldn't find elsewhere. But in December, folks came in on all days and at all hours to find useful gifts.

A few customers were browsing the clothing racks, looking happy to do so unassisted. Earl was helping a sturdy-looking cowboy find a pair of boots that fit his feet and budget. Stephanie Cochran, Chandler's ex, had looped her way around the aisle with the basics in underthings and feminine care. She looked frustrated.

Izzy came out from around the sales counter. "Hey, Stephanie. Can I help you find something?"

"Oh... I..." The tall brunette folded a paper, cheeks pinkening. "Honestly, Izzy. I think I'm going to have to head over to Friar's Creek."

Izzy had always liked Stephanie. She delivered the mail to downtown businesses during the week and often stopped by for a quick chat or to refill her water bottle.

Sensing a sensitive topic, Izzy came closer to the woman. "Tell me what you're looking for."

Stephanie sighed. "Compression pantyhose."

"Compression pantyhose? Not socks?" Izzy considered other options for Stephanie. "Doc Nabidian would have compression socks for sale at his office. And the drugstore has support pantyhose."

Stephanie shook her head, biting her lower lip. "I've been offered a job that requires compression pantyhose. I was curious as to how much they cost."

Izzy's curiosity was piqued. Compression wear was for athletes, old or sick people and those who flew often. Izzy ran through the possibilities when it came to Stephanie. "Do you have your pilot's license? I heard the crop duster company in town is looking for a pilot." Flying was the only job Izzy could think of that required compression wear.

Stephanie smiled, a joyous, secretive smile. "The job is as a flight attendant," she whispered.

"Oh, wow. Congratulations." But her confession only gave rise to more questions. "Is this at a commuter airport locally?" Although Izzy couldn't think of any nearby.

"Well, I haven't actually accepted yet, so I shouldn't say," Stephanie admitted. "And the list of things I need to buy beforehand is daunting. Not to mention, compression pantyhose sound..."

"Uncomfortable." Izzy nodded, adding quickly, "But safe."

"Right? But... What am I thinking?" Stephanie laughed self-consciously, gesturing toward herself. "Do I look like I'm cut out to be a flight attendant?" She wore a white hoodie, a pair of blue jeans and sneakers. Her brown hair was in a messy ponytail on top of her head. She looked like a mom out running errands.

"Put you in a uniform with those compression hose and you would absolutely pass as a flight attendant." Izzy didn't mention the hair. She figured Stephanie knew that would have to be spruced up, too.

"You always brighten my day." Stephanie wrapped her arms around Izzy and gave her a warm hug. "Thank you."

It was a quick hug and Izzy ended it by saying, "I think you need to take that list and shop online for this new job of yours."

"I hope I didn't hear the *O* word," Earl called

from the boot department, voice carrying over a country version of "Silent Night." "I taught you better than that, Izzy Adams. We can order whatever you need, Stephanie."

"Thanks, Earl but… No, thanks." Stephanie headed toward the door, walking backward. And she walked right into Chandler.

How long had he been standing there?

"Oh. Hey," Stephanie said to him, blushing furiously. "Didn't see you there."

"Hi, Mom. Bye, Mom." Sam raced around Stephanie and toward Izzy. He had on his church clothes. "Is Della-Mae here?"

"Not yet. She was at a sleepover." Izzy adjusted Sam's cowboy hat, which was about to fall off.

When she glanced up, both Chandler and Stephanie were looking their way.

And Chandler's hand was on Stephanie's arm.

Izzy HAD BEEN hugging Steph.

And Izzy had told Stephanie to shop online for *"that new job of yours."*

Chandler had stopped by the feed store at Sam's insistence, telling himself it was best to rip off the bandage and get this first post-kiss meeting over with, never expecting to find Stephanie or overhearing that his ex-wife was leaving town. Talk about adding fuel to an already tense fire.

"Steph." Chandler's hand somehow found his ex-wife's arm without him taking his eyes off the woman he'd kissed last night. "Is there something you need to tell me?" He almost didn't recognize his own voice. It had a cold, defensive quality in it that he hadn't used in years.

Because of change and uncertainty.

There was safety in the status quo. But the very wood beneath his cowboy boots felt unsteady.

Because of potential moves and unforeseen mischief and knee-knocking kisses.

Admittedly, the latter had been his doing, but the rest... What had gotten into everyone around him? Mom... Sam... Steph... Izzy...

I have to keep everything under control. I am the rock here.

The peacekeeper. The problem-solver. The cowboy who was steady in a crisis.

"Nothing's been decided, Chandler." Steph shifted away from him, and Chandler's hand dropped away. "You'll be among the first to know when I make a decision." But she didn't leave.

Chandler spared Stephanie a glance. She was staring toward Sam with her heart in her eyes. With *regret* in her eyes.

She was planning to leave, all right. Chandler's shoulders tensed. Perhaps fittingly, Elvis's "Blue Christmas" began to play over the store's speaker system.

"But Della-Mae told me she'd be here this morning," Sam was saying to Izzy, whining a little. "She told me we'd look at the bulletin board with puppies."

No.

"Puppies?" Stephanie breathed the word with animosity. Her attention shifted to Chandler and her mood to anger. "You thought a puppy would make me stay?"

"Nope." Chandler tipped his hat to Steph and then joined Sam in front of Izzy, vaguely registering his ex-wife leaving. "What's this I hear about a puppy board, Sam? Is this one of Della-Mae's *ideas*?"

"*Dad.*" Sam tapped his chest. "Puppies are my idea."

Chandler grunted, not believing him. His gaze drifted toward Izzy. He'd been hoping that seeing her in her usual feed store setting and garb— cowboy hat, gray Clementine Feed hoodie, blue jeans and boots—would vanquish his fascination with her.

He took a good long look. Gone were the perky Christmas sweaters and the cheerful, bouncing headbands. No antlers. No jingle-jingle. No garland or tinsel. And yet, he could still feel her kitschy Christmas cheer. He could still feel the near-tangible attraction. He could still feel the magnetic pull of *her*.

Crud.

Was it because he knew how she kissed? Or that he wanted to kiss her again? He suspected both were true.

Double crud.

Chandler wasn't supposed to be mesmerized by a female at his age. That was a teenage boy's purview. He hadn't searched for this. He hadn't asked for this. Like everything else in his life lately, Izzy made Chandler feel unsure of the outcome. Doubts about the future were why he'd never been a good rodeo competitor. There were too many variables outside his control—a bull with a bee in his bonnet, a steer that zagged when a rope was thrown, a balking horse spooked by a rowdy crowd.

The tension had taken hold of Chandler's neck now, too. He'd worked himself into a snippy mood. Yep, good and proper. And now, he needed something to reverse that mood.

Kisses?

He averted his gaze from Izzy, rejecting that notion.

Puppies?

He averted his gaze from Sam, rejecting that notion, as well.

"What a good friend you are, Sam." Izzy gave him a candy cane from a Santa mug on the sales counter. "I'm proud of you for admitting puppies were *your* idea."

"Dad always says I'm a good boy." Sam performed a goofy dance, kicking up his heels and waving his candy cane.

"Almost always," Chandler murmured.

"Even good boys get into mischief sometimes." Izzy tipped back her cowboy hat, a grin forming on those delicate features of hers. A grin directed at Chandler, inviting him to let go.

Chandler was focused on Izzy's cowboy hat instead. He couldn't remember her riding a horse, even during Santapalooza. And yet, she always wore a cowboy hat and boots.

Izzy's grin widened. "Sam, aren't you lucky that you're in the same class as your best friend? You'd never want to switch classrooms, would you?"

Chandler's mouth dropped open. Izzy wasn't respecting his wishes. This woman… She… She didn't understand how important it was to keep the peace. She didn't supervise scores of cowboys with erratic pasts and varying levels of ego. She didn't manage hundreds of stock. She didn't realize it was best to head things off at the pass early, to keep everything and everyone on the same even keel.

The number of cowboy terms floating in Chandler's head didn't escape his notice. Cowboying was ingrained in Chandler. *Herd first* when making ranch decisions. *Family first* when making life decisions.

The cowboy way…

Perhaps that was why Izzy didn't understand those two kids of theirs needed separation. She lived in town. She worked at a feed store. She may wear cowboy boots and a cowboy hat as if she was familiar with the cowboy way. But she didn't know.

"I am lucky to have my best friend with me all day." Still dancing, Sam beamed up at Izzy as if her opinion mattered most. Her opinion, not Chandler's.

That was the last straw. Chandler couldn't rein

in his frustration any longer. "Izzy, have you ever owned a horse?"

"Me?" Izzy's smile fell. Around these parts, questioning someone's Western legitimacy was like tossing down a gauntlet. "I had a horse when I lived with my dad. But he sold A.J. before he left town. Are you... Are you questioning my cowgirlness?"

"Are you two fighting?" Sam stopped dancing.

"No, honey," Izzy was quick to reassure Chandler's son. "We're talking about the cowboy code."

"Oh." Sam shifted his cowboy hat to a jaunty angle on his head. And then, he recited, "Every cowboy needs a hat, a horse and a dog."

"And an understanding of how to manage a herd," Chandler said, still frustratingly unsettled because this slip of a woman had somehow managed to trot into his life, bells ringing, and upended his quiet, orderly, predictable existence. Even now, just meeting her unflinching gaze made him want to...want to...

Kiss her again. Longer this time.

Chandler scoffed and shifted his feet on the wide wooden planks beneath him. *"Cowgirlness."* He frowned. "Is that a word? Is it from one of those old books you read?"

"Answer my question," Izzy demanded softly, chin rising. "Are you saying you're more of a cowboy than I am? That just because I don't currently own a horse that I have no right to wear cowboy boots and a cowboy hat?"

"You are fighting." Sam righted his cowboy hat. "That's not good."

"He started it," Izzy murmured.

"Dad," Sam chastised in a big-boy tone of voice. "If you hurt someone's feelings, you have to say sorry."

"That's very wise," Izzy told Sam. "You must have lots of friends at school."

Sam bobbed his head. "Sometimes stuff happens that's an accident. And I always say sorry." His clear brown eyes found Chandler's. "That's why I have lots and lots of friends. Just like my dad."

Chandler had been backed into a corner by his own testiness. "I'm sorry," he mumbled, not feeling remorseful but needing to do the right thing when his son was watching.

"You're not sorry," Izzy said, peering at him with those big blue eyes.

Sam gasped. *"Miz Izzy!"* He called her out the same way he did Chandler.

Izzy rushed on to explain. "I mean, your dad is probably sorry if he hurt my feelings, but he looks like someone put too much wood in his fire and he needs to blow some smoke."

Sam looked confused.

Chandler felt humbled. "Well, now I am truly sorry."

Someone came through the front door and said in a small voice, "Hey, everybody."

"Della-Mae!" Sam ran toward the front of the store to greet his bestie, who wore the same red outfit she'd had on yesterday and carried a backpack, sleeping bag and pillow. "I'm here, Della-Mae! And look. My dad's here, too. With your mom."

"All present and accounted for," Izzy said softly enough that only Chandler would hear. "Including the cranky kissing bandit."

Chandler choked on a laugh, dark mood taken down another notch. He was discovering that Izzy had the power to drag him—or prod him—out of his funks.

While the kids were wrestling with Della-Mae's stuff, he leaned over to say to Izzy, "Will you forgive me if I admit that I woke up on the wrong side of the bed this morning? I was confused about what happened last night, and then I walked in to hear my ex-wife talking to you about a job that will take her away from Sam. And I... I let myself get overwhelmed."

"And you got cranky." Izzy tsked, looking like she was fighting a hint of a smile. "When I get overwhelmed, I panic."

"Good to know." Chandler straightened. "Should we start the day over? You can still call me a miserabilist if it makes you feel better."

"My day starts with coffee and chocolate." Izzy waggled her finger. "That's the only way to earn a do-over."

"I'm taking notes," Chandler promised. "Coffee and chocolate." He plucked a bar of chocolate from a nearby display and handed it to her. "My treat."

"You're impossible," Izzy muttered, but she accepted the bar.

Sam towed Izzy's daughter forward, dragging her sleeping bag, which had unrolled, across the floor.

"Are you here to buy something?" Della-Mae asked, looking at Chandler with a tired yet hopeful expression.

"We're here to see you!" Sam crowed in answer, dropping the unrolled sleeping bag and bouncing around like a bunny on a sunny spring day.

"Tone it down, squirt." Chandler scooped up the sleeping bag and began rolling it up neatly.

"What are you here to buy, Mr. Cochran?" Della-Mae asked, less hopefully, looking at her mother this time.

Chandler's mischief radar kicked on. There was something going on here. He studied the faces of the two kids, searching for clues the way he did when something hinky was going on with his ranch hands.

"What's this all about, bug?" Izzy asked, kneeling in front of Della-Mae, perhaps having suspicions of her own.

Della-Mae stared at Chandler over Izzy's shoulder, lower lip starting a pout.

"Just say it, Dad." Sam tugged on Chandler's hand. "Tell Della-Mae why we came."

"To see you," he said in a gruff voice, barely stopping himself from saying it like it was a guess. But it was.

Della-Mae threw herself into Izzy's arms. And then she hugged Chandler's leg and said, "Merry Christmas, Mr. Cochran!"

Chandler's gaze sought out Izzy's, looking for answers.

She shrugged, apparently having none. And before he could interrogate the kids, they were interrupted.

"Hey, Izzy. Can you ring up Kevin's boots?" Earl dropped a boot box on the sales counter. The old man wore a black denim vest with the Clementine Feed logo over his blue flannel shirt. He tipped his black porkpie hat at the young boot buyer. "Thanks for coming in." He clapped his hands and caught the children's attention. "While Izzy rings him up, I'll show the kids the puppy board."

"Puppies," Chandler murmured. And then he plucked Sam's small cowboy hat off his head. "Do we really need one, Sam?"

"Dad..." Sam didn't qualify the issue. He simply took back his hat.

Evie Grace stepped into line behind Kevin, holding a large blue dog toy.

"Earl..." Izzy picked up her daughter's sleepover stuff, then returned to her position behind the register. She smiled brightly at the cowboy purchasing boots, but her words were for her boss. "Earl, I'm not getting a dog."

"Me, either," Chandler echoed.

"Every cowboy needs a horse and a dog," Earl

said in a preachy tone. "Along with boots and a hat. Everybody knows that's a law in Oklahoma."

"If that were true..." Izzy scoffed, catching Chandler's gaze. "It must be why Chandler doubted my cowgirlness."

"I deserved that," Chandler admitted, trailing after the kids.

"You certainly did," Izzy said tartly but with a hint of a tease.

Chandler followed Earl and the kids into the room behind the sales counter, which was the break room. There was an office on one side with a desk cluttered with papers. A glass-paned door revealed the large warehouse crammed with goods—bags of feed, bales of hay, red-and-white metal posts, stacks of boxes and rolls of wire.

"Folks from around these parts email us their puppy litter pictures." Earl's hair was going white and his shoulders were bent with age, but his voice was as steely as ever. "We print them out and tack them up here. They bring the staff joy."

"And puppies presumably," Chandler said under his breath, earning a dark look from Earl.

The break room smelled of green hay and popcorn. There was an old oak table in the middle with four ladder-back chairs. The floor was clean, and the light was bright. A bulletin board was hung on the wall next to a nearly full coffeepot.

Smelling fresh brew, Chandler poured himself a cup while the kids perused the board.

"Mr. Earl, we're looking for a puppy family."

Sam pushed a chair over to the board and then climbed upon it.

"A brother and sister, Uncle Earl," Della-Mae clarified, lifting her arms to Chandler...kid speak for *pick me up*.

Chandler set his coffee mug down and lifted her to his hip. "We're just window-shopping, Earl."

"It's Christmas," Earl grumbled. "Are you or aren't you a cowboy in need of a dog?"

"He's a cowboy." Della-Mae poked Chandler's chest. Then she leaned over and patted Sam's hat crown, trusting Chandler not to drop her. "And he's a cowboy. And someday, I'll be a cowboy, too." She slung her little arm around his shoulders.

"Cowgirl," Chandler corrected. His heart warmed. No matter how he wished otherwise, Della-Mae didn't seem like the instigator of school mischief, not that he'd admit it to Izzy so quickly.

"What about me?" Earl asked Della-Mae in the gentlest tone Chandler had ever heard him use.

"And you're a cowboy, too." Della-Mae reached over to pat his gray-stubbled cheeks with both hands. "Even though your horse is retired, Gator crossed the rainbow bridge and you wear a funny hat."

"Do you have kids, Earl?" Sam studied the old man from head to toe.

"I've got Izzy and Della-Mae," Earl said by way of answering. "They're going to run the feed store one day."

"Mama and me run it already," Della-Mae showed a little sass that her mother would probably be tickled to see. "I feed all the baby chicks and bunnies. And Mama does everything else."

"I suppose you're right," Earl told her with a wink. And then he fixed Chandler with a threatening look. "But I'll deny it if you tell anyone else in town. I've got my pride, you know."

"Dad won't tell no one," Sam promised.

"Cuz he likes Mama." Della-Mae hugged Chandler.

And darned if Chandler's heart didn't melt again. So much so that he felt a reluctance to refuse Della-Mae anything. And she wasn't even his kid!

Earl harumphed in a way that could only be taken as disapproval over Chandler's liking of Izzy.

And even though Chandler didn't want to like Izzy, he resented Earl's reaction.

With one last disapproving look at Chandler, the old man cleared his throat. "Back to the business at hand, folks. And that's—"

"Puppies!" the kids cried.

"Yes, sirree. There's a litter of terrier puppies over in Friar's Creek." Earl pointed to a picture of scruffy little brown pups tumbling across green grass.

"That's what ranchers call a coyote snack," Chandler stated as the kids cooed over the pups and their cuteness.

Earl scowled at Chandler, but allowed, "Point taken. We need something bigger."

Sam gasped, slapping his hand on a picture of roly-poly puppies. "Are these Labradors?"

"The doodly kind." Earl nodded, rubbing a hand over gray stubble. "Pricey, if you ask me. Are you allergic to pet dander?"

"What's that?" Sam asked.

"He's not." Chandler adopted his most serious expression. "But we're just looking."

"My Della-Mae isn't allergic, either," Earl said, taking the girl from Chandler. "I'm partial to a hunting dog, though."

"We don't hunt," Chandler grumbled.

"Hunting dogs are smart. Short-haired don't shed a blanket of hair every week," Earl continued. "Got this picture of some German shorthair pups from a breeder just over the county line. What do you think, sweet thing?" he asked Della-Mae.

She examined the picture with a serious expression while twirling a lock of white-blond hair. "Do they have girl pups?"

"Might," Earl said.

"What about boys?" Sam leaned in for a close look, practically pressing his nose on the picture.

"Might," Earl repeated.

"Are they free?" Chandler wondered aloud, thinking of Izzy saving for her daughter's fancy bed.

Sam gasped, turning on the chair and losing his balance. He would have fallen if not for Chandler grabbing hold of his arm. "Dad, can we have a puppy if it's free?"

"Now isn't the right time of year to bring a pup home." Chandler tried to evade, shifting his feet on the old floorboards. "They say puppies are more likely to be hurt at Christmas, choking on chewed bows and glass ornaments because they don't know any better."

"Even the Grinch had a dog." Frowning, Earl pointed out another photograph. "Here are some cocker spaniels."

"They look like Lady," Della-Mae whispered. "I love that movie. Lady falls in love with the Tramp."

Sam didn't look impressed, possibly because his taste in movies ran more toward cartoon superheroes.

"Earl." Izzy stuck her head in the break room. "No dogs."

"Amen," Chandler echoed.

"Oh, man." Sam looked at Della-Mae. "We're in trouble. What moms say goes." And Izzy wasn't even his mother.

"Have a heart, Izzy," Earl called toward the now-closed door. "We could use a dog at the feed store."

"A pretty dog?" Della-Mae asked sweetly.

"Any kind of dog you want, Della-Mae." Earl chuckled. "We'll find the right dog for you. Just don't tell your mother I said that."

Sam set his finger on the picture of Labradoodle puppies, then pouted at Chandler. "If Della-Mae gets a puppy, I want one, too."

A SMALL, FAMILIAR body took hold of Izzy's leg as she was helping Dix Youngblood select outdoor extension cords.

"Mama. Mr. Cochran said no to Lady and Tramp. But Uncle Earl said—"

"Bug, I told you we aren't getting a dog. We have chickens." She gave Dix an apologetic smile. "Do you need anything else, Dix? Replacement light bulbs? Maybe a star made of lights for your front window?"

"Just the extension cords." Dix knelt to her daughter's level. "Don't give up on a puppy, Della-Mae. Santa Claus is coming to town."

"But I didn't ask Santa for a puppy," Della-Mae moaned.

"What did you ask for?" Izzy was curious but her daughter pressed her lips together and ran toward the back of the store.

Dix stood, grinning. "Now, Izzy. You know that requests for Santa are secret."

"Thanks, Dix," Izzy said dryly. "But that works both ways. Better watch out if you bring your littles into the store. I may show them the adorable baby bunnies." She rang him up and sent him on his way, nose still bent out of shape. *"Puppies."*

Della-Mae and Sam were playing checkers at the small table behind the sales counter, debating the merits of different pups, as if they were indeed getting a pair.

"Izzy, can I talk to you?" Chandler had been leaning against the wall near the break room while she was busy with Dix. He pushed away, staring at her in that manner of his that she couldn't read.

Apprehension skittered through Izzy's veins as

if she was the one who didn't like surprises, not Chandler. She needed to draw some boundaries. There would be no more kisses. She was banning them along with puppies.

"Why are you still here? I'm working," Izzy told Chandler, moving into the boot department and away from their kids. "If you placed a call asking about puppy availability, I'm going to go all Scrooge on you."

"This isn't about puppies." His gaze grazed her mouth.

And suddenly, the powerful kiss they'd shared the night before was top-of-mind. Izzy lost some of her bluster. *Evade. Evade.* And tried to emotionally regroup. Her chin came up. "Do you finally agree with me that the kids shouldn't be separated at school?"

Chandler shook his head. "Earlier... When we came in... Stephanie was saying something to you about a new job?" He wasn't looking Izzy in the eye. He straightened out a display of boots.

Chandler wanted to know about his ex-wife? Not their kiss? That was a relief, although Izzy wasn't going to blab.

"Chandler..." Izzy began. "If you have questions and you're feeling overwhelmed, you should ask Stephanie. She was excited and seemed like she really wanted to talk to someone about her job."

He gave a barely perceptible nod.

"Izzy, do we have any inflatable Santas left in

the back room?" Earl called from the front of the store.

"We're sold out," she called back. "We still have abominable snowmen, though." And then she placed a hand on Chandler's arm, just a brief touch before his gaze moved to it. She removed her hand and took a step back. "I know you're not a chatterbox. But I imagine you're a good listener. Listen to her."

Actually, that was Izzy's new hope—that Chandler preferred listening to speaking. A talker would ask about that kiss. Over and over until he got answers. And the last thing Izzy wanted to do was talk that through. She couldn't even think it through on her own. How was she supposed to put it into words?

"I did listen to her." Chandler straightened more boots on display. "She told me she was thinking about taking a job in Texas. And..." His gaze drifted in the direction of his son. "If she took the job in Texas, does that mean she wants to take Sam, too? In which case, I need to assert my parental rights. Or is she taking the job and leaving Sam behind, in which case... He'll be crushed."

The way I was when Dad left me. And I was an adult.

"I'm sorry. I hadn't realized the implications to Sam," Izzy said sympathetically. For a man who didn't like change, Stephanie's decisions had a huge impact on Chandler. "No wonder you're worried. If you ever want to talk, I'm good at listening."

Chandler glanced at her hand on his arm again.

Izzy quickly removed it. "How did that get there?"

"That's what I wondered, too…" Chandler murmured, gaze moving from his hands to Izzy's lips. "…when *I* kissed you."

"Oh, no. You're not allowed to take the blame." Izzy backpedaled, practically leaping away from him and toward the corner of the store.

Chandler matched her step-for-step, a smile growing on that attractive face. "Maybe we're both to blame."

Izzy scoffed, coming to a stop with her back to a display of hat and boot bands. She grabbed a leather hatband with a peacock feather decoration, holding it in front of her like a shield. Although that might have been hypocritical because she was taking inventory of Chandler's lips.

He had a wide mouth, well-suited for smiling. And he was clean-shaven, well-suited for prolonged kisses. And unlike other times he'd been in the feed store, he wasn't looking distant and distracted.

It's been a long time since a man has looked at me like that.

"Dad, I'm hungry," Sam called.

"Me, too," Mae seconded.

"Me, three," Chandler said softly, although it was clear to Izzy that he wasn't hungry for food but for kisses.

Izzy couldn't catch her breath.

"Dad?"

"Mama?"

Chandler took the hatband from Izzy and returned it to the display. "There's something going on between us but…" He looked deep into her eyes. "… I'm not looking for something."

"Me, either," Izzy wheezed.

Chandler turned and walked away.

But she was afraid whatever this was between them wasn't over yet.

CHAPTER TEN

"UNCLE CHANDLER, we have to stop at Clementine Coffee Roasters for hot chocolate," Ginny said from the back seat of Chandler's truck on Monday after school. "I have coupons. Buy one hot chocolate and get one free. That covers me and Sam. Right, buddy?"

"Right," Sam piped up.

Chandler was hoping to head back to the ranch to work on the new year's rodeo schedule. Requests were already coming in from rodeos to provide them with stock for their events. It was a balancing act since Chandler had to make sure he didn't overpromise and be short on bucking bulls or roping steers or underbook and have stock sitting idle.

Chandler inched forward in the slow-moving pickup line without seeing Izzy's blue-gray SUV, either in front of him or behind him.

Not that I'm looking.

After seeing Izzy at the feed store yesterday and confessing that he felt something pulling him into her orbit, and also stating that he was going to resist that pull, Chandler planned to give the woman a wide berth.

If only he didn't keep having conversations with her in his head.

I'm going to a rodeo in Denver this spring. The wildflowers will be in bloom. Have you ever seen them? Would you like to?

Romantic nonsense. Chandler had better things to do with his brain cells than to think about Izzy.

"Can we stop, Dad?" Sam sat behind Chandler, repeatedly tossing his cowboy hat to the ceiling. "I heard a lot of kids are going to use their coupons."

"Which means it's going to be crowded and take a long time." The Grinch was back, sitting on Chandler's shoulder.

What would Izzy think of me ixnaying hot cocoa?

"You're something, all right," she'd told him Saturday.

For his own peace of mind, Chandler had to get Izzy out of his head.

Chandler sighed. "I suppose since you didn't get called into the principal's office today that we can stop for hot chocolate."

"Yay!" Sam cried, high-fiving Ginny. And then he tossed his cowboy hat too enthusiastically. It bumped against Chandler's hat and then ricocheted into the front seat. "Oops. Sorry, Dad."

"Not cool or safe." Chandler made the turn toward the center of town, not looking for a blue-gray SUV or white-blond hair with antlers floating above. "Now, just so we're clear. We're not staying to drink our hot chocolate. It's to-go." The stress of scheduling pressed on him but he'd give the kids this special treat.

Chandler found a parking spot on the street a block away. "Sam, cowboy hats aren't for tossing," he told his son before plopping the stray hat back on Sam's head.

Sam pulled down the brim on either side of his ears. "My hat is for everything."

"Your hat will be in the trash bin if you don't take care of it." Ginny gently pried Sam's hands clear. "My dad says cowboy hats don't grow on trees."

Chandler chuckled. "He told you that after yours was chewed on by those goats, Ginny."

"There was nothing left!" Ginny settled her straw cowboy hat more firmly over her brown braids. And then she stuffed her hands back into her pink puffy vest, which was the same color as her pink boots. "A cowgirl has to have a hat."

Sam made a go of jumping over all the cracks in the sidewalk. "I'm so glad Ginny had a cocoa coupon."

"I got them from Mom." Ginny slowed to check out the merchandise in the local boutique's window.

There were lots of holiday doodads on display, including a snow globe with a music box base, which made Chandler want to think of Izzy. But he refused to think of Izzy.

Even when Sam asked, "Can we get a Christmas tree today?"

Nope. Chandler did not think of Izzy.

Because I'm a man in control of my own destiny.

"This week is kind of busy, squirt," Chandler told Sam, thinking that at some point, he'd have to pull himself out of the divorce funk, haul up his anchor and put up Christmas at the house. "We'll do it soon."

"That's what my dad says when he doesn't want to do something ever," Ginny quipped. "I could decorate for you, Uncle Chandler. Me and Mama Ronnie already put up our decorations."

"That's kind of you to offer, but no thanks."

"You could pay me." Ginny was just as industrious as Ronnie. Or Izzy for that matter. "Mama Ronnie said I'm old enough to babysit and get paid for doing other stuff, too."

"I bet you are, but I've got to clean and move furniture around first," Chandler said.

"I could clean," Sam said, stepping over Ginny trying to say the same thing.

"It's just something I've got to do myself," Chandler said, more firmly this time.

The two kids looked at each other and exchanged shrugs. They were too young to understand that it was the past holding Chandler back, not cleaning or furniture moving. Still, his reluctance to leap into Christmas with an eager embrace made him feel sullen. Something had to be done. And he was the only one able to do it.

When they reached the coffee shop, Chandler opened the door to let the kids in first, and spotted Izzy, Christmas personified, in line with her daughter.

I've been set up. By two kids, no less.

But Chandler didn't feel as grumpy and stressed for time as he had a minute ago.

He'd like to attribute that to the wreath with bells on the front door or the decorated Christmas tree by the front window. But he was afraid that he knew the truth behind this cheerier mood.

And his truth had hair the color of tinsel.

"Della-Mae!" Sam sprinted to the little girl's side, as much as a gangly boy in cowboy boots could sprint. "We're here, too!"

The pair hugged. Ginny joined them in line, laughing and whispering, as if she was in on the joke.

Chandler mostly ignored them. He drank in Christmas Izzy. She'd changed out of the feed store garb he'd seen her in this morning. Now, she wore gray jeans beneath a red-and-white-striped sweater, topped with red-and-white-striped earmuffs, currently hanging around her neck. "Miss Candy Cane, fancy meeting you here."

Izzy wore a quizzical expression where he'd come to expect a smile.

"Did you have a coupon for a free hot chocolate, too?" Chandler asked, giving Ginny—who was clearly up to something—a stern look.

Course, it couldn't be too stern of a look.

Chandler didn't go telling the world, but he was fond of candy canes, especially life-size ones. That may have explained why his stern expression had been broken apart by what felt like a broad smile. For Izzy.

"We have a coupon, too," Izzy confirmed. She glanced at Sam and Della-Mae. "Did you two plan this?"

"No," the younger kids chorused innocently.

But Ginny... Ginny didn't wear guilty well. She blushed furiously.

"Yep, there's nothing for it, I guess, but to..." Chandler glanced toward the exit, hoping to make the kids suffer a little by making them think they were leaving empty-handed. And then he tilted the brim of his cowboy hat back and grinned. "There's nothing for it but to get our hot cocoas."

The kids cheered.

And truth be told, Chandler was cheering a little inside, too. So much so, that he allowed himself to be talked into drinking their hot chocolate with Izzy and Della-Mae instead of taking it to go.

"WHY ARE WE sitting at this little table *alone*?" Izzy asked Chandler, torn between enjoying herself and being a grump because there was matchmaking in the air but no Ronnie around to blame it on. "And why are the kids sitting way up at the front without us?"

"We're suckers." Chandler shrugged, but he was smiling a smidge, like a man who'd surrendered to his fate and found it wasn't horrible. "Didn't you take a good look at those drink coupons? On the bottom, mine said, '*Complements of Ronnie Keller, Matchmaker.*'"

"You think this was Ronnie's doing?" Izzy tossed and turned that idea around in her head for a minute, staring into Chandler's warm brown eyes as if she had a right to. "Did *you* hire Ronnie?"

"Me?" Chandler chuckled. "I did not. And I can't imagine you did, either. You'd have told me this morning when I picked up my feed order if you'd hired her. I hear her clients go out of their way to make small talk."

"So your theory about the drink coupons is…"

"Oh, Ginny took them. No question." Chandler glanced at the kids as the opening verse of "The Twelve Days of Christmas" filled the coffee shop.

"Have you ever sung this song?" Izzy wondered aloud.

He quirked a brow. "What kid hasn't belted out the five golden rings part?"

"There are eleven more gifts to sing about."

"No one remembers gifts seven through ten." Chandler slowly spun his hot chocolate cup. "I bet you another kiss that our kids will sing the line about the gold rings in a minute. And *only* the line about those gold rings."

What a tempting bet. Izzy chewed her lip. "Are you…?" She leaned forward, filled with suspicion. "Are you sure Ronnie didn't put you up to this?"

"Ronnie has nothing to do with this conversation and…" Chandler held a finger in the air and sang along with every kid in the room, *"Five golden rings!"*

He had a strong singing voice. Deep and rich. And that smile…

"You owe me a kiss," Chandler whispered, smiling in a way that made kissing him seem as natural as breathing.

"I never agreed…" Izzy trailed off when Chandler laughed. She slapped a hand on her forehead.

He laughed some more.

"That's not fair." She was the one trying to come out of her shell and here Chandler was *outshelling* her. A week ago, she'd never have imagined him laughing so freely with her, singing in a place that wasn't church or kissing a woman he barely knew with complete and utter abandon.

Izzy tugged at the neck of her candy-cane-striped sweater and tried to make small talk. "I decorated Harper Dye's place before picking up Mae from school today. Harper is going through a Christmas gnome phase. But she hasn't quite let go of her white turtledove phase. I think we hit the right balance in her living room."

"Of gnomes and turtledoves?" None of the amusement had drained from his face.

She nodded, still fighting the urge to accept his kisses in her future. Kisses—plural—promised things. Dates—casual, formal, legal. A Saturday night dinner, a big wedding, a wedding certificate. Izzy shook her head at her thoughts. "How was your day?"

"We're tabling bets?"

"Yes," she said nervously, still thrown by thoughts of dates and marriage.

"Okay. I'll play along," Chandler capitulated. "I've got a crick in my neck from bending over the computer." Chandler rubbed a hand around the back of his neck. "I was trying to figure out the schedule for the new year, but Dad kept interrupting me."

"Earl does the same when I'm trying to manage our inventory." Izzy sipped her hot chocolate.

"Five golden rings!" the kids chorused.

"You missed that one," Izzy couldn't resist teasing Chandler.

"I was thinking about…" Chandler stared into her eyes without speaking, as if he'd lost his train of thought. "Truth be told, I was thinking about checking in with Ronnie when I got back to the ranch. And that made me think of Wade, who's flying out tomorrow to compete at the national championships in Las Vegas. And that reminded me to check in with our ranch hands who're transporting a couple of our bulls to that competition. And that had me wondering how I was going to have time to work rodeos in person next year if Stephanie takes that job and I have custody of Sam every week." He sat back with a defeated sigh.

And here Izzy had imagined he'd been lost in romantic thoughts about her. Not that having a romance with him was her goal, far from it. But this was a reality check.

Izzy reached for her sense of humor. "That sounds like what goes on in my head. But it's more like... Shoot, Mae has a stain on her leggings. Am I out of laundry detergent? I should probably stock up. And speaking of stocking up, did I remember to place an order for summer bulbs at the feed store? Those always sell out quickly, just like Christmas merchandise. Which reminds me that I haven't ordered a fruit and nut basket to send to my father and stepmother this Christmas. And I should put in a request for a babysitter the Saturday before Christmas for girls' night out. But shoot... Mae has a stain on her leggings."

"Five golden rings!" the kids and Chandler chorused.

Izzy and Chandler shared a laugh, a laugh with everyone in the coffee shop actually.

"And here I thought I was the only one carrying too many responsibilities to think straight." Chandler's gaze was warm, but also tender.

The way he looks at me...

It probably doesn't mean what I think it means.

"We're having a normal conversation." Izzy picked up her hot chocolate cup. "Did you notice?"

"Yep. No disagreements about where ornaments, trees or lights usually go." Chandler smiled.

"No discussion about separating our kids in school." Izzy nodded. "You know what this means."

"I do *not*." Chandler set his cup aside, expression turning serious.

"It means that we're becoming friends." As soon

as Izzy spoke the words, she knew this was true. She leaned forward and whispered, "We don't need to be something more."

Chandler opened his mouth but said nothing.

"Five golden rings," the kids and Chandler chorused along to the music, creating another cascade of laughter afterward.

"We'll be fine like this," Izzy went on, reassuring herself.

Chandler tapped his finger on top of his cup, keeping time to the music. "Are you coming out to the ranch later?"

"Yes." Izzy noticed Chandler changed the subject. That was a tactic they both used when they wanted to avoid the sticky conversations.

He continued tapping his cocoa cup. "Maybe you could…help me put up lights or decorations at my house."

"Outside or inside?" Izzy held her breath, thinking about how Mary had told her Chandler hadn't put up any Christmas anything since his divorce.

Chandler's gaze roamed toward the kids. "Inside? Sam's been wanting a tree."

"Do you need me to buy a tree for you?" She had for some of her older clients.

Chandler frowned, attention coming back to her. "No. That's something Sam and I should do together."

He's a good man.

But Izzy wasn't in the market for one. Christmas would be here before she knew it and she had to use every spare minute to earn money for Mae's Christmas gift. She couldn't afford to be distracted by Chandler.

"I suppose if I want you to help me today, I've got to buy a tree now." How Chandler-like. The Chandler that she used to know. Stoic. Business-like. Pragmatic.

Izzy laughed. "Well, Mr. Grinch, if it's Christmas that's gotta be done, you wouldn't want to make it fun, would you?"

"So, you'll help me?"

"Just today." Izzy nodded. She had time. And she wouldn't accept payment. Sam would be over-joyed.

"There's just one thing we need to agree on, though," Chandler said slowly, pausing to join the kids to sing, *"Five golden rings."*

"Oh, here we go." Izzy sat back in her chair and crossed her arms over her chest. "Is this about the bet you offered me earlier? The one I didn't agree to?"

"Not that… It's two things, really," Chandler allowed. "First, we decorate my way."

Izzy might have been slower than usual to nod her agreement. She was Team Mary first, after all, when it came to shaking things up at the ranch. Any decor at all was a win. "And second?"

"And second, I'm not sure this *something* between us is going to hit Pause in the friend zone." At Izzy's gasp, he added, "We'll either be *some-*

thing to each other or we won't be *anything* to each other."

Izzy didn't answer.

She didn't want to admit that he might be right.

"CHANDLER, ARE YOU ready for me?" Izzy called across the dark ranch yard near dinnertime. The sun had set. She carried a large cardboard box.

The bright Christmas lights and colorful yard decorations lit her way from the main house to Chandler's. Although with her candy cane sweater and white-blond hair, she looked like she could be a part of the cheerful display.

And Chandler might have been cheered to see her if he hadn't been suspicious of the box she carried. "Did my mother send you over here with decorations?"

"She did." Izzy came into the glow of the lights Zane and Ryan had hung around Chandler's front porch earlier that afternoon.

"I thought we agreed that we'd do things my way." Chandler took the box from Izzy. "These aren't my decorations."

"Mary didn't think you had enough." Izzy had her sights on that box Chandler was holding. She should have been concerned about the cold. She wasn't wearing a jacket, just that candy-cane-striped sweater. And the temperature was quickly dropping below fifty. "We don't have to open the box if you have sufficient decorations at your place."

"Sufficient?" Chandler rolled his eyes toward the white twinkling lights outlining his front porch. "Why do I get the impression that your idea of sufficient and my idea of sufficient when it comes to holiday baubles aren't the same?"

"Because you're one smart cowboy."

Chandler grunted. "Now you're just trying to butter me up."

"Is it working?" She grinned. And even though she wasn't wearing any bells, Chandler thought he heard the soft jingle-jangle of sleigh bells.

"Is it working?" Chandler echoed, thinking about all the undone tasks on his to-do list.

Instead of working on the rodeo stock schedule for the new year, Chandler had bought the first tree Sam chose, put the Christmas tree in a stand in the living room and done a quick clean of the house. Not that his house wasn't always orderly and relatively dirt- and dust-free. It just hadn't been giving a guest-cleaning recently. And while he'd cleaned, Chandler had fretted about the work he wasn't doing, wondered how Izzy would see his house and chastised himself for throwing down the relationship gauntlet at the coffee shop.

We'll either be something to each other or we won't be anything to each other.

Izzy probably thinks I'm a pompous jerk.

And that bet about the kids singing *five golden rings…*

She hadn't taken him up on it. And he'd brought up his reward.

Again, jerk.

"Is something else bothering you?" Izzy seemed to have switched tactics. She'd apparently given up on reclaiming the box of decorations and was inching toward his front door.

"Something else is always bothering me." The workload. His ex-wife's plans and intentions. Keeping Sam happy and well-behaved. And Izzy... She'd recently taken up too much of his mental space and he wasn't the better for giving in earlier today to spend time with her when she very clearly wanted to park him in the friend zone. "But if you must know, I promised Dad I'd go with him tomorrow to check out some livestock."

"Which meant you were trying to do double your work managing the ranch today." Izzy nodded, hand reaching for his doorknob. "And now, you can't catch up tonight because of Christmas frivolity. Is that what you're thinking?"

Without answering, Chandler eased over to block Izzy's easy entry. Truth be told, he'd had second—and third—thoughts about her coming inside. "At least there's one place where we're on the same page."

Izzy's brow quirked. "You don't want me inside your house."

"Correct. It seems like an important step." Chandler hesitated before pushing on. "And since we don't know what to do with each other, I'm not sure I want to open myself up to your judgment."

"Is that what you think I'd do?" She crossed her

arms over her candy-cane-striped chest. "Explain yourself, cowboy."

Chandler drew a deep breath. "When I see a cowboy and his horse, it gives me a good idea of who he is."

"Really." Izzy gestured for him to continue.

"Is his tack well taken care of? Is his horse well-behaved? Does he respect his livestock?"

Her brow was wrinkled. "Did I judge Harper Dye for her gnome and turtledove obsessions? I think not."

She had him there. He opted for honesty. "I don't really know what message my house gives off. No one's been inside except Sam and my parents since Stephanie moved out."

Izzy nodded slowly. "And you prioritize taking care of this ranch and others more than you do sprucing up the place where you lay your head at night."

"Exactly."

"Ah." Understanding dawned in her pretty blue eyes. "You're like Earl. Utilitarian."

"Earl?" The stooped-shouldered, white-haired, slow and crotchety old man who owned the feed store. "You're likening me to Earl?" Chandler's ego was bruised.

"It sounds as if you're just like Earl." Izzy was nodding, moving closer to him and the door as she warmed to her topic. "Let me assure you that Earl has nothing on his walls. No throw pillows on the sofa. No guest soaps in the bathroom. And do you know what? I don't feel any different about Earl. He's a smart businessman with a big heart. When my dad left town after I graduated high school, Earl offered me a chance to turn a part-time job into full-time work. Plus, he let me rent out the studio apartment over the office." She glossed over what was surely a rough time in her life.

And that made him like her all the more.

"He's good people," Izzy said matter-of-factly. "And guess what? You're good people, too. Why does it matter if you've only got the basics inside your living space?"

He'd run out of excuses.

"Don't say I didn't warn you." Chandler nodded toward the door. "Let's go in." And if she was turned off by what she found, this *will they, won't they* feeling might hit a hard stop.

A small, foolish part of him pulled for *will they*.

They entered his house.

"You need a wreath outside on the front door," Izzy said, almost like an afterthought.

Chandler reluctantly agreed, setting the box of decorations down on the entry bench. They removed their boots before going any farther. Standing next to Izzy in his socks in his home felt somehow…intimate. But then his gaze went to the visible parts of the house—the couch almost completely blocking the entry, the bare walls, the sparse collection of mismatched furniture. It was definitely a bachelor pad, furnished with castoffs.

Izzy didn't pull a face or make a quick exit. She

moved slowly inside, inching around the too-large couch. "The tree has got to be in front of the big window facing the ranch yard. You should have something Christmassy that Sam can play with in the living room, like Mary's village."

"A train set? But isn't that a little much? It's just me most of the time."

"Sam is seven." Back to Chandler, she ran her fingers along the Christmas tree branches. "Christmas is still magical to him. A train would create a wonderful memory for him." She turned to the fireplace. "And you should have candles on the mantel with some garland woven in, plus a Christmas blanket on the couch."

"I'm surprised you didn't say I needed Christmas throw pillows." Chandler kept his distance from Izzy, standing behind the couch, still in the foyer.

"Christmas should be comfortable for you, too." Izzy turned and removed her candy-cane-striped earmuffs, hanging them around her neck the way she had at the coffee shop. "I like pillows but if you don't…" She shrugged. "And then stockings on the mantel, of course."

Chandler was still dwelling on Izzy liking Christmas throw pillows. It took a moment for her last words about stockings to sink in. "Stephanie does the stockings with Sam on Christmas morning. And Mom fills one for me at the main house."

Izzy studied him. "That doesn't mean you shouldn't hang some stockings in here for both of you. Remember what you told me about Mary making Christmas special for you. You can make Christmas special for you and Sam. What I saw in your eyes when you talked about Christmas that day told me it was important to you."

"Like what might be ahead for us," Chandler murmured.

That something between us.

With a guarded expression, Izzy moved into the dining room where three small cardboard boxes of Christmas decorations sat on the table. "A table-cloth and some kind of holiday centerpiece would liven this up."

Chandler followed her, drawn as if connected by a string. "Why? We don't use the dining room at all."

Izzy gave him a questioning look. "Don't tell me you eat in the living room all the time?"

"Most of the time we eat at the main house." She was making him reevaluate his parenting style and his bachelor habit of eating in the kitchen standing up.

"Forgive me. I'm not here to judge." Izzy moved on to the kitchen. "You might hang a pine garland between these rooms. Mary has some plastic ones you could use. A Christmas cactus on the counter over there would bring some festiveness into your kitchen. And maybe a holiday dish towel if you can stand it." Before Chandler could stop Izzy, she was marching down the hallway.

"The rest of the house doesn't need holiday

cheer." Chandler hurried after her, heart pounding. She wasn't going to go into his bedroom... Was she?

"Really? Mae and I each have little Christmas trees in our bedrooms. As for the bathrooms—"

"That's Mae and you. Sam and I—"

"He's going to love a little tree in his man cave. You can get some twinkle lights and let him put whatever he wants in the branches." She smiled at Chandler the way he liked, easy and unguarded. "When spring comes, you can plant it in a bigger pot outside so that you can use it again next Christmas."

This was all new territory to Chandler. "Is that what you do?" He wasn't even sure if that's what Stephanie did.

Izzy nodded. "We've replanted our little trees twice since we got them. They were almost too heavy to bring in this year." She glanced around Sam's room. "Do you know what else you're missing? An advent calendar. Kids love those, especially the ones with chocolate. We still have a few at the feed store. I can set one aside for you."

"Sam isn't here every day." Chandler rubbed his neck. "I mean, he might be if things change and..."

"He'll happily eat the chocolate on the days he misses." Izzy seemed to sense she'd waded into uncertain waters. She moved passed Chandler, headed toward the living room. "What are you getting Sam for Christmas?"

"There's a mini-quad in the ranch garage. It doesn't go very fast."

"He'll love that." Izzy chuckled. "And frankly, I love that you aren't getting him a puppy." She leaned against his couch, gaze roaming the room once more. "Mae would never let me hear the end of it."

"Are you sure Earl isn't giving Mae a puppy?"

"You called her Mae." Izzy smiled, blinking watery eyes. "Twice since we've been in here."

"Seemed natural, I guess." Chandler leaned against a bare wall, hands behind his back so he wouldn't reach for Izzy. "Is it okay that I do?"

"I… I'd like that." Izzy smiled. But it was a careful smile. "And here we are again. Dancing around *something*."

Chandler nodded. He felt it, too.

"Or maybe we're dancing around the furniture in this room." Izzy looked from one end to the other. "It's laid out weird. There's no flow. You can't walk inside and directly into the hall or the dining room. There's no space for that Christmas tree. Where it is now, if you light a fire in the fireplace, you might start a fire. Did you lay it out this way on purpose? Or leave it the way the previous foreman did?"

"I arranged it like this." Chandler wobbled gently against the wall, which was probably because he wasn't sitting. If he was sitting, his knee would have been bouncing.

"So…you…like it this way?" Izzy's gaze fell on him, causing what felt like a significant *ka-thump* inside his chest.

"Yes." Chandler rubbed a hand over his chest. *This.* This was where he should stop. Instead, he said, "Like this."

Izzy opened her mouth, closed it, and then said, "You wouldn't like it better if we rearranged it?"

"No."

"Why not?" Izzy took a few steps until she stood in front of Chandler. She touched his arm, something she'd done frequently over the past few days, a connection she barely seemed aware of making. "You don't have to tell me, but I'll ask again. You're so utilitarian. Why would you keep your furniture arranged in a way that slows you down?"

I don't have to tell her. I can change the subject.

Relief unstuck the shoulders Chandler hadn't realized were approaching his ears. But what she was offering…not having to tell her… It was an easy out. And yet…

"I do have to tell you." He had to tell someone. And he'd never told Stephanie. "My dad was a drinker. He used to tell my mom that he could handle it." Chandler rolled his shoulders back. "And maybe he could. He showed up to work every day on time. Didn't drink a drop while on duty as a construction worker." Or so he'd claimed. "But come five o'clock, it was time to hit the bar. And he didn't come home until whatever game was on TV at the bar was over. Dad was like a cat. He could walk into our apartment in the dark—no matter where we lived—" and they'd moved around a lot "—and navigate his way to the bedroom without bumping into furniture." It was something of an art form. "But he always woke Mom up when he got to the bedroom. And then the yelling would start." Waking Chandler up. Making him tense into a ball on his bed, listening, waiting. For the crash of something fragile, human or otherwise.

Izzy gave his arm a gentle, understanding squeeze.

Chandler covered her hand with his own. "They were competitive. Mom didn't like Dad drinking. Dad didn't want to give in. I never knew what the night would bring. What would be broken. What situation I'd be greeted with in the morning." He'd felt so small back then. So helpless. "I tried to be invisible."

"Oh, Chandler."

"Mom started moving the furniture around before Dad came home, but she'd always deny doing it. She'd tell him he was so drunk that he couldn't remember. Things…escalated. And I… I didn't help matters. Sleep deprived, on edge, I had a short fuse at school. Hence my aversion to the principal's office the other day."

The angry words of his parents, shouting at him, shouting at each other, reverberated in Chandler's head, tunneling his vision, tensing his shoulders.

But through the brain fog, one voice reached him. A calm voice. A caring voice. Izzy's voice.

"It's okay, Chandler."

And surprisingly, with a deep breath, it was better. Chandler focused on Izzy's face. Those empathetic blue eyes. Her delicate features framed by that silver-blond hair. The nod of her head. "One time, my mom shoved all the furniture in front of the door. Dad couldn't get in. Not without things hitting the fan anyway."

"Those days are long gone." Izzy slipped her arms around Chandler's waist and gave him a hug, laying her head over his heart.

It seemed natural to bring Izzy closer, to feel the steadiness of her breath, to picture her as the oar he needed when he was adrift because he'd lifted his anchor, sailing into uncharted waters. With her.

"Is that why you arrange your furniture to block the entry?" Izzy spoke into Chandler's chest. "In case your dad shows up?"

Chandler nodded, realized she probably couldn't see or feel him nodding since her head barely reached his sternum, and said, "Yep. I know it's not likely but it makes me feel better."

"That's sad."

"Yep." It wasn't something to be proud of, either. Chandler tried to make a joke of it. "You should see my bedroom."

Izzy stiffened.

"That was a joke," Chandler said gruffly.

"I knew that." But Izzy eased out of Chandler's embrace and turned her back on him. "How about we change things now in the living room? Are you up to moving furniture?"

"Yep."

But he suspected they both knew he was lying.

CHAPTER ELEVEN

"HOW ARE YOU FEELING?" Izzy asked when they'd rearranged Chandler's living room into something that had more feng shui.

The couch was opposite the fireplace, not blocking the entry. His chairs faced the tree, which they'd moved in the middle of the big front window. Now, anyone could come in and reach the hallway or the kitchen without having to shimmy around the couch.

Chandler hadn't spoken much while they moved things around, perhaps because he was uncomfortable with how much he'd shared about his past.

Or the length of their hug.

Or the comment about his bedroom.

Why was the room silent?

Izzy realized Chandler hadn't answered her question. He stood near the Christmas tree, staring at the carpet and the clear path to the door.

"Hey." Izzy waved at him. "Are you woolgathering?"

He blinked slowly. "Wool *what*? Is that another of your historical terms?"

"Yes, sir." Was it nice that he remembered her love of reading historicals? Izzy decided it was. "Woolgathering. It means you're lost in thought."

"I was." Chandler's warm brown gaze was encompassing.

Like his hug.

It had seemed so natural to embrace him.

And when he'd looked at her... It was as if he could stare into her eyes all day.

I know I'd be able to do the same.

"Now who's woolgathering?" Chandler's smile was infectious. "Aren't you going to ask me what I was thinking about?"

"Nope." Izzy was afraid to. "I asked you how you were feeling about removing your defense against the past. I'm still waiting for an answer. We can move it back if we need to."

"One thing at a time," Chandler murmured, a small smile on his lips. He came over to her side of the couch. "I was just noticing the deep imprint of the legs in the rug and thinking how I wasn't able to do this when I was married. Not the talking. Not the moving."

If he couldn't do this when Stephanie was here, that must mean...

Izzy's cheeks began to feel hot. She pressed her hands to her face. "We should get your Christmas decorations out. Or at least the lights for the tree." She took a step toward the dining room.

Chandler caught her hand. "You're changing the subject."

"We're both good at doing that," Izzy said softly, not daring to look at him.

Voices and the sound of feet on the porch stairs announced the arrival of others.

Slipping her hand free, Izzy hurried to open the door. "Sam! Mae! Come see the tree."

The kids barreled in, not even removing their boots before running into the living room.

Moving at a slower pace, Frank helped Mary ascend the stairs.

"Thought we'd see what was taking you so long." Frank didn't look up. He had one arm around Mary's waist and a hand supporting her arm.

"Took us ten minutes to get out the door." Mary wore black snow pants and a very thick white parka. From what Izzy could see of Mary's face beneath a knit cap and infinity scarf bundled over her chin, the older woman had a healthy burst of color. "Frank wanted me swaddled tighter than a newborn. Can't hardly move my arms and legs."

"A chill does no one any good." This was Frank at his best. Patient and unflappable. Must have been why he was such a success at taking in dozens of teenage foster boys over the years. "You'll thank me tomorrow, Mary."

"Oh, I'm grateful," Mary grumbled, reaching the front door. "Overheated and exhausted. But grateful. You will always be the best of my blessings, Frank."

"And you, the love of my life." Frank kissed his wife's cheek.

Izzy was humbled by their comfortable love for each other. It was out in the open for everyone to see.

Izzy's love for Mike had been a private thing. They whispered endearments but only when they were alone. And those words came less and less often the longer they were married, until Izzy had felt that she didn't know what love was. That she'd been attracted to Mike and to his ambition because she wanted something more—more financial stability, more emotional stability and a future that included being a mother. But she hadn't loved Mike as deeply as Frank and Mary loved each other.

And maybe that was why the feelings she had for Chandler were so frightening. Would their feelings grow like the Harrisons? Or wither as her feelings toward Mike had? She didn't know.

Frank helped Mary over the threshold. "Well, will you look at that. Do you see that pretty tree, Mary?"

"I do." Mary leaned on the doorjamb, staring at the rearranged living room. And then she reached for Izzy and whispered, "Thank you for this change."

"It was him," Izzy whispered back.

"If it was Chandler, it would have happened long ago." Mary tugged off her knit cap and scarf. "It was you, Izzy. Now, help me shed these layers, Frank. My son needs a little expert advice creating Christmas cheer for my grandson."

Izzy's phone beeped with an alarm. She'd set it to remind her when it was time to go, so that she could get Mae to bed at a decent hour and limit her time with Chandler, if necessary. And boy, was it necessary. She was at risk of getting too close to Chandler before she thought things through. "We've got to go. It's getting late."

She needed time to figure out what love was supposed to be. And if love was possible with him.

"I'LL WALK YOU OUT, IZZY." Chandler practically bolted to the front door for his hat, boots and jacket. Only Izzy's wary gaze had him slowing down and saying, "Come on, Mae. Wouldn't want you out late on a school night."

"*Della*-Mae," Sam said. "Her name is *Della*-Mae, Dad."

"My mama calls me Mae," Izzy's little girl said in that innocent voice of hers. "Your daddy can call me Mae, too."

"Oh, like family," Sam said as if understanding was dawning. "Should I call you Mae?"

"I think I'd like that." Mae beamed.

Chandler had no time to dwell on his son's re-action. Izzy had her boots on and was in possession of Mae's hand. He stumbled after her, heels finding purchase in his boots, arms punching into jacket sleeves, his hat left behind.

"While you take care of that fire, Chandler," Mom called after him, sounding like her precancerous self, "we'll talk about what decorations Sam wants on his tree."

"Monster trucks!" Sam cried. "And apples, in case I get hungry."

His son was anything but traditional.

"Izzy." Chandler stretched his legs to catch up to Izzy and Mae with only a vague notion in his head about what needed to be said. His heart was racing in circles, urging him to slow Izzy's departure. "I think… I think we need to talk."

"About what?" Mae asked, all adorable and sweet. The winter wind tossed her long white-blond hair this way and that.

"Can't talk right now." Izzy was working those short legs of hers double time. A candy cane escaping through the ranch's winter wonderland. "It's a school night. Gotta get home. I'll be back here tomorrow afternoon."

"Did I…say something wrong? Or…say too much?" Chandler's movements felt stiff, wooden, yet wobbly. "Like you said at the feed store. I'm more of a listener. Probably put my foot in my mouth." Scared Izzy off, more like. A man who didn't feel comfortable moving his furniture? Izzy was probably wondering what else was wrong with him.

They reached her SUV.

Izzy opened the back door. "Mae, get in and buckle up, please." When her daughter was safely inside and the door shut behind her, Izzy faced Chandler, arms crossed, shoulders hunched against the cold prairie wind. "You didn't say too much. I'm… I'm *honored* that you told me about your dad.

But this…this *something*…" She gestured back and forth between them. "I have no foundation to judge it with. I don't have the depth of experience—*successful experience*—to trust these feelings. I have responsibilities… Mae… Earl and the feed store… my holiday decorating… Christmas. I'm already stretched too thin. And then you…"

"Put you over the edge." Chandler nodded. "I get it." It made his chest ache, but he understood. "Not rushing in… It's a sensible decision." The wrong one, he was sure.

She sighed in apparent relief. "Thank you for understanding."

Chandler nodded again.

Izzy turned, taking hold of the car door handle.

And that's when an urgent feeling took hold of Chandler, a feeling that propelled him forward and had him taking gentle hold of Izzy's arm covered in red-and-white knit.

Izzy paused, glancing up at him over her shoulder.

"We won't always be this stressed out and time crunched." Chandler released Izzy's arm and put her candy-striped earmuffs over her ears, holding them out so she couldn't claim not to hear his next words. "We should keep the channels of communication open." And then, he settled those round muffs over her ears. "Good night, Candy Cane Izzy."

She stared at him in silence for another moment before nodding briefly and opening her SUV's door. "Good night."

"Good night, Mr. Cochran!" Mae called from the back seat.

Chandler waved, and then waited for them to drive off before he walked back to his house. Along the way, he admired the exterior lights hung where they'd always been. There was permanence in those lights. And safety.

Not surprisingly, when Chandler looked at Izzy, he didn't feel any of that permanence or safety. Instead, nerves trotted along a repeating, circular path in his stomach. When Chandler looked at Izzy, he didn't know where she fit in his life.

But when he'd held her in his arms... The nerves came to a halt, dropping anchor. And certainty... Certainty settled in his chest.

Izzy could mean something to me.

He was afraid she already did.

"Everything all right, son?" Dad asked Chandler when he'd shed his boots and jacket and joined them in the living room.

"It could be." Chandler took another look around the open layout of his space.

On the couch, Sam and Mom were exploring the treasures in the box Mom had sent over with Izzy earlier, the one Chandler had taken from Izzy for fear she'd use every last item in that box to decorate his home. Now, he wished she'd stayed to do just that. If they spent more time together, she might figure out how she really felt about him.

"There's a fresh feeling in here since you re-arranged the furniture." Mom blew dust, real or imagined, off a red bird ornament before handing it to Sam to hang on the tree. "Like a fresh start."

Chandler grunted.

"Gives the room balance with the tree in here," Dad said, still studying Chandler. "Speaking of the tree, I tossed a string of lights on it because young Sam was determined to put ornaments on tonight."

"Christmas trees can't be naked, Grandpa." Sam was putting all the ornaments in a one-foot-square area on the tree. The rest was bare. "That's what Grandma says."

"I do, indeed." Mom spared Chandler a smile. "Everything about Christmas should make you feel joy."

Chandler nodded. From now on, he wouldn't think about the holiday without also thinking of Izzy—her over-the-top Christmas spirit and tinsel-colored hair. And speaking of... "We need tinsel."

"I might have some in a box somewhere." Mom's gaze found Dad's. "Frank, would you—"

"Nope." Dad got to his feet. "Izzy had the right idea. It's time to head home. Chandler and I can pick up tinsel in town tomorrow when we go look at that stock."

"I suppose you're right." Mom allowed Dad to bundle her up again while Sam continued to put ornaments in a one-foot radius on the tree. "Big day for you today, Chandler. Can't tell you how proud I am."

"Of what?" Sam piped up. "Of our tree? Does it look pretty, Grandma?"

"Sure does." Mom patted Chandler's cheek. "Nothing is easy. Not even love."

"It was easy the first time." And Chandler bet Izzy would say the same.

"But look how that turned out," Dad pointed out, not unkindly. "No offense but easy isn't always forever."

"That's a shame." Chandler nodded, opening the door for them. "Easy is something you look for when you get older."

Mom tsked. "Easy should only be something you look for in a chair."

CHAPTER TWELVE

"Izzy, YOU'VE GOT the face of a woman burning the candle at both ends."

Izzy grumbled something in the affirmative to Earl early Tuesday morning.

Earl handed Izzy a cup of coffee. And then gave bright-eyed Mae a mug of hot cocoa, ushering her to the table in the break room. "Usually, it's Mae who drags her feet in before school."

"I'm wide awake," Mae said. She wore a bright blue dress with yellow tights, colors as wide awake as she was. "I woke Mama up this morning. She didn't hear her alarm."

"You worried about something?" Earl stared at Izzy, raising his bushy white eyebrows.

"I'm counting down the days to Christmas is all," Izzy said. And counting every penny toward buying that princess bed. If only the furniture store in Friar's Creek offered layaway. It would be one less thing to worry about because Chandler... He expected them to figure this *something* out after the holiday. He was willing to wait. That had to mean their *something* could lead to something real.

"This month is flying by," Izzy said. December was nearly half-gone.

"The best days often do," Earl remarked.

Izzy chugged half her cup of coffee, hoping it would chase away the cobwebs in her head where thoughts of Chandler had stuck last night. And this morning. And threatened to stay all day long.

In the warehouse, Stan was driving the loader, filling the store's delivery truck with pallets of hay. The steady hum of the Bobcat matched the steady thread of thoughts regarding Chandler in Izzy's head.

He's a good man. He's a good father. He's a good kisser.

Izzy performed an imaginary eye roll as she drained the rest of her coffee.

A good kisser didn't guarantee a future together.

Mae stared into the contents in her mug. "Can I add marshmallows, Mama?"

"Of course," Earl answered for Izzy, reaching for his stash of mini-marshmallows, undoing the rubber band sealing the bag. He was like a grandfather to her. Always spoiling Mae.

Chandler's suspicions might be right. Earl could get Mae a puppy for Christmas.

"That's a lot of sugar before school, Mae," Izzy felt compelled to point out. Point out. Not reject. She wasn't feeling up to snuff in regards to winning any argument, no matter how small.

"Sam says sugar makes you run faster." Mae held out her mug for Earl.

"Tell me when." Earl poured the white puffs into her mug until the hot chocolate couldn't be seen. "Or we can stop here." He closed the bag when Mae would have taken more. "Wouldn't want to get into trouble with your mama."

Mae began eating the marshmallows one at a time off the mountain in her mug. "I'm going to be the fastest kid at school today."

Earl refilled Izzy's mug with coffee. "I hear someone in the front. You look like you need a distraction."

Izzy shed her jacket, picked up her coffee, settled her cowboy hat more firmly on her head and went out to face the day. She stopped just on the other side of the door, shocked to see her ex-husband standing at the sales counter. Not being a cowboy or a rancher, and not living in Clementine anymore, Mike never came in the feed store.

But here he stood in front of her in his unwrinkled khakis, crisp blue polo shirt and black leather jacket.

"Mike." Izzy hurried forward, keeping her voice low. "What are you doing here?"

"Is Della-Mae around?" he asked, voice nearly a whisper.

Izzy nodded, set her coffee down, grabbed hold of the edge of the sales counter and braced herself for bad news. A death. A disaster of some kind. Conversations with Mike were rarely about the weather. And then, she realized what else he might have come for. "Did you check the school's online messaging system?"

"No. Should I have?"

Izzy shrugged, trying to ignore the guilt of not telling him Mae had been in trouble. "I can never sign in and you said you were going to."

"I've been too busy." Her ex-husband shifted his weight, checking a message on his phone before pocketing it.

Izzy reached for her coffee, needing to hold something. "Mike, why are you here?"

"First, I want to thank you for not being difficult about the divorce or the custody agreement." Although Mike's voice was low, Izzy recognized that tone. It was his deal-closing tone—smooth, nonthreatening, trying to establish trust while he laid out the terms that benefited him. "We've had a good few years of co-parenting."

The hair on the back of Izzy's neck rose. Mike hadn't come to deliver bad news. Mike was here to renegotiate. But what? All Izzy could decipher was that Mike considered this a potentially difficult negotiation. "And…"

"Second," Mike continued in that easygoing liar's voice. "You had to know that at some point, our relationship status would change for one or both of us. And that change will affect Della-Mae."

"It shouldn't." Annoyance—*or perhaps main-lining caffeine*—heated Izzy from the inside out. She let go of the sales counter and crossed her arms over her chest. "And…"

"I'm getting serious about someone." Mike was still in negotiation mode. "And she doesn't want to have kids."

"Does she have a dislike of kittens and puppies, too?" Izzy blurted, laughing nervously.

Mike shoved his hands in his black leather jacket pockets, frowning. "Izzy."

"I'm sorry. That was uncalled for." Izzy's arms stayed locked tight over her chest because she had the oddest suspicion that Mike wasn't done. But what was she missing?

And then a thought surfaced. And her stomach dropped.

She'd been in this situation before. With her own father.

"This woman you're serious about doesn't just not want children, she doesn't want stepchildren, either." Izzy's voice trembled. "And since you're here, you've *chosen*..." She choked on the word, swallowing before she could start again. "You've chosen *her* over your own daughter."

Oh, those words hurt to say, if only because they'd break Mae's heart. *He'd* break her little girl's heart. *Just like Dad did mine.*

"What kind of man are you?" Izzy whispered, voice strained, releasing a hand to tip her cowboy hat back.

"I want to change our custody agreement." Mike tried for his salesman's smile, but it didn't fool Izzy. She'd gotten under his skin and made him feel uncomfortable.

Good.

"Are you relinquishing all rights?" Izzy's temperature changed from hot to cold. Her toes stung with it in her cowboy boots. "Or are you only going to see her once in the summer and once at the holidays? Is that what kind of father you're turning out to be?" Izzy lowered her voice. "How could you do this to Mae? This is low even for you."

"Let's keep this civil." Mike's voice had taken on a gravelly quality, a warning of sorts if one knew him well.

Which Izzy did. "Oh. I can be civil. That doesn't mean I won't judge you." She sucked in a breath, blinking back tears. "I'll gladly take Mae most of the year. I won't fight you on that. But I won't make excuses for you."

Mike scowled. "I'm not asking you to make excuses for me."

"But you expect me to talk about you in a good light." Izzy grabbed her coffee cup, wishing she was the type of woman to give vent to her anger by dousing him in coffee. But she wasn't. She was just Izzy, a woman who avoided confrontation.

Candy Cane Izzy.

That's what Chandler had called her last night.

Chandler. His tall, steady, *honorable* presence came to mind. The strength of his arms when they wrapped around her. The sturdiness of his torso when she leaned into him. He wouldn't abandon his child for a woman. How she wished he was here beside her to tell Mike to get lost.

To tell Mike that he'd adopt Mae.

Izzy's breath caught. She shouldn't be thinking such things.

"Have your lawyer contact my lawyer," Izzy told Mike coldly. "And get out of here before Mae sees you and I make you tell her how coldhearted you are to her face."

"*Della*-Mae," Mike said, clearly being ornery just because. "Her name is *Della*-Mae Adams."

Zane entered the store carrying what looked like a frayed pair of braided reins.

"Move along, Mike." Izzy gave her ex-husband a shooing motion. "When Mae's older, she'll decide what she wants to be called. And what she thinks of you."

"Turn here," Dad instructed Chandler late Tuesday morning. "This is the place. Sooner Wagon Wheels."

The turn put them on a weedy, dirt road lined by barbed wire fences. Pastures on either side held large draft horses with swaybacks and long white whiskers. Those old horses had literally been put out to pasture.

"Sooner Wagon Wheels." Chandler scoffed after hitting a deep pothole. "They should have called it the Retirement Home for Draft Horses. I hope the wagons are in better shape." He and Dad were shopping for a horse and cart for Mom to ride in on Christmas Day. Ever since Izzy had mentioned it, Dad had bitten into the idea and wouldn't let go.

"I called around." Dad was smiling. He'd been smiling all morning.

And if buying a horse and buggy gave the older man's smile back to him after Mom's cancer battle, Chandler was willing to consider it. He'd been considering a lot of things he wouldn't normally lately. Moving things around in his well-ordered life. Opening his heart to Izzy. Keeping it open while she sorted through things.

"Sooner Wagon Wheels has a good reputation," Dad continued. "And you know how your mother loves a horse with character. I bet every one of these big fellas has character to spare." He leaned to look out the passenger window. "Look at them. They're trotting along with us."

Sure enough, the horses were keeping pace with Chandler's truck. He had to admit, it was magical.

"What if I slow down?" Chandler took his foot off the gas and coasted.

The horses paced him, slowing.

He sped up again. And so did they.

Sam would love to see this.

And Izzy. She'd love it, too. She and Mae.

"Your mother would love to see this," Dad said in a thick voice, echoing Chandler's thoughts. He sat back in his seat. "We aren't leaving until we get what we came for."

The ranch was a mile down the road. The horses followed them the entire way.

When they reached the ranch yard, Chandler was impressed by the grandeur. Two double-decker barns, a covered arena, an outdoor racetrack—all in good repair. A large sign on the side of the barn proclaimed it as Sooner Wagon Wheels, Established in 1950, C.D. Sutton, Proprietor.

A man of unusual height and girth strode out of one barn with an aura of authority. His boots and jeans were worn and faded, nearly as colorless as his shaggy white hair. *Was that a new plaid shirt?* His narrow-brimmed straw cowboy hat looked as if a horse had nibbled its crown.

"I'm Clarence Dwayne Sutton." The big cowboy was taller than Chandler and had a firm handshake with hard calluses. "But you can call me C.D."

"Impressive operation you have here." Chandler knew how difficult it was to stay on top of maintenance on a large spread.

C.D. chuckled. "Quite a difference from our driveway, ain't it? Most folks forget the potholes when the herd escorts them here."

Chandler nodded.

"I'm not interested in one of them," Dad told C.D., hitching up his blue jeans. "You've got more to offer than our escorts, I'm hoping." And instead of waiting for C.D. to respond, he hurriedly added, "I want a well-trained, well-behaved cart horse with personality and I'm willing to pay extra for it."

"No sense spilling your hand." Chandler shook his head at his father's naïveté. "What happened to my father? Frank Harrison, master stock negotiator?"

Dad crossed his arms over his chest. "This is an important purchase for your mother. When you think about the woman you love, the woman you almost lost to the Big C, you'll spare any expense to make her happy."

"Merry Christmas to me is what I'm hearing." C.D. chuckled, hooking his thumbs in his belt loops. "Never fear, Chandler. My family hasn't been in business for three generations because we take advantage of our buyers."

"That's a relief." Dad clapped a hand on Chandler's back. "Isn't it, son?"

"Yep." Chandler gestured to C.D. "Let's see what you've got."

"I've got two different horses and rigs ready for you to check out in the arena." He led the way toward the open gate to the covered arena. "Dinah is a Clydesdale. She's in her prime at ten. She enjoys pulling a bigger wagon. If you've got children or grandchildren, or you're interested in taking a group of folks for a ride on the regular, she's the way to go."

They entered the arena. A large chestnut Clydesdale with huge hooves was hitched to a wooden wagon that looked like it could sit eight burly cowboys.

"Much as I like to include the family in everything we do," Dad said, planting his boots in the loamy arena soil, "my Mary would treat that like a cubic zirconia."

C.D. scratched the gray hair at his temple.

"Translation…" Chandler began. "My dad wants Mom to be as thrilled with this gift as she would be if she received a real diamond."

C.D. pivoted toward the other end of the arena toward a large gray horse hitched to a black buggy with two forward-facing bench seats, yellow wheels and a black fringed canopy on top. "If you want a fancier rig, you'll like the surrey and Shirley."

The gray whinnied, making C.D. chuckle, which given how often he'd chuckled since they arrived didn't seem such a hard thing to do.

"She knows her name?" The enthusiasm in Dad's tone matched that of his smile. Despite his shorter legs, he hurried past Chandler.

"Sure does," C.D. said with a nod. "She's a Percheron. Knows she's a beaut and likes to prance. Gets impatient if you go too slow."

"Can't prance when you walk," Dad agreed.

"Is she headstrong?" Chandler was going to reject her if she was. "Mom isn't—"

"My Mary would sure like something with flash and character." Dad walked up to the mare and reached up to run a hand over her withers, and then down her front leg. She politely shifted her weight so that he could pick up her large hoof. "That's my girl. I like her."

That's my dad. Forgetting how to negotiate.

"Dad." Chandler sounded as put-upon as when Sam used the moniker. "You don't buy a car without a test drive. Same goes for livestock."

"He'll get his test drive, Chandler." C.D. had his

thumbs hooked through his belt loops again. He rocked back on his boot heels. "You both will. And since you told me in your call that you didn't have driving experience, we'll do a bit of training first."

"Sounds good," Dad said, happily running his hands up Shirley's neck. The mare lowered her head, nudging Dad's chest like a cat seeking attention. "We've got all day."

All day?

Chandler's eye twitched. He checked the time on his cell phone, mentally rearranging his afternoon schedule. Zane could swing by and pick up Sam from school, if necessary. And if things dragged on here, what did it matter? It was probably for the best that Chandler didn't see Izzy as she went about decorating the ranch tonight.

"Snowy white horse, yellow wheels, fringe." Dad was practically singing. "I feel like Curly."

"I have no idea what that means." Chandler walked around the mare assessing her confirmation, which seemed excellent.

"It's an *Oklahoma!* reference." Dad laughed. "Our parents were fans of a good musical and *Oklahoma!* is one of the best, especially if you live in Oklahoma."

Chandler was vaguely aware of the musical.

"There's a song where Curly sings to Laurey about a rig and pair of horses fit for a bride to ride in." Dad stroked beneath the gray's forelock. "And Shirley—"

The mare whinnied, nudging Dad and pushing him back a step.

Chandler rushed to his side, grabbing his arm to prevent him from falling over.

"—Jones played Laurey in the movie version. This is Curly's buggy and Shirley..." Dad paused, grinning.

The mare blew a raspberry and pawed the ground.

"Why isn't she named Laurey or Curly?" Dad wondered aloud.

"Laurey was this girl's mama." C.D. climbed into the front seat with surprising grace for being such a large man. "Hop in, gents. I'll take you for a ride and then teach you about driving."

Chandler made sure his foster father was in the front seat safely before he scooted into the back, ducking a little when the crown of his cowboy hat brushed the canopy above him. His knees bumped the backside of the front seat. "Not much legroom back here."

"These surreys are made for women." C.D. picked up the reins and signaled for the cowboy holding Shirley's headstall to release her. "And off we go."

Shirley leaped into action, jerking the buggy forward before settling into a bouncy trot, a pace Chandler assumed was the prancing the owner was talking about.

"You fellas should note how I'm holding the reins. I've got them coming below my ring fingers, up and over my index fingers, and I hold them in place with my thumbs." The owner showed his hands to Dad. "Shirley—"

She whinnied.

"—has a light mouth. So, if you want to go left, don't saw on the reins. Ease her into it." C.D. guided her to the left, crossing the arena. "Same when you bring her to a stop. Whoa, now. Whoa." He eased the reins back.

Shirley came to a bouncy halt, tossing her head a little as if she was annoyed at being denied her prancing.

"You feel like trying?" The owner handed Dad the reins.

"I'm game." Dad threaded the reins through his fingers. "Giddyap, Shirley."

The large mare lunged forward with a shrill whistle, practically giving Chandler whiplash.

"Not so much rein when you start," C.D. advised.

"Let's see what she can do." Dad drove the buggy the way he drove a motor vehicle—too fast and like he had a death wish.

C.D. white-knuckled the bar at the front of the rig.

"Slow down," Chandler cautioned when Shirley broke into a gallop.

"This is like a ride at one of those amusement parks!" Dad shouted. "*Hoo-whee!* Mary's going to love this."

"Dad!" Chandler clapped a hand on his foster father's shoulder. "Reel it in."

Someone was going to have to act like the adult. And Chandler was afraid that role was on him.

"WE NEED MORE WREATHS." Mary held a pine sprig to her nose on Tuesday afternoon. She sat at the kitchen table across from Izzy, wearing a gray sweatshirt appliquéd with a teddy bear and a sprig of mistletoe. "This smells like Christmas. And we need more of it."

Izzy agreed. "I can pick up some more wreaths tomorrow before I drive out. You can never have too much Christmas cheer." Although Chandler might argue that.

Or he would have last week. He was…different now.

But maybe, so was Izzy. Every time she heard a truck pull up in the ranch yard, she held her breath, waiting for Chandler to enter. She wanted to tell Chandler about Mike. She hadn't even shared the news with Earl. What Mike was doing… It sent her blood pressure soaring.

"Never have too much Christmas cheer. That's what I always say this time of year." Mary gazed around the kitchen, smiling contentedly. She seemed to have more energy than she had on Saturday. "The house is shaping up, thanks to you."

"My pleasure." Izzy smiled. "We've done a lot in just a few days."

The tree was up and decorated in the living room, along with the Christmas village and lighted boughs on the mantel. The vintage candle lights were in the front windows and twenty stockings had been hung from the mantel—one for every foster cowboy spending Christmas at the ranch this year.

And the kitchen…

There were ceramic reindeer at one corner of the counter and jolly knit gnomes tucked in between the sugar and flour canisters, while white twinkle lights sparkled beneath the upper cupboards and around the large kitchen window. A red-flowering Christmas cactus sat in a pot in the middle of the kitchen table, sporting bright red blooms. A bright red tea towel hung from the oven handle, alongside a green hot pad with a Santa on it.

And that was just the inside.

Mary reached over to squeeze Izzy's hand. "I've been enjoying your Christmas outfits. Just seeing them lifts my spirits."

Izzy's sweater today was also pink, decorated with a team of pink flamingos sporting antlers and pulling Santa's sleigh. She wore her antlers, and they jingled as she helped the two kids prepare felt cowboy hats to be hung on the bunkhouse Christmas tree. Izzy was gluing turtledove ornaments onto two wreaths Mary had selected, chuckling to herself about how Harper would appreciate this. Mary was supposed to be signing and addressing Christmas cards, but she was easily distracted and had only done a few.

"I changed after school so me and Mama match." Mae's white knit dress had pink flamingos and presents in an alternating pattern around the skirt.

She was gluing gold cords on the felt cowboy hat ornaments Izzy had found in a box in the garage.

"I don't have any sweaters for Christmas." Sam's job was to glue green ribbon hatbands over the crown of the felt cowboy hats.

"Maybe you should ask for a sweater for Christmas," Izzy suggested, then lifted her head because she thought she heard another truck pull in.

"I wrote my letter to Santa already." Sam coated his fingertips with glue from the glue stick, then stuck them together and pried them apart. Repeatedly. "We both did. Miz Stodimeyer was going to mail them to Santa."

"That was the day Miz Stodimeyer had her baby." Mae gasped. "Do you think she mailed our letters?"

Sam's eyes widened. "What if our letters don't get to Santa on time?"

"I'll get in touch with Mrs. Stodimeyer," Izzy promised. She'd been meaning to anyway. "I'll try tonight after dinner."

"I'm sure she mailed those letters," Mary said reassuringly, but she gave Izzy a worried glance. "She knows how important they are to all you kids."

"If you don't write a letter to Santa, do you get a lump of coal?" Sam whispered, big brown eyes wide.

"No." Izzy laughed, taking the opportunity to wipe the boy's glue-covered fingers. "Coal is for kids on the very naughty list." Like Mike, who deserved a stocking full of coal.

"Are we on the very naughty list?" Mae looked scared.

"You've been in trouble, but I don't think it's enough to put you on the naughty list." Mary was still trying to reassure the kids.

"And besides, I hear they give you cauliflower nowadays instead of coal if you've been misbehaving." Izzy did something with the cookie dough. "If you get a stalk of cauliflower, Sam, Mary will cook it."

"But… I don't like cauliflower." Sam turned up his nose.

"Do you know the best way to make sure you aren't on the naughty list?" Izzy asked them. When they shook their heads, she said, "Stay out of trouble at school and be a blessing at home."

The kids went back to mixing. Still worried, if their pouts were any indication.

"I'll send Mrs. Stodimeyer a text now in case the baby is sleeping later." Izzy opened her phone screen and scrolled through her contacts with only a twinge of guilt for not trying to use the school's online messaging system, which she had yet to try and figure out. "If your teacher hasn't mailed your letters, I'll swing by on the way home and get them."

"And my mom will get them in the mail," Sam said happily, referring to Stephanie. "I can't wait to show her my Christmas tree. I had Dad take a picture with his phone and send it to her."

"That's half the joy of the holiday." Mary nodded. "Seeing what other folks decorate with."

Her words reminded Izzy of another conversation about folks enjoying the festive displays at the Done Roamin' Ranch. "Mary, have you ever considered opening up your holiday display to friends and family?"

"Ronnie mentioned that the other night." The older woman tsked. "She seems to think it would do me good. Everyone has an opinion about what would do me good."

"Think about it." Izzy gave up on Chandler arriving and focused on Mary. "I bet you'd have fun seeing people enjoying your decorations. If we rearranged the trucks in the ranch yard, we could make a loop so that your friends could drive past, say hello and then drive back out."

Mary thought about that for a moment before saying, "I don't know. Frank will complain if they come at all hours. He likes to go to bed early." She chuckled. "Or fall asleep in his recliner early in front of the TV."

"We could post a sign saying the lights switch off at ten." Izzy hadn't thought this through but for every argument Mary presented, she seemed to have an answer. "Maybe nine if you prefer."

"Can my friends come, too?" Sam asked.

"Oh, and me." Mae perked up.

"All right. I'm making an executive decision." Mary chuckled. "If I don't go for it, Chandler will never agree. Let's get it going before the boys get back."

"Why don't we call them?" The last thing Izzy wanted was to upset Chandler and his status quo.

"I'll call and have *you* ask Chandler." Mary's eyes twinkled with mischief.

Izzy's cheeks heated. "What makes you think I have any sway over Chandler?"

Mary laughed louder, but she wouldn't answer the question.

And it was a moot point. Neither Chandler nor Frank answered their phones.

CHAPTER THIRTEEN

"WHAT'S GOING ON HERE?" Chandler drove into the ranch yard after sunset on Tuesday.

After taking the horse and buggy for an extended test drive, receiving a time-consuming tour of C.D.'s operation and haggling with the Sooner Wagon Wheels owner, Chandler and Dad had purchased a horse and buggy for Mom. Shirley and the rig were to be delivered next week. All he wanted was a hot meal and a little rest and relaxation with Sam before bed. But there was mischief afoot at the ranch.

"Looks like someone's rearranging the yard." Dad picked his white cowboy hat from the dash and put it on his head. "And look at all those tires. Are they supposed to be round pyramids?"

"Snowmen," Chandler mumbled, recalling Izzy's idea from days before.

Zane waved his arms, directing Chandler to park nearer the side pasture.

"What's going on?" Chandler demanded as soon as he'd parked and his boots had hit the ground.

"We're making a turnabout." Izzy came into the

glow of the ranch yard lights, wearing several tones of pink and looking like she was ready to celebrate Christmas somewhere tropical.

And if Chandler hadn't been upset over things changing without his or Dad's approval, he might have spent more time dwelling on thoughts of pretty, tropical Izzy.

But he was upset and so images of bikinis and umbrella drinks were banished. "Izzy, why didn't you think to check with me? The ranch foreman?" Chandler pointed at the many stacks of old, bald tires that formed the circle he assumed vehicles were supposed to drive around. "I told you that we save those tires until we have a truckload and then we haul them to the recycle center."

"You can still do that." Her antlers jingled, defying his sour mood, encouraging him to join in the joyous spirit of Christmas and change. "We're going to spray-paint them white, use black markers to make blocks of coal for a face, and *voila!* We'll have recyclable snowmen defining the turnabout. Mary suggested we put the nativity scene in the middle."

"Haven't seen the nativity here in years." Dad was noticeably not entering this fight.

"All this effort for more holiday cheer?" Chandler washed a hand over his face.

"Chandler..." Izzy's voice softened. "If you want to help Mary recuperate this season, you need to be supportive. We thought it would be fun to open up the ranch a few hours after sundown a few times a week for the community to do a drive-through. Zane and Dylan moved a couch from the bunkhouse onto the front porch so Mary can wave or talk to friends who swing through. It'll lift her spirits."

"In the cold." Chandler huffed, looking to Dad for support. Getting none.

"She's agreed to bundle up," Izzy assured him, also appealing to Chandler's foster father. "Plus, Zane found her a portable heater."

"We *have* gone along with Mary being a hermit during and after her treatments," Dad allowed. "These outdoor visits might be good for her spirits. It was her idea, you say?"

Izzy looked uncertain for the first time since their arrival. "It was Ronnie's and my idea first. But when we floated it by Mary, she wanted to run with it and..." Izzy blew out a breath. "Frank, when you hired me, you did say you wanted me to go the extra mile. And when Mary tried reaching you two this afternoon, she rolled to voice mail."

"We had no signal where we were," Dad admitted.

"She didn't leave a message," Chandler stated. He'd texted Zane, asking if there was an emergency. Zane had indicated everything was fine.

And that would be the last time Chandler trusted Zane. He should have clued Chandler in.

"Dad! Come see what we did!" Sam appeared out of the darkness and crashed into Chandler's legs. Sam stared up at him with one hand holding

his cowboy hat on. "Mae and me have been working on bunkhouse decorations so we won't be on
the naughty list."

And Sam was so happy...

Chandler very nearly gave this Christmas Tree
Lane idea of Izzy's his blessing.

"And Miz Izzy brought me a chocolate calendar." Sam pranced around. "Yummy, yummy,
yummy. Happy, happy, happy tummy."

"I guess that's what's important," Chandler told
Izzy, leaving her and Dad and submitting to Sam's
tugging. "Happy, happy, Sammy."

"I'm sorry!" Izzy called after him.

"Give it a chance, son," Dad hollered after him.

"Give it a chance, Dad." Sam bounced happily
next to him.

Chandler's son led him to the bunkhouse, where
white lights outlined the wreath-adorned door. Inside, there was a small tree decorated with red-
and-green paper chain garlands, white lights and
cowboy hat ornaments that Chandler had never
seen before. Stockings with each ranch hand's
name were pinned to each bunk bed. A small pillow with a reindeer had been tossed onto each bed.
A red plaid runner crossed the length of the dining
table. White lights, red glass balls and fir boughs
made a cheerful centerpiece. A glass jar on the
small kitchen counter held candy canes. Another
held sugar cookies. Next to that was a stack of
paper napkins with Santa printed on them.

"I bet Grandma Mary was happy with this."

Even if it wasn't what she normally did. Chandler bet the other ranch hands were happy with it, too.

"She was." Sam looped an arm around Chandler's leg. "I glued so-o-o-o many cowboy hatbands on these ornaments."

"All by yourself?"

"Mae helped." He used Chandler's leg like a pole and swung around.

"We'll have all the ranch hands thank her." And Izzy. The space looked warm and welcoming, just the way he, Zane and Dylan had described to Izzy. She'd come through for them. And what had Chandler done? Nitpicked. Harping on about the same old place for lights and decorations. Snapping at her about the drive-through. "Where is Mae?"

"We were playing with the Christmas village inside with Ginny and Grandma." He laughed. "I like Della-Mae. Do you?"

"Why wouldn't I?" He lifted Sam to his hip. "Mae's your best friend."

"Yep. She's practically family." Sam placed his hat on top of Chandler's.

"That's good to hear," Izzy said from behind them, having entered the bunkhouse without Chandler noticing. "I've got to get Mae home. We haven't eaten yet."

"Why not stay for dinner?" Chandler surprised himself by asking. So much for giving her space.

"Yay!" Sam leaped to his feet and dragged Chandler toward Izzy. "We're having pork chops and potatoes." Sam stopped an arm's length from Izzy and tried to join her hand with Chandler's, something he used to do when Chandler and Stephanie were together. "Come on, everybody."

Chandler's fingers brushed against Izzy's before they each pulled back. Her cheeks turned an appealing shade of pink. Appealing, because it was Chandler's touch that had created that blush. Pride filled his chest.

I'm not so old, after all.

"Wait until I tell Mae she's eating with us." Sam ran out of the bunkhouse calling, "Mae! Mae!" Chandler's son ran on a long-lasting battery. His energy and enthusiasm never seemed to wane.

Izzy snuck a glance at Chandler…at his lips, reminding him of how combustible their kiss had been, making him want to kiss her again. Maybe on a tropical beach given her hot pink holiday attire.

"I guess we're staying for dinner," Izzy said softly, still blushing, still not quite looking Chandler in the eye.

"Pork chops and potatoes." Good thing the rule at the Done Roamin' Ranch was to always make extra. "I guess I should give the roundabout my blessing." Because Dad didn't seem to mind, and the last thing Chandler wanted was to start a fight with Izzy.

"Are you sure you don't want to talk about it some more?" Izzy's soft blue gaze finally met his, tentatively. At his shaking head, she added, "I'm so glad. Mary is excited about it."

"She knew I'd cave in." Chandler shook his head, feeling the tension inside him ease. "Have you decorated all the outbuildings? Mom won't want to throw open the gates to visitors until you do."

"No. Honestly, I haven't even been inside anything but the main house, your house and here." Now that he'd given the roundabout his blessing, the more she talked, the more comfortable she seemed with him. "Do the barns and outbuildings really need decoration?"

"Mom would insist." They should be moving toward the kitchen and dinner. But Chandler wanted more time alone with Izzy. "Let me give you a brief tour of the barn to give you a chance to come up with some new ideas."

"New ideas? I thought you didn't want anything that hasn't been done before?" Her gaze turned wary. "Or does the tour include you trying to talk about *something…*?" Izzy gestured between them.

"Your suspicion wounds me." Chandler held the door for Izzy without answering her question. The cold air and chill wind wrapped him in its chilly embrace. "I heard you before when you said now wasn't the time to pursue anything."

"Good." She walked out past him.

"But it's nice, isn't it?" Chandler moved to her side as they headed for the large barn, head bent to catch anything she might say, be it muttered or murmured. "This *something*?"

"You're fishing." Her antlers jingled. "We're not pursuing whatever this is, remember?"

"Talking isn't really pursuing." If they never talked about this hum between them, they'd never kiss again. And Chandler had an inkling that never kissing Izzy again would be a crying shame.

"Are you flirting with me?" Izzy gave Chandler a quick glance before hurrying onward. "You don't flirt."

"Like I shouldn't flirt with you...ever?" Oh, this was completely not like him, but he couldn't seem to stop. "Or you don't want me to flirt *with you*?"

Izzy huffed, accented by her antlers jingling. "How can you be flirting with me? Weren't you annoyed with me fifteen minutes ago?"

"Yes, but then the way you looked at me reminded me of Saturday night, obviously because it was one of the worst experiences of your life." And if that wasn't a blatant play for a compliment, Chandler didn't know what was. "Regardless of who kissed who, it sounds like you were disappointed."

"It wasn't bad." Izzy walked faster. Her white-blond hair shimmered in the overhead ranch yard lights. "And that's as much as I'll say."

It wasn't bad. From Izzy, that was practically high praise. Chandler's chest swelled with unexpected pride. *Go, me!*

"And that's why we aren't going to talk about it," Izzy continued, hanging on to her antlers when the wind nearly blew them off.

He recognized that tone of voice. It was the efficient tone Izzy used when handling his business calls at the feed store. That wouldn't do. "Well, we have to talk about something." Even if it wasn't the spark between them.

"Tell me what your mother usually does in terms of decoration in the barn." Izzy practically broke into a jog.

"I can't talk to you when you run away." Unfortunately, Izzy wasn't stopping. "I know I make you nervous and we've been in awkward situations the past few days but…"

"But?" She slowed, glancing up at the barn looming before them.

Izzy not running away was a win Chandler would analyze later. Instinctively, he knew that he'd miss sleep while taking his feelings and her words apart tonight. For now, it was time to put her at ease. "Outside the barn, there are wreaths and lights. Mom loves her wreaths and lights. And mistletoe."

"Why is there mistletoe at the barn?" Izzy asked, still studying the barn.

Chandler took a moment to think about that, having never really considered it before. "I think it's Mom's way of encouraging opportunities for romantic moments. Ronnie isn't the only starry-eyed woman on the ranch."

"We didn't need mistletoe to…" Izzy turned to him, cheeks blooming with color, revealed by the exterior barn lights. "Never mind. It's been a long day, starting with my ex."

A gust of wind kicked up. Izzy shivered, not surprising given she only wore that pink sweater. That seemed like her work uniform and if she wasn't careful, she was going to burn too many calories shivering outside at night. That could lead to dangerously low blood sugar levels.

"Let's get out of the wind and get you warm." Chandler opened the barn door for her. The smell of hay and horse greeted them. Up and down the breezeway, horses poked their heads over stall doors. "You saw your ex-husband this morning?"

"Yeah. He wants to change our custody agreement." Izzy's voice had a fragile note in it. "He's getting serious about a woman who doesn't want to be a mom. Not to Mae. Not to anyone."

"The good news is that you'll have Mae more often." Chandler frowned, making a mental note to check in with Stephanie.

"And the bad news is that she'll realize at some point that Mike was willing to give her up." Izzy had stopped. Her shoulders drew inward. "For a woman. Just like my father did with me."

Chandler dared rub the small of her back. "Hey. Don't crawl into your shell over this. We can get through it. Together."

Izzy drew a shaky breath. "You're right. I can get through this. With the help of my friends. Like you. I can only control so much, right? The rest… The rest I have to weather with grace, the way you all do here at the ranch."

Chandler couldn't speak. No one but his foster parents had ever spoken so powerfully about what he'd overcome, the way he moved forward. He and his foster brothers.

"You honor me…us…" But Chandler didn't want to talk about strength and perseverance. He didn't want to talk about ex-spouses. They were alone. And they were so rarely alone that he wanted to make the most of it. He pointed upward. "Here's where the first sprig of mistletoe goes."

Izzy glanced up, and then at him. "You're teasing me."

"A little. But I'm also telling the truth." He led her to the first stall, which held Baby Bear, the pony Ginny had ridden until a few years ago, and was now Sam's. "Mom hangs a sprig of plastic mistletoe outside each stall door, too."

"Plastic?" Izzy's brow wrinkled.

"Real mistletoe can give a horse colic, which can be deadly."

"Wouldn't want that." She nodded, ruffling Baby Bear's dark forelock. "My mother loved Christmas. And since money was tight, she had a ton of plastic decorations we reused every year. It was my job to clean the dust off the wreath for the front door." She glanced up at Chandler. "Did your mother love Christmas? Your biological mother, I mean."

Chandler's throat clogged unexpectedly with the sharp pain of abandonment. It made no sense. That had been over twenty years ago.

One glance at his face and Izzy withdrew, inching away from him as if sensing he needed space. "I didn't mean to pry or upset you."

Chandler nodded, moving because he needed to, walking away even if his heart didn't want him to put distance between them. He was used to evading questions about his past, including with Stephanie. But if he'd learned anything from his failed marriage, it was that you couldn't open your heart to a woman without opening the door to your past, as well.

Chandler stopped at the stall of Cisco, a palomino, making a low noise to call the horse over. And while he gave the gelding pats on the neck, Izzy joined him at the stall. Cisco tried to nibble on her antlers.

Izzy removed her headpiece with a sleigh-like series of jingles and held it out of reach. "Hey, not edible, young man."

Cisco blew a raspberry.

"About my mother…"

Izzy's blue gaze met his. She waited for him to say more.

"My biological mother was a coffee shop waitress. She always worked on holidays, like Christmas. She said the tips were better. And I…" Chandler drew a bracing amount of air in his lungs. "I already told you about my dad. Neither one was interested in celebrating Christmas the way a lot of families do, like my ranch family does."

Izzy touched his arm briefly, making him wish her hand remained. "You were only a child. That must have been terrible."

"Some kids who were lucky enough to end up

here experienced worse." Chandler speared his fingers through Cisco's thick mane, grabbing hold, trying to find emotional balance. "The thing about kids is… They're really good at adapting." To loneliness, to hunger, to lack.

Izzy stared at Chandler with those big blue eyes that he'd forever associate with Christmas. "*You* were good at adapting. None of this third-person stuff. You. And you shouldn't let them haunt you."

Cisco stretched his head over the stall, making another play at nibbling on Izzy's antlers.

Chandler gently pushed the gelding back. "My mother doesn't haunt me. In a way, I have a lot to thank her for. She went to work one day and never came back." Leaving Chandler with only the memory of her words—*take care of yourself, kiddo.* "I kept going to school. At least they gave me two meals a day. And then Dad had a streak where he couldn't stay out of jail. Social services found out and… Here I am."

"Oh, Chandler." Izzy laid her hand on Chandler's arm once more. "Don't ever make light of it."

"I guess we shouldn't judge Mike's new girlfriend." Chandler tried to smile. Failed. Placed a hand over hers. Kept talking. "It might be for the best."

"My dad wasn't a drinker, but he wasn't interested in raising a kid, either," Izzy said in a faraway voice. "Especially not a grieving one when he'd already moved on."

"Kids deserve better than they get sometimes." That seemed like a gross understatement.

"Agreed." Izzy had moved closer as she spoke, brows slanted with curiosity, gaze trained on his mouth.

Chandler was curious, too. And Izzy was too close not to kiss.

He leaned forward, pausing with his lips a hair's breadth away from hers, waiting for Izzy to meet him halfway.

And on a sigh, she did.

It was a gentle kiss this time, a kiss that didn't burst with barely contained heat. This kiss said there was more between them than a surprising attraction. There was a sense of shared experience, of shared values, of respect.

But underneath that tender kiss, there was a growing unease inside Chandler. Because this attraction…this connection… It required change. And change made him twitchy.

So, it made no sense that Chandler kept kissing Izzy. Or that he held on to her as if he never wanted to let her go.

The barn door opened.

Their kiss didn't end. Chandler imagined Izzy didn't hear.

"Oh, hey, Chandler. *Dinner?*" Zane's voice. Surprised.

And then the barn door closed.

CHAPTER FOURTEEN

"WHAT WAS THAT?" Izzy hurried to the main house, trying—*and failing*—to outwalk Chandler after she'd belatedly realized they'd been discovered kissing and had bolted out of the barn. "No. Don't tell me. I don't want to know. It was bad enough you said that Zane saw us. Go back to looking at me like I'm an alien in Christmas clothing."

Because that kiss had been gentle but powerful. Emotionally powerful. She was just regaining her internal footing after the divorce. She didn't want or need to be plunged into the turbulent waters that love brought.

Izzy suspected Chandler would argue or laugh off her reaction. But they passed beneath the twinkle lights illuminating the trees without speaking. They walked between an inflatable Santa and Frosty without speaking. The main house loomed with gutters and gables lit up with colorful lights. Sam's Christmas tree on the front porch had racing lights. And still, they didn't speak.

She risked a glance at Chandler as they walked

across the path toward the stairs and the mudroom. He looked as shell-shocked as she was.

Their gazes met. And it was just as Izzy had requested. Chandler regarded her as if she was an alien dressed in Christmas clothing—shocking, surprising, someone to be wary of.

Be careful what you wish for, Izzy.

"Kissing isn't supposed to be like this," Izzy muttered, charging up the stairs. "Like the Buffalo Diner gave me a double-slice of Coronet's famous pecan pie when I've sworn off desserts."

"If you liked it that much, it means we should be kissing, and kissing frequently," Chandler muttered back, matching her step for step. Still, he managed to reach the mudroom door first and open it for her.

"That's not what it means." Or at least, it wasn't what Izzy wanted it to mean.

There was chatter in the kitchen that quieted to whispers as they removed their boots.

Great. Zane blabbed about what he saw.

She couldn't bolt. Mae was in there. But her cheeks were heating and her courage failing.

A touch on her hand made her jump. But Chandler didn't recoil. His fingers curled about hers.

Izzy lifted her gaze to his. She saw understanding there. He knew she wanted to run.

But she'd heard the reputation of the Done Roamin' Ranch boys. And she knew many of them. They didn't run from hard times.

And I won't, either.

Izzy straightened her boots, hooking her jingling antler headband in one, and then entered the kitchen, head held high. "Sorry to keep everyone waiting." She slid into a chair next to Mae.

"We didn't wait." Sam had a pork chop and a mountain of potatoes on his plate with a lake of gravy on top surrounded by a forest of green beans.

"Mr. Zane said you were talking to Mr. Cochran in the barn." Mae had only a dollop of mashed potatoes and five string beans on her plate. She ate like a bird.

Izzy ladled green beans on her plate, and then took two pork chops from a serving tray, placing one on Mae's plate. She quickly cut the meat into Mae-sized bites.

"Mae, why are you calling Zane by his first name and my dad by my last name?" Sam broke the dam on his potato lake, sending gravy streaming onto his plate. It flooded his pork chop and green beans.

"I don't know Mr. Zane's last name." Mae ate a dainty bite of pork chop.

"You don't have to call me mister," Zane said from down the table. "Zane will do."

"And you can call me Chandler." He with the power of drugging kisses took a seat across from Izzy.

"You want me to call you Chandler because you and Mama were talking in the barn?" Mae asked in a hopeful voice.

Zane suffered a coughing fit, resulting in cowboys on either side of him slapping his back.

Zane, who'd most likely witnessed that kiss.

Izzy's cheeks heated once more.

"Everyone at the Done Roamin' Ranch is family," Mary told Mae. "And that means there's no mister or ma'am."

"Oh..." Mae drew out the word, small brow furrowed. And then she brightened. "Family? Does that mean they're married now?"

"Yippee!" Sam cried, raising his fork in the air.

Those who'd started dinner before Izzy stilled. Only their heads moved, shifting focus toward Chandler and Izzy's end of the table.

Izzy didn't dare look at Chandler for fear she'd die of embarrassment. "Mae, allowing you to use Chandler's first name doesn't mean we're married. We were just...talking in the barn. About holiday decorations." No one but the kids would believe that whopper of a fib.

"Were you talking about me and Mae?" Sam asked.

"Or about getting married?" Mae asked.

"Or about holiday decorations?" Mary jumped into the fray with a barely contained smile.

"Or about the Christmas turnabout?" Frank asked, better at hiding his amusement than his wife.

"I bet they were talking about specks of dirt in someone's eye," Zane managed to choke out.

Izzy wished there was a way she and Mae could disappear. This not-running stuff was hard.

"What does it matter what we were talking

about?" Chandler grumbled, filling his plate with the last of the mashed potatoes. "Pass the gravy, please."

"Oh," Mary said, looking pleased.

"Oh?" Frank said, looking speculative.

"Oh, yeah," Zane said, looking smug.

Izzy wouldn't have thought it was possible, but her cheeks grew hotter. This was worse than the time she tried to ask Tate Oakley out only to find he was in the midst of a date at the time. "Anyway, it's nice to be included in the Done Roamin' Ranch family without having to marry into it."

"Although that's still on the table," Zane said in a stage whisper.

"Sweet." Sam nudged Mae with his elbow. "Now, is anyone going to get me and Mae puppies for Christmas?"

A CONTINGENT OF Done Roamin' Ranch cowboys escorted Izzy and Mae to their SUV after dinner.

The stars were out and the night was crisp and cold. The prairie wind buffeted the inflatable Santa Claus.

And if he was being honest with himself, Chandler wasn't upset about not having time alone with Izzy. He hadn't counted on their kids assuming their time together meant there was marriage on the horizon. That was too much, too soon.

"Well…" Dad turned after Izzy's taillights disappeared over the first rise separating the ranch from the main road, holding on to the top of his cowboy hat when the wind tried to carry it away. "Never a dull moment around here."

"I'll say." Zane covered Sam's ears with his hands, tucking them under his hat brim. "Are you staking a claim on our Christmas flamingo?"

"Hey!" Sam squirmed free.

Chandler frowned at Zane. "We're navigating *something.*" He didn't know how to describe what was going on between them. "There's no claim." *Yet,* a voice whispered in his head.

"Then you won't mind if I ask her to dance next time we're both at the Buckboard." Zane had always been comfortable dancing at the edge of fire.

"I won't stand in anyone's way if that's what you mean," Chandler growled.

"What?" Sam scaled three stacked tires that were soon to be snowmen. "Who are we talking about?"

Chandler lifted Sam into his arms. "Not who. What. We were talking about Christmas decorations."

Zane snorted.

"Dancing ones?" Sam snuggled close, nearly knocking off his hat.

"Yep." Chandler took hold of it.

"Our decorations sure look pretty," Dad said, playing along. "That was a good call on my part. Hiring Izzy, I mean. Why if I hadn't, we might have been stuck."

Chandler grunted.

Laughing, Zane bid them good-night, heading for the cheery lights in the bunkhouse.

"Do you want to talk?" Dad asked Chandler.

"Nope." Chandler headed for the main house. "We're just walking you home." His job was to make sure his parents were safely tucked in at night, same as their stock.

"We could go inside for a few of those Christmas cookies." Sam tucked his head on Chandler's shoulder, beneath the brim of Chandler's cowboy hat, a sure sign that his batteries were running low. "Nothing puts me to sleep better than milk and sweets."

"You made cookies again today?" If so, Chandler hadn't seen the evidence.

"Ronnie and Ginny made fudge." Sam was drooping, limbs turning slack. He yawned.

"You should follow your instincts," Dad said. "If you find something you like that makes you feel good inside, you should stick with it."

"Are we talking about fudge?" Chandler teased.

Dad chuckled. "If you want to be."

"I think this is going to be the best Christmas ever." Sam yawned again. "Decorations, puppies, family. Can we have fudge, Dad?"

"Nope. Time for bed. Plenty of time for fudge at Christmas." Chandler smirked. Sometimes he couldn't believe the parental dreck that came out of his mouth. Chandler stopped at the first porch step.

Sam snored softly.

Dad rubbed Sam's back. "You and Izzy seem to be getting along."

"You've got to preheat an oven, Dad." Chandler didn't want expectations about the two of them to race ahead of their actual progress.

Dad nodded his head. "Well, that's the thing about getting in the kitchen. Sometimes you whip things right up. And sometimes you take hours to create a masterpiece. Don't always know what you'll get as a result."

"You're always so optimistic." And unless Chandler was kissing Izzy, he didn't share that sentiment where they were concerned.

"I know my glass is half-full, son." Dad smiled, slowly scaling the porch steps. He turned when he reached the top. "But the fact remains that if you never go back in the kitchen, you'll never know what happiness awaits you at the dinner table."

CHAPTER FIFTEEN

"Izzy, DO YOU have a Santapalooza costume?" Earl led Lois Pierce through the jeans section of the feed store on Friday morning toward the sales counter. "You and Mae?"

Earl was walking with noodle legs, and he kept glancing over his shoulder at Lois with an unusually large smile. He'd had a crush on Lois since Izzy couldn't remember when. Lois had taken up dying her grays last Christmas when she began dating again. She usually went around town in worn ranch clothes, carrying a tote with whatever craft project she was working on. In the summer, it was knitting. And with Christmas approaching, she'd be working on costumes for the annual Santapalooza ride on Christmas Day, where all participants had to dress like Santa or his missus.

"A Santapalooza costume?" Izzy set aside the Christmas-scented candles she'd been pricing and thoughts of Chandler. Who would have thought that beneath that stoic exterior lived a man who was so passionate and impulsive? Probably the same folks who would have predicted Izzy would go around town in holiday-themed outfits getting paid to decorate for Christmas.

"Izzy," Earl said, bearing down on the sales counter. "Do you have a Santapalooza costume?"

"Nope," Izzy said. "Why do you ask?"

"Last year, we broke the record for the most Santas in a parade ride." Lois set her large purple tote on the counter. It was stuffed with red velvet and white faux fur trim. "Now some yahoo town in New Mexico is trying to break our record. We're recruiting riders, preferably those who already have costumes. Clementine must defend Santapalooza."

"We don't have horses or costumes." Izzy smiled apologetically. "My last ride was when I was a teenager. When my dad sold my horse, I gave my costume away." And every year since, she'd watched with just a twinge of envy.

"I asked Frank over at the Done Roamin' Ranch if we could borrow some horses." Lois stared at Izzy from beneath a worn brown hat. "And I'm going around town this morning to recruit Santas. If I can make you costumes in time, can we count on you and Mae?"

"Course you can," Earl answered for Izzy. "You can count on me, too. Whatever you need. You just call me. Day or night. You have my number, don't ya?"

"I'm glad you said that, Earl." Lois smiled at him without a trace of reciprocal opposite-sex admiration. "I've never been able to get you to ride in Santapalooza. Can we count on you this year?"

"I... I... I... I..." Earl stammered. He hadn't ridden for years due to a bum hip he kept putting off replacing. Riding for him was a bit painful, not that anyone but Izzy knew it. But after being blindsided by Lois's offer, he recovered, standing taller. "Course, I will. If you need me."

Izzy hid her amusement behind a small cough. "If someone has a wagon, Earl, Mae and I will gladly climb on board in our Santa costumes. We'd be proud to represent Clementine."

Earl beamed at Izzy. "That's a right good idea. Count us in for a wagon ride."

A few minutes later, having taken note of their clothing sizes and promising to deliver costumes next week, Lois made her leave. No one else was in the store. Stan was out making deliveries.

It was the perfect time to tease Earl about his crush.

"You should ask Lois out." Izzy returned the priced candles to their display box. "You'd make a cute couple."

Earl removed his cowboy hat and ran his hand through his white hair, scoffing. "She's been dating Chet for a year."

"Then you should attend some of those socials at the retirement home to find yourself a dance partner." Izzy carried the box toward the Christmas aisle. "Studies show that men live longer with a romantic partner. Love keeps you young."

"I've got you and Mae to keep me young," Earl

stated matter-of-factly. "Speaking of, when are we going to set up Mae's princess bed?"

Mae's Christmas gift. Izzy bit her lip. "Mike is supposed to have Mae on Christmas Eve." Izzy made room for the candles on the shelf, wondering if her ex-husband would still want Mae given the self-serving choice he'd made. "And I need a few more payments to come in from my holiday services before I can buy that bed."

"Our girl's going to have big dreams beneath that canopy," Earl mused.

"I hope so." Satisfied with the way the shelf looked, Izzy returned to the sales counter, still thinking about Mike. "Earl, why didn't you ever get married and have kids of your own?"

His back to her, the old man was restocking the candy display. He didn't answer for some time.

Izzy opened a file on the store's computer to check online orders.

"I wanted to have a family," Earl said, turning slowly to face Izzy. His eyes were filled with sadness. "I never met the right woman at the right time. It's like this attraction I have to Lois. She wasn't ready to date for years. And then when she was ready, I didn't notice." He snapped his fingers. "And just like that, she got snapped up."

"I'm sorry." Was that how it would be with her and Chandler?

"Don't be." He carried empty candy boxes to the counter, breaking them down until they were flat. "I have you and Mae."

"That you do. We're lucky to have you." Izzy's father lived in Oklahoma City and had little interest in staying in touch other than with birthday and Christmas cards. But who would take Mike's place as a reliable father figure for Mae? Chandler? He was a good father.

Izzy bit her lip. Love shouldn't be judged by the other attributes a man brought to the relationship.

"Izzy..." Earl pressed his palms on top of the stack of flattened boxes. "If you feel something for little Sam's father the way I think you do, don't wait."

"Whose team are you on?" Izzy tried to make light of Earl's advice, even as a tiny voice in her head agreed with him. "Haven't you ever heard the phrase about fools rushing in?"

"Try telling that to all those friends of yours who've gotten engaged in the past year or so." Earl's chin thrust out. "They're rushing in, the same way customers barrel in here on Black Friday for our annual cowboy boot sale. And why? Because they know a good man is as hard to find as the right pair of boots."

Izzy laughed. She couldn't help it.

Her laughter riled Earl all the more. "Mark my words, Izzy. If you hesitate, you'll end up like me. Alone. Sending signals to the person you pine for but whose radar is oblivious to your frequency."

"Don't you worry about me." Izzy came around the counter to hug Earl. "Or my love life."

"That's just it, girl." When Izzy would have pulled away, Earl clung tight. "You're all I've got to worry about."

"THERE'S MY LITTLE MAN." Stephanie opened the door and smiled at Sam, who stomped past her and headed for his room. "What's wrong with him?"

It was Friday night and dark outside even though it wasn't yet dinnertime. The prairie wind had died down but there was promise of cold in the air.

Chandler handed Stephanie Sam's duffel. "Sam is super excited about things going on at the ranch." The Christmas roundabout, the decorations inside his room at the ranch and the fact that Mae was there practically every day. "He really wanted to stay the weekend."

"That's not like Sam." Stephanie frowned, tugging at the collar of her mail uniform. Her thick-soled work boots were in a heap next to the door. "He's always so good-natured."

"There's a lot going on everywhere right now, including you and that job offer." Chandler tipped his cowboy hat back. "Sam told me he wanted to buy you a suitcase for Christmas. Seems like he might know something that I don't."

"He might have heard me and Mom talk about it on Thanksgiving." Stephanie crossed her arms over her chest. "You'll be happy to know that she doesn't approve of the job, either."

It felt petty to acknowledge how happy that statement made him. "Have you made your choice?"

"That's what I wanted to talk to you about." Stephanie hugged herself tighter, a stubborn look in her eyes. "I took next week off to go to Fort Worth for orientation. Monday through Friday."

"Steph." Frustration at his ex, worry for his son's heartbreak and annoyance that Steph could be this selfish... Those emotions tangled up inside Chandler, tighter and tighter until he thought his control might shatter. That he might rant and rail at Stephanie for throwing away their son's love and trust.

"You're freaking out. I knew this would happen." Steph drew a deep breath. "It's just five days. And I might not like the work, or they might not like me. But if I do move to Texas, I want to take Sam with me."

"No!" Sam cried, running for the front door. "I won't go."

And before either of them could stop Sam, he'd bolted out the door into the darkness.

"Sam!" Stephanie shouted, eyes filling with tears. She reached for her shoes.

But Chandler had already crossed the threshold. He turned back. "Wait here. I'll talk to him."

Steph stood, wiping a tear from her cheek. She looked away, and then slowly closed the door, shutting him out.

Chandler hurried to the sidewalk, then walked down the street, calling for Sam. He didn't have to go far. Christmas lights were shining up and down the avenue, all except at one house. But there was activity on that lawn. Chandler could just make out the silhouette of a ladder and beside it a small figure, possibly a child.

"She wants to take me, Mae. Can you believe it?" Sam's voice carried to Chandler, who was still a few houses away. "I won't go. I won't."

A crack, like a branch snapping under unexpected weight, cut through the air.

"Take a breath, Sam. You're not going anywhere right now until I can get out of this tree." Izzy's voice. "Mae, can you shine that flashlight up here. *Ugh, n*ot in my eyes, bug. There. That's better."

"Your dad won't let you go, Sam." Mae sounded worried. "Will he, Mama?"

Another crack was followed by Izzy's cry of, *"Ouch!"*

Chandler broke into a jog, heading for Paula Lincoln's house. She was a retired schoolteacher and a member of the Santapalooza planning committee, always cheerful with a kind word for Sam. And it seemed she'd hired Izzy to help her put up lights. Why Izzy was working in the dark and in a tree, no less, was beyond Chandler.

"Ouch!" Izzy cried again, followed by the slightest of jingling bells.

"Are you gonna fall, Miz Izzy?" Sam's voice. "Do we need to get out of the way?"

"Yes," Chandler answered for Izzy, charging across the lawn and into the meager light spilling out of Paula's front windows.

"Do you want me to climb up there, Mama? I can get those lights untangled for you." Mae now sat on the bottom rung of the ladder. She shined the flashlight at Chandler, luckily not into his eyes. "Hi, Chandler."

A branch cracked. Izzy made a sound that was half gasp, half curse.

"Hey." Chandler took one of Mae's cold hands and drew her to her feet. And then he took possession of her flashlight. "Sam, if that's you hiding behind the tree trunk, kindly step out where I can see you and Izzy won't fall on you. I want both you kids to move over by the front door."

"Dad, I'm not going back. I'm going to live with you at the ranch." Sam leaned his head around the tree trunk.

"We'll talk about this in a minute, squirt. Right now, I need you and Mae on the front walk." When they did as he'd directed, Chandler glanced up into the tree. "Trouble, Izzy?"

"Nothing I can't handle." Izzy was balanced precariously on a branch above Chandler that bent to support her weight a few feet from the trunk. She was dressed as Rudolph, whose nose blinked like a beacon. And she was struggling to free a section of lights tangled with a branch. "I've got this. I just need to get a little farther out."

Chandler aimed the flashlight into the tree, assessing the bouncy bend to the branch every time Izzy moved and the determined look on her face. "I thought you didn't do circular lights in trees."

"I had a client request." Izzy's frustration was showing. Her chin was out. Her sweater had a big

snag with a small branch stuck in it. And her antlers had sunk to the back of her head and were at
risk of sliding off. "Now, don't say another word."

"Where's that fancy pole we used the other day
at the ranch?"

Izzy made an indecipherable noise. "That's
twelve words, Chandler. And I have three words
for you. *At the ranch.*" Izzy was losing her cool,
lunging more precariously for the stuck strand of
lights every time.

"I think she can do it," Mae said. "Mama does
everything she says she will."

Sam made a sound of disgust. "My mom, too.
And she wants to take me to *Texas.*"

Chandler ignored them. "Come down, Izzy. You
can tell Paula that you'll finish tomorrow. I'll bring
the pole into town first thing in the morning." He'd
even untangle the strand from the branches for her.

"You'll come in at dawn?" Izzy scoffed. "Paula
wants her lights up before her grandkids arrive for
lunch. I promised her we'd be done tonight and..."
Izzy swiped her hand out toward the stuck strand,
but the foot she was standing on slipped. She con-
torted, seemingly balancing midair. And then she
plunged, torso landing on the branch where her
foot used to be. And her feet...

One boot kicked Chandler's hat off.

Her hands flailed toward him. But she was out
of reach, sliding off the branch backward.

Young cries filled the air, accented by Chandler's
flashlight beam highlighting the fear in Izzy's eyes.

"I've got you." Chandler held out his arms, grabbing Izzy's legs as she fell, but lost his balance and toppled backward onto the ground.

Oof.

"I'm okay," Izzy wheezed but it sounded as if she was taking her last breath.

"Mama!" Della-Mae dogpiled them. "You're safe."

Oof.

"Dad!" Sam fell on top of them all. "You saved her."

"I can't breathe," Izzy wheezed, fainter this time.

Chandler slowly rolled over, sending the kids gently tumbling to the grass and Izzy listing next to him.

"Can't..." Izzy repeated, not gasping, just wheezing, like a hooked fish taken from water.

"You've got the wind knocked out of you." Chandler had seen it often enough when someone got thrown from a bull or bronc.

"Mama?" Mae sounded woeful.

"I've got you." Chandler moved to his knees, bringing Izzy with him, pushing her into a crouched position. And then he wacked her on the back with the flat of his hand. "It's all right. It's all right." But he was scared to death that he wouldn't be able to get her lungs working properly again.

"What are you doing?" Mae hollered, moving closer. "Don't hit Mama!"

"Dad, what are you doing?" Sam scrambled to his feet, sounding aghast.

Chandler kept giving Izzy bracing backslaps. "Come on, honey. Fill those lungs with air."

"What's going on out there?" Paula Lincoln opened her front door, sending light spilling out to the lawn. "I can't hear *Jeopardy*."

Izzy drew a deep, raspy breath.

And without thinking, Chandler wrapped his arms around her. "It's okay. It's going to be okay."

He'd save the lectures for later—after he was certain Izzy was fine, after he calmed the kids and reassured Paula that her lights would be up on time in the morning, and after he and Sam drove Izzy and Mae home.

"I'm FINE." Izzy couldn't count how many times she'd told Chandler those same words in the past hour.

He'd insisted on driving them home, insisted on coming inside, insisted on staying. "I've seen plenty of cowboys get the wind knocked out of them when they get thrown. There's a possibility that your diaphragm will cramp up again, seizing up your lungs. Just so you're aware. You shouldn't be alone."

"Dr. Cochran," she'd scoffed. But while he'd ordered pizza and found a movie suitable for the kids to watch, Izzy had searched for information on follow-up care on her cell phone and was humbled to find Chandler was correct. "Thank you," she told him when he sat next to her on the couch. "I appreciate you watching out for me. But it's been nearly an hour."

"I don't mind staying." Chandler settled her red-and-green Christmas blanket over his legs, too, and slid his arm behind her neck. "Better safe than sorry. How are your ribs?"

"It hurts to breathe," she admitted. And because he'd been her hero, she added, "If you hadn't been there…" Her voice cracked and her heart clenched because she couldn't imagine how she would have survived if Chandler hadn't been there. "I could have…"

"But you didn't. I was there. Mae and Sam were troupers, just like when Mrs. Stodimeyer's water broke. If I hadn't been there, Mae would have pounded on Paula's door. As a teacher, Paula would have received medical training. She'd have come to your rescue."

What-if scenarios continued to swirl through Izzy's head, but eventually she had to admit that Chandler was right. And about that time, the pizza arrived.

Chandler didn't let Izzy get up. He found plates. He brought them drinks. And when they were all seated around Izzy's small dining room table, it seemed so natural, like they were a family, and Izzy started to cry.

"Mama?" Mae abandoned her chair for a seat in Izzy's lap.

"It's okay. I promise not to cry for long." But when she wrapped her arms around Mae, more tears fell than dried up. The pressure of the week had caught up to her—the expensive bed for Mae, Mike's startling announcement, all her running around without proper rest, Chandler's confusing kisses and that horribly scary fall.

Her meltdown didn't stop the males at the table from devouring their pizza.

"Dad?" Sam asked when Izzy blew her nose in a napkin. "I don't want to go with Mom. Not anywhere. Not ever again."

Suddenly, Izzy remembered how Sam had shown up, bursting out of the shadows full of upset. She glanced at Chandler.

He took Sam's outburst calmly, laying a hand on Sam's shoulder. "Do you remember what Grandpa always says about bull riding?"

Eyes wide, Sam nodded. "You gotta hang on and roll with whatever happens."

"That's right." Chandler's smile looked brittle, and Izzy's heart went out to him. "Your mother was offered a job in Texas and—"

"I'm not going." Sam's lips thrust out.

"I don't want you to go, either," Chandler said quietly. "But this is just like a bucking bull suddenly putting on a spin move. We've got to hang on to each other and figure this out."

"I'll tell somebody I want to stay with you." Sam wasn't ready to be mollified. "Just like you told somebody you wanted to stay with Grandma and Grandpa."

"A judge," Chandler murmured, gaze drifting Izzy's way.

"That's right." Sam gained steam. "You told a judge cuz your mom came out of nowhere and wanted you back."

Izzy gasped. Taken to court and forced to choose between that family he'd dreamed of and a mother who'd left him behind. What a horrible position to be put in.

Chandler ran a hand through his hair. "I was older than you, squirt. And it wasn't easy to look my mother in the eyes and tell her I was better off where I was."

"I could." Sam picked a pepperoni from his pizza, and then stared up at Chandler. "But maybe you could do it for me?"

"This is something your mom and I have to work out." Chandler moved his hand from Sam's shoulder to his hair, giving it a playful ruffle. "And who knows? She may spend next week in Texas and realize she hates it."

"I can't leave." Sam laid his arm on the table and then put his hand on Chandler's. "My life is ruined. I had it all planned out."

Mae slipped off Izzy's lap and worked her way around the table to Sam's side. She patted his head. "We'll figure this out, Sam. The same way we work on math in school."

That seemed to cheer Sam up.

Later, after the pizza had been devoured and another movie found for the kids to watch, Izzy and Chandler still had the couch to themselves. He'd texted Stephanie. They'd agreed that Sam would spend the night with Chandler at the ranch. Hopefully, by morning the worst of Sam's rebellion would have passed.

Izzy snuggled closer to Chandler, trying not to breathe too deeply and make her ribs hurt, or too shallowly and give herself a panic attack for thinking her lungs weren't working the way they should. She replayed Earl's conversation about missed opportunities in her head. Decided that was demoralizing and somehow replayed Chandler talking about their something either being fabulous or ending up a bust all around. Since that was depressing, her thoughts went to someone else's problems— Lois and the need for more Santas on horseback, the unexpected run on tinsel at the feed store and Stephanie deciding to follow her dreams.

"I need to think about something other than my ribs," she whispered to Chandler. *Or problems in general.*

"You want to talk?" he whispered back. "About what?"

"About something that doesn't matter." Oh, that wasn't it at all. She wanted to talk about important things, topics that would help her decide if there was hope for a future with Chandler or if they were doomed to fail. She needed to be careful that Mae didn't get too attached to Chandler. Her daughter was already attached to Sam. But was this the right time for romance?

The kids were sprawled out on pillows on the floor, engrossed in their animated movie. She was tucked in next to Chandler as if they were a real couple. It was very domestic, almost...safe.

"Actually, the truth is... I was angry with my mom for dying," Izzy admitted in that same whisper. "Probably the same way you were angry at your mother for leaving without saying goodbye."

Chandler said nothing. But he didn't push her away or bolt for the door.

So, Izzy continued. "Other people go through cancer successfully, with their kids or spouses by their side. But my dad... He couldn't handle adversity of any kind. He worked for the power company when I was a kid until he got a bad performance review." She'd overheard Mom telling someone that he'd quit because of pride. "And then he managed a grocery store in Friar's Creek but when someone else was promoted over him, he quit. Each time, he tried to explain things to me. And even though I didn't really understand..." She'd been a kid, after all. "I wanted to believe in him. You know, to root for him. But then, Mom got sick, and I realized that he couldn't stand loss of any kind." She'd tried talking to him but that hadn't worked.

Chandler said nothing. The kids still looked engrossed in their movie.

"I was relieved when Dad left town but also sad, the way I imagine you felt after choosing your foster family over your mother. But my dad didn't give me a choice. Stay here, he said." And that had made Izzy feel relief, as well. Her father had lost her respect and she'd wondered how long it would take for her to lose his, for him to turn his back on her the way he had on Mom. "But there was a happy ending. Because of Earl..." Izzy drew too big a breath and winced, taking a moment to allow the pain to fade before continuing. "I had a place to call home and someone to watch over me. And then... I fell in love with Mike."

Chandler grunted.

"Mike had a life plan. Find a woman with the same work ethic as he had. Start a family young so that he could enjoy his later years as an empty nester." It had all sounded good to Izzy, like they were on the same team.

Chandler released a deep breath.

"Are you listening?" Izzy glanced up at him. "Should I stop?"

"Don't stop." Chandler shook his head, compassion in those soft brown eyes. "I heard every word. Mom. Anger. Dad. Anger. Mike. Getting to the anger."

She supposed he was right. "The point is... We've both had our share of folks breaking our hearts. I never wanted that for Mae."

He made a deep sound in his throat. "Or me for Sam."

Their gazes met and held. And she knew... Izzy knew that neither one of them wanted their hearts broken again. Not by family. And not by the person who promised to cherish you till death tore them apart.

There was a long pause, during which time the hero in the movie disappointed everyone important to him. And the difference between that character and someone like Izzy's father was that the animated hero was self-aware enough to realize he'd made a mistake and apologize.

Izzy eased away from Chandler. The movie would be ending soon, and she didn't want to give the kids ideas about weddings again.

But Chandler drew her back to him, turning his head to whisper in her ear. "I resented my mom for disappearing. Well… I told the police my dad might have done something to her. But that turned out to be untrue."

"The spouse is the first suspect on every police show I watch," Izzy whispered back. "And from what you've told me, they were a volatile couple."

Chandler nodded. "I bounced around in foster care. Hurt. Angry. Resentful that no one wanted me."

Izzy found his hand and gave it a squeeze. "Unlike me, you probably let it all go."

"Yep."

"I can't imagine leaving Mae."

"Or me, Sam."

His statement warmed Izzy's heart immensely.

"Mike canceled having Mae this weekend because there's a big car sale at his dealership." She was afraid that was the end of him taking Mae for anything. The revised custody agreement was sitting on her bedroom dresser awaiting her signature.

"Can I call Mike a jerk?"

Izzy smiled, but it was a sad sort of smile. "Why not? I do. Can I call Stephanie scared for wanting to take Sam with her to Texas?"

"She's selfish," Chandler said quietly. "Not scared."

Izzy shook her head. "She's afraid and I'll tell you why. You understand how scary change is. I know you do because you hate change so much that you hadn't moved a couch that disrupts the flow of traffic in your house."

He made a face. "So what?"

"Stephanie wants to take Sam because she's scared, too. Scared of reaching for a dream and falling flat on her face. And there's nothing that makes a parent feel better than a hug from their child."

And even if Chandler said nothing, Izzy could tell by the way his brow was furrowed that she'd given him something to think about.

CHAPTER SIXTEEN

"DAD." SAM PADDED into Chandler's bedroom and crawled into bed with him while it was still dark outside. "Are you awake?"

"Yep." Chandler had merely been waiting for his alarm to go off in…another twenty minutes. Funny how just thinking about Izzy made him lose sleep. Funnier how he didn't feel sleep-deprived. He felt energized, ready to see her, curious to know how she was feeling today.

"Can we go into town for breakfast at the Buffalo Diner?"

"Yep." Chandler didn't move, though. If they went into town, he'd need to let Stephanie know and broker peace between her and Sam. Considering he wasn't a neutral party in the negotiations— he wanted Sam to stay in Clementine—that was a conversation he wasn't looking forward to.

Sam kicked out his feet and moved his arms as if he was swimming in bed. "Dad?"

"Hmm?"

"You're not moving."

"Right." Chandler rolled out of bed. It being Saturday, he didn't need to feed stock or manage work on the ranch.

He didn't shower. He didn't shave. He just threw on some clothes, same as his kid. He stepped out on his front porch, taking stock of the ranch buildings, the Christmas decorations, the roundabout with its snowmen surrounding the nativity scene.

It was dark. The Christmas lights were still on.

That wasn't unusual. Mom liked her light show on all night. Said it reminded her that there was good in the world and that there would be good in the world when she got up the next day. Sometimes those lights got too much for Chandler's brothers in the bunkhouse and they unplugged a strand or two in the name of a good night's sleep. But this morning, the lights were all still on, still bright and cheerful.

Enduring cheerfulness. Enduring...love.

When Chandler thought of his foster mother, that's what he thought of. When he thought of his biological mother, he thought of selfishness, of weakness, of bitterness. Thinking of her left a bad taste in his mouth.

But last night, when he and Izzy were sharing confidences, she'd said something about Stephanie that had given Chandler pause.

Stephanie wants to take Sam because she's scared.

Was my mother scared? Scared she'd be stuck in that unpredictable, unhappy life?

Chandler had washed his hands of his biological mother out of self-preservation. If she left him once, who could promise she wouldn't leave him again? No one, that's who.

"Dad?" Sam took Chandler's hand. "Are you gonna look at the lights all day?"

"Nope." But he'd like to. Chandler didn't think he'd look at Christmas lights again without thinking of his foster mother and Izzy. "But we need to find that pole Izzy used to string lights in the high places. I think Zane and Ryan used it to put up our porch lights."

Sam whooped. "I know where it is!" He ran down the porch stairs, pulling Chandler along behind him. Across the ranch yard. Into the roundabout. "Zane said it looked like a shepherd's staff."

Sure enough. Izzy's wooden pole was in the lean-to shielding the baby Jesus from the elements.

Sam used it like a staff as they walked to Chandler's truck. Staff in the truck bed, Cochran fellas buckled in, they drove into town. The sky to the east was cloudy, a mixture of purple and red.

"I'm not going to Texas," Sam said from the back seat. "Not ever."

"Not ever?" Chandler glanced in the rearview mirror, making out the shadowy features of Sam. "What if I'm working a rodeo in Dallas?"

"You never take me to rodeos." Sullen.

"You're old enough now to compete in junior rodeos."

"I am? Wow." Sam was less sullen now. "Can I ride bulls?"

"Most kids start with sheep."

Silence. It stretched for a mile or so.

"Mom doesn't like rodeos."

There was a test for Chandler in that statement. Sam might just as well have asked, *"Whose side are you on, Dad?"* Chandler chose his words carefully. "Your mom doesn't want you to get hurt."

Silence. The pastures of the Oklahoma prairie gave way to smaller ranchettes. The horizon showed a sliver of yellow.

"I'm not going to Texas," Sam said, less sullen, more feisty.

"Not even to visit your mom?"

"Do you want me to leave you?" Small, booted feet kicked Chandler's seat back. Small fists bumped the truck's ceiling. "Are you trying to get rid of me?"

Chandler slowed down, pulled over. Put his truck in Park so he could turn and face his little mini-me. "Sam, I love you. I don't want you to go anywhere." His arms were long enough that he could rest a hand on Sam's jean-clad leg. "But your mom… She wants to do something more exciting than deliver the mail. And she can't do it here."

"I'm not—"

"Going to Texas," Chandler finished for him. "Yeah. I know. I'm going to talk to your mom. But you have to understand that if I can convince her to let you stay with me that it's going to break her heart to leave you."

"Then she shouldn't go." Sam crossed his arms over his chest. "She's supposed to take care of me."

Chandler nodded slowly, trying to channel Izzy. She always seemed to know what to say and when to say it. Even if it wasn't what Chandler wanted to hear. "Sometimes you have to make hard choices, squirt. Like your uncle Wade. He had to leave Ronnie and Ginny home to compete in bronc riding."

"They could have gone."

"Nope. They had responsibilities and commitments. To work and school."

"Then Wade could have stayed."

"But then he wouldn't be able to do the thing he loves."

Sam slumped in his seat. "I don't want to grow up."

"But you will, squirt." Chandler turned around and put the truck in gear. "And when you do, you're going to make me proud."

Sam was quiet the rest of the ride into town.

Of course, as soon as Sam's boots hit pavement, he ran for the Buffalo Diner's front door. "Come on, Dad!"

Chandler hadn't taken two steps into the coffee shop when a young, feminine squeal rose in the air, bringing Coronet and her coffeepot to a halt midpour.

"Look! It's Sam!" Mae cried, rising to her knees in a window booth.

"Look! It's Mae!" Sam cried, running toward his bestie, who sat with her mother.

With Izzy.

The sky outside seemed to lighten.

Chandler felt the beginnings of a smile. And of a thought…

What are the chances that this was a coincidence?

But when Chandler's gaze connected with Izzy's, he didn't care if fate was lending him a hand in winning her heart or if two seven year-olds were in cahoots and trying to set them up. Izzy was his ray of sunshine. She made change worth the risk.

Sam scooted into the booth, taking a seat next to Mae. "Come on, Dad." He glanced back at Chandler and pointed to the seat next to Izzy.

Oh, yeah. There was mischief afoot.

Chandler eagerly walked across the diner to join them.

Chandler's boots came to a stop at Izzy's booth, their tips nearly touching the base right where there were scuff marks on the linoleum. Someone had bolted into or out of this booth lickety-split. *Bolting into…* That had practically been Chandler. "Sam, were you invited to take a seat? Maybe Izzy and Mae want to eat alone."

Mae and Sam bumped shoulders and giggled… *nervously?*

What did it matter what mischief was afoot when Izzy was smiling so warmly at him?

"Invited? *Dad*," Sam said after their laughter died away. "It's Mae. We have to sit with her."

"Because we're best friends," Mae echoed, smiling so sweetly…so innocently.

Maybe I have an overactive imagination.

"Best not to paddle upstream." Izzy patted the seat next to her. She was dressed to decorate houses today—green sweater with a squirrel on the front and a Santa hat. The squirrel had antlers and...

"I see you're finally owning up to the fact that tangling Christmas lights is your holiday superpower." Chandler chuckled, taking a seat next to her. The squirrel on her sweater was tangled in blinking lights.

"Hardy-har." Izzy sipped her coffee. "Did you bring my pole?"

"Yep." Chandler sat back to give Coronet room to slide a steaming mug of coffee in front of him. She also dropped off crayons and place mats to color for the kids. "Not that you're going to use that light-stringing pole. I'll put up lights for you today." He cataloged Izzy's posture. "How are you? Sore?"

She nodded. "Now I know how bull riders feel the day after they've been thrown."

"Then you need to learn the secret to a speedy recovery, sworn to by every Done Roamin' Ranch cowboy." Chandler smiled at Sam, not that his son noticed. He was playing tic-tac-toe with Mae. "It's pancakes and bacon." *And love.*

He didn't dare say that last part out loud.

LATER, AFTER A filling breakfast and an hour spent preparing Paula Lincoln's front yard with enough holiday cheer to please any Scrooge, Chandler stood on Stephanie's front porch with Sam. Izzy and Mae had moved on to decorate Destiny Rogers's room inside the retirement home.

Chandler glanced at Sam. "Remember what I said."

Sam nodded, staring at the front door. "Mom is scared and needs us."

The front door swung open. Stephanie looked a right mess—dark circles under her eyes, uncombed hair ends sticking out from under a knit cap, baggy gray sweats. She dropped down to her knees and opened her arms. "Sam…"

Their son propelled himself forward, throwing his arms around Stephanie. They both started to cry.

After a moment's hesitation, Chandler knelt on the ground next to them, drew them close and said the most natural thing. "We're going to figure this out. Together."

"WE PULLED IT OFF." Ronnie gave Izzy a side hug on Saturday night. "Cars are beginning to pull through the First Annual Done Roamin' Ranch Christmas Roundabout." She squeezed Izzy harder.

"Ouch." Izzy grimaced through a wave of rib pain, easing a step away from her friend where they stood on Ronnie's front porch.

"Sorry." Ronnie's mittened hands hovered over Izzy's midsection. "I forgot you're among the walking wounded."

Izzy drew a careful breath. "No hugs until the

new year. Doc Nabidian said it'll takes weeks to heal." He'd wrapped Izzy's ribs in gauze, prescribed rest and pain pills. "He wants me to slow down."

"To which you vaguely nodded, all the while thinking you'll slow down after Christmas." Ronnie fussed with Izzy's heavy coat, gently pulling the ends closer together before zipping it closed. "I know how you think."

"That's because you and I think alike." As many single mothers were wont to do. Izzy watched the first truck make the U-turn around the circle of tire snowmen ringing the nativity scene.

The ranch was ablaze with light and color. Every building outlined in lights. Every tree ringed with the same. Wreaths on every door. Inflatable Santa and Frosty waving toward visitors. Christmas music was playing on a speaker set on the main house's front porch, currently playing "Deck the Halls." All they needed was snow to make folks think they weren't in Clementine, Oklahoma, anymore.

Ginny, Mae, Sam and some kids from the junior rodeo team were working a hot chocolate and cookie station at the beginning of the circle, overseen by Bess and Griff, the high school team's coaches. That had been Mary's idea, very much last minute. But she'd contacted various local teams and clubs offering to let them take over for a night to raise money. Or, in the case of Lois and her quest for more horseback riding Santas, a chance to recruit volunteers.

Chandler, Frank and a few other cowboys flanked Mary, who sat bundled in a chair between two tire snowmen. She was covered in several layers of blankets, wore Christmas-themed knit—cap, scarf, mittens—and was ready to greet visitors as they pulled through. She'd rejected the idea of sitting on the front porch as being too far from her visitors.

Chandler glanced Izzy's way and waved.

And then the visiting truck rolled to a stop between them, blocking Izzy's view of Chandler and Mary.

"You've got an admirer," Ronnie teased, fussing with the pink scarf around her neck before slipping her hands into her purple swing jacket pockets. "How's that going?"

Two more vehicles appeared on the rise, their headlights sweeping down on the ranch as they approached. Laughter emanating from those around Mary filled the air.

"Things with Chandler are...confusing." Izzy drew another careful breath. "For me more so than him, I think. I've been trying to remember back to when I thought I was in love with Mike because I don't want to be in a relationship just because a man is nice to me and kisses my socks off. If I'm going to do this again, I want it to be real and lasting, like what Frank and Mary have. Or what you found with Wade."

"Love doesn't come with checkboxes." Ronnie smiled gently.

"If this isn't the kind of love songs are written about, it isn't fair to Mae. She's fond of Chandler."

More vehicles were arriving.

"Not to mention she and Sam are suddenly best friends." Ronnie nodded. "I understand where you're coming from. But nothing worth having comes without a risk. And if what you're feeling for Chandler and he's feeling for you has the foundation of deep, everlasting love, it's worth taking a chance."

Izzy nodded. "A few weeks ago, I wouldn't have been open to risking our safe little life." And then Mae had turned down a role in the Christmas pageant. "I wouldn't have ordered a week's worth of ugly Christmas sweaters or matching headgear."

"Or fallen out of a tree?" Ronnie asked. "Perhaps never kissed a tall, handsome cowboy?"

"There are disadvantages to you knowing me so well." Izzy tried to laugh, but that still hurt. "One of which is that it's hard to keep a secret from you. But... What would you do if you were in my boots?"

The roundabout was filled with trucks and the Done Roamin' Ranch cowboys had spread out to greet them. The hot chocolate and cookie table looked to be doing a good business.

"What would I do..." Ronnie began, then laughed. "I'd think about it and then go for it. It's what I did with Wade—all in." Ronnie rubbed a hand across

Izzy's back. "But that's me. We may think alike but you've treaded carefully since your divorce. If you have doubts, slow things down."

More vehicles were coming over the rise now. Mary was due to have lots of visitors tonight.

"I have doubts, but..." Izzy leaned her head on Ronnie's shoulder, thinking of Earl. And letting the warm, excited emotion toward Chandler roll through her. Was this love? "I'm worried that this is something I could lose out on if I don't take hold of it now."

CHAPTER SEVENTEEN

"MERRY CHRISTMAS, IZZY."

The female voice first thing in the morning had Izzy looking up from reconciling feed store inventory to find Della-Mae's teacher holding the handle of a car seat cradling a thickly bundled newborn. The woman's normally smooth brown hair stuck out in spots and she had the air of exhaustion about her.

Truth be told, Izzy was having a hard time concentrating on checks and balances. She hadn't seen Chandler in two days, but he was never far from her thoughts. Partly because he texted her several times a day, asking how she was feeling. Her ribs didn't ache as badly as they had but the holiday decorating business wasn't helping. Nor were her worries about earning enough to buy Mae that princess bed or the wait for a new set of papers from Mike. If it wasn't Chandler keeping her awake at night, it was her achy ribs, the size of her checking account or the revised custody agreement she and her lawyer were waiting for.

So, the appearance of Theresa Stodimeyer was a joyful and welcome distraction.

"Merry Christmas, Theresa." Izzy hurried to usher the new mom to a chair behind the sales counter. "What can I get for you? Water? Help shopping for Christmas gifts? Wrapping paper? Dog food?" Izzy ran through a litany of things Theresa might need.

"I'm not here to trouble you with requests, Izzy. I brought you Della-Mae's letter to Santa. I meant to deliver them two weeks ago...but..." Theresa stared lovingly into the face of her baby boy. "I was interrupted. And since some parents in our class didn't want me to mail them to the North Pole, I knew it was important to deliver them to parents as soon as I was cleared to drive." She reached into her diaper bag and withdrew an envelope with *Santa* written on the front in big, wobbly letters.

"For the record, I voted to mail them to Santa," Izzy told her. She opened the envelope carefully, trying not to rip it. "It's risky getting these letters back. Heaven forbid Mae finds it in my possession." She took a moment to read her daughter's Christmas wish before looking at Theresa in shock. "This is unexpected."

"I bet." Theresa nodded, swaying side to side in her chair. "I helped her and Sam with the wording."

"They wrote these after Thanksgiving? Together?"

"Yes. They wrote the same Christmas wish." Theresa smiled warmly at Izzy. "It's not a bad wish."

"Says you." Izzy shook her head. "If you have Sam's, I can save you a trip to the Done Roamin' Ranch and give it to Chandler myself." She'd call and see if he could make a trip into town. This seemed important. It was certainly unsettling.

But first, Izzy spent a few minutes visiting with Theresa. Luckily, she had her Christmas gift under the sales counter. It was always fun to hear moms talk about their babies. Thankfully, it was slow at the store, allowing them some privacy.

Finally, when the baby started to fuss and Theresa got slowly to her feet, Izzy was about to wish Theresa a Merry Christmas when she remembered something.

"Did you hear about Sam and Mae getting into trouble the week you gave birth?"

"I did." Theresa smiled apologetically. "They're good kids. But even good kids get caught up in the moment once in a while."

"They were caught up in moments five days in a row," Izzy felt compelled to point out. "And Chandler seems to think one of them should be moved to a different classroom."

"Oh, I wouldn't do that." Theresa reached for the diaper bag, but Izzy got there first.

"I'll carry this out for you." It was lighter than a baby in a car seat and it didn't hurt her ribs to heft it. "And not only because I'm hoping you'll tell me why the kids shouldn't be separated."

"They're really a good influence on each other." Theresa chuckled, heading toward the door. "Sam is a dynamo and Mae is too much in her head. They balance each other out."

Mae is too much in her head? That didn't sound good. But Izzy wanted to wrap up one conversation before starting another. "You don't think they egg each other on?"

"I think their experiences after Thanksgiving were a product of a new and surprising found friendship. They haven't misbehaved since, have they?"

"No." But then again, Izzy hadn't checked the online message system. She made a mental note to ask Ronnie to help her log in.

After Izzy got Theresa to her car, she came back inside and called Chandler, feeling tense and out of sorts.

"Yeah." Chandler sounded distracted when he answered his phone.

Izzy explained about the Santa letters their kids had written and how she had them in her possession. "Can you swing by the feed store and take a look at Sam's before school gets out? I don't feel right opening his. But if his wish is the same as Mae's… Well, there might be trouble." If what she felt for Chandler wasn't love.

"What's this I hear about letters to Santa?" Earl came out of the back room after she'd disconnected. He carried a box containing multiple sets of outdoor holiday lights.

Izzy put her hand on her hip. "Were you eavesdropping?" The man was as bad as Ronnie when it came to keeping a pulse on other folks' business.

"Nope." Earl set the box down on the counter and picked up the envelopes addressed to Santa. "I saw these. Did Mae ask for a puppy in that letter?"

"No." At this point, Izzy would have loved it if her daughter had. She was feeling a bit panicky.

"Hasn't been the same since we lost Gator a year ago." Earl's beloved Labrador. He made as if to read Mae's letter.

Izzy grabbed the envelope before he could open it. "You feel free to get a dog, Earl."

The old man gasped. "She *did* ask Santa for a puppy. You wouldn't snatch it if she hadn't."

Izzy picked up the box he'd brought and placed it in his arms. "Butt out, Earl."

"We're on the same team." Earl stomped off and disappeared down the Christmas aisle. "A dog will always be there for Mae, even if that car salesman isn't."

"A dog will always be there…" Izzy picked up the stack of paper invoices but couldn't concentrate on them. She stared at the two Santa envelopes. What had come over those two?

There were sounds of Earl restocking the shelves. A few minutes later, he returned with the empty box. "I don't suppose we can get in any more tinsel before the holiday?"

Izzy shook her head, glad for the interruption. "It would take more than a week. We'd be stuck with it until next year. I'll make a note to buy more next summer when we order." She scribbled on her calendar.

"You should also make a note of this." Earl leaned on the counter and tipped his porkpie hat back. "Mae needs something permanent to take from one house to another. And a puppy—"

"You think Mike will care for a puppy properly?" Izzy slapped her pen on the counter, so touchy about the situation that she had an unusually short fuse. "Mike can't even pick up his daughter from school when it's his week. Not to mention he's giving up custody."

"What?" Earl's mouth dropped open.

"He was here a few days ago. He's found someone new and…" Izzy sighed. But that wouldn't get rid of the uneasy feeling in the area of her heart whenever she thought about Mike abandoning Mae. "I signed his paperwork. He'll only see Mae a few days a year. If that."

Earl tossed the empty box toward the break room door. "All the more reason to get Mae a dog." Earl shook his finger, first at Izzy, then pointing up at the ceiling. "A dog can get you through the worst of times."

"Earl… I can't… I can't think about puppies right now. Or… Or…inventory." Izzy was horrified to find herself near tears. "There's so much uncertainty in my head. And I just… I don't know what to do."

"Oh, darling, come here." Earl threw his arms around her and held her close.

"You needed somewhere?" Scotty, the Done Roamin' Ranch's regular blacksmith, asked Chandler when he tucked his cell phone back in his pocket.

"I need to go into town." Although why Izzy sounded so panicked over letters to Santa Claus was beyond him. And yet… Chandler was worried because she was worried. "I can help you finish shooing Baby Bear before I leave."

The pony always misbehaved when shod. He tried to lean his body weight on Scotty while the man balanced Baby Bear's rear hoof between his thighs.

"Hey, none of that." Chandler gave the pony a few pokes in the ribs when he tried to misbehave again.

Baby Bear adjusted his center of gravity with an impatient puff of air.

"Ponies and draft horses are always a shooing challenge." Scotty finished fitting the pony's shoe and then set his hoof down.

"Draft horses? Why?" Chandler thought about Shirley and the buggy arriving tomorrow.

"Those large breeds have very thin hoof walls." Scotty heated the pony's shoe and then pounded it with a hammer to achieve a shape closer to Baby Bear's hoof. "It's better to let them go barefoot and develop calluses on the bottom of the hooves than to have nails split the hoof wall."

"Interesting." Chandler trusted Scotty's opinion. He'd been their farrier for over a decade. "Does it take long to develop calluses?" A key question since Shirley had been shod when they'd bought her.

"It does. At least a season. In the meantime, once their shoes are off, they need rubber boots if they do any work—riding or pulling." Scotty finished hammering Baby Bear's rear shoe on. "Are you thinking about adding a draft horse around here?"

"More than thinking. It's a surprise, but..." Chandler told Scotty about Dad's purchase of Shirley.

"My next visit is scheduled before Christmas. I'd love to take a look at her hooves and come up with a plan for care. I can order boots for her, guaranteed to fit."

Chandler thanked him.

A few minutes later, Scotty was done, paid and loading his tools in his van. Chandler headed out of the barn and toward his truck.

"Chandler, are you going into town?" Dad caught him in the ranch yard. "I sure wouldn't mind a lift."

Chandler agreed and soon the pair were on their way.

"What errand are you on?" Dad asked, plopping his wide white hat on the dashboard.

Chandler explained about the letters to Santa. "Izzy wouldn't tell me what was in Mae's, but she sounded upset."

"Those kids aren't in trouble again, are they?"

"Not as far as I know." Izzy would have mentioned it to him... If she'd been able to log in to the school messaging system. He couldn't begrudge her that. Chandler was guilty of not trying. He made a mental note to ask Ronnie about it tonight.

Dad fiddled with the brim of his cowboy hat. "Nice to see you with a woman in your life."

"*Dad.* You're jumping the gun." Chandler had respected Izzy's request to go slow. "I can't even label what this is as dating."

"I'm not planning your wedding." Dad chuckled. "Although I think young Sam wouldn't mind it if you did and made his best bud his sister. Still, you can enjoy Izzy's company. She's sweet and good-natured. And your mother is growing very fond of her."

Chandler kept silent.

"Whatever it is you're feeling for Izzy deserves to be explored. And weathered." Dad turned his wedding ring on his finger. "True love weathers the good and the bad. And in life, there's always the good and the bad. Why can't you just go with the flow where Izzy's concerned?"

"Because Izzy…" Chandler slowed as they approached the center of Clementine. "Izzy's reduced the flow down to a trickle. She's being careful where her heart and Mae's are concerned, which makes me…"

"Overthink your feelings, too." Dad nodded slowly, seemingly considering the problem at hand. "If there's one thing I've learned about life, it's that you can't rely on it to be predictable. And when things between you two get unpredictable, you'll know."

"Know what?"

"If she's the one."

IZZY HAD JUST realized she'd entered alfalfa under the oats code in the computer program when Chandler entered the feed store.

It's about time.

His boots rang out on the hardwood floor as he approached the sales counter. He wore a blue flannel shirt beneath a sleeveless tan jacket. He looked stressed, yet when their eyes met, he smiled.

And it was in the glow of that smile that Izzy felt the world slow down, felt the moment stretch, felt again the inner pull to smile back, to meet him halfway, to offer her hand to twine with his and say they were stronger together.

The feed store phone rang, jolting Izzy back into the present, turned her attention to the laptop screen in front of her.

"Clementine Feed." Earl's voice drifted to her from the break room.

"Thanks for coming in, Chandler," Izzy said in her best businesslike voice as she closed the laptop. Then she opened a drawer beneath the cash register and took out the two envelopes with letters to Santa, handing them to him.

She waited for Chandler to read both, listening to a bouncy rendition of "Jingle Bell Rock."

"Well…" Chandler returned both letters to their envelopes. "That explains a lot."

Izzy nodded. "They both wished for a new parent—a mom for Sam and a dad for Mae. This explains why Mae asked me if I liked meeting the principal after we saw him in his office. And you. She wanted to know if I liked you."

He grunted but didn't reply.

Chandler stared at Izzy without speaking for so long, that she had to ask, "What's going on in that handsome head of yours?"

Shoot. She hadn't meant to add the word *handsome.*

Chandler's guarded smile appeared, making him look more handsome, more…kissable. "I'm thinking that the reason the kids have been behaving at school ever since their mischief-making spree is because you've been working out at the ranch, often with me. And this also explains how we ended up having breakfast with you on Saturday. And…a half-dozen other things that didn't seem like a coincidence." Chandler leaned over the counter, bringing those tempting lips closer. "They'd be absolute angels if they knew about *our kisses.*" He whispered those last two words.

And those last two words made Izzy shiver, made her want him closer.

The sound of a phone being dropped back in a cradle reminded Izzy that they weren't alone.

"But the question is… What do we do about it?" Izzy whispered, trying not to be overheard. "Because they want us paired up and committed by Christmas. That's ridiculous."

"Is it?"

There were no customers in the store. It sounded as if Earl was making another pot of coffee in the break room. Stan was off delivering feed. The store was unusually quiet. Except for the blood rushing in Izzy's ears.

Because no matter what I just said about commitment being off the table by Christmas, I wouldn't mind it.

And Chandler seemed to suspect as much. He hadn't budged from midcounter. He was within reach, barely smiling, letting Izzy decide.

Is commitment off the table?

Impulsively, Izzy rose up on her toes and planted a kiss on Chandler's cheek. And then she dropped down on her heels, jarring her ribs.

"What was that?" Chandler didn't relinquish the ground he'd taken.

"Merry Christmas," Izzy said breathlessly. "But... We have to be careful considering those letters."

"Hmm." It was when Chandler was stingy with his words that Izzy suspected there was a lot going on behind those warm brown eyes.

Izzy had plenty of words, enough for both of them. She'd had lots of time to think about their situation. "We should write letters back, telling our kids that there are some things Santa can't deliver for Christmas."

"Hmm," Chandler repeated.

"You're not taking this seriously," Izzy complained.

"If you knew how seriously I'm taking this, you wouldn't peck me on the cheek." He smiled. Wickedly.

Oh, my.

Izzy's heart pounded faster. She'd never seen Chandler smile like that. He was Mr. Staid. Mr. Tall and Silent. Mr. Frown at My Antlers.

Where was that Chandler? Izzy could resist that Chandler.

"Something's happened," she murmured.

"Besides these letters?" Chandler asked.

She nodded.

And then Chandler did draw away, resettling his cowboy hat on his head. "I dropped my dad off at the pharmacy. I'm paraphrasing. He told me that when things got unpredictable that we'd know what to do and how to feel about each other." Chandler tapped the Santa letters on the counter. "This could be our sign. Our sign to move forward."

"I disagree." Izzy barely got the words out, mind spinning with the idea that Chandler had talked to his father about her. "We barely know each other."

Chandler shook his head. His gaze was gentle, as if he knew this conversation would scare her. "I know you, Izzy. I know you're honest and trustworthy. You work hard and love to dance. You're a good mom. You have a deep love of Christmas. You don't always take yourself too seriously, but you don't always take care of yourself the way you should." He gestured toward her ribs. "Men who were supposed to love you didn't do a good job. And that makes you afraid to trust me, even when your kiss says you want to." He paused, walking around the sales counter to stand in front of her. "Am I close?"

Her eyes were filling with tears and her breath was ragged and all she could manage was a whispered, "Yes."

"You set aside your dreams when your mom died but you want your daughter to be free to dream and to pursue them, too. And I…" Chandler took one of her hands. "I'm afraid that you'll swoop into my life like a colorful, chattery finch, only to flit away when you finally realize that you have dreams that need cherishing just as much as Mae does."

He was afraid she'd be like Stephanie, harboring dreams that could only take flight elsewhere.

"I don't have dreams," Izzy said in a hoarse, subdued voice because it felt like a betrayal of herself to admit that. "I don't have the luxury to have dreams."

Chandler took hold of her other hand, standing with her behind the outdated cash register like it was an altar and they were about to exchange vows. "You have dreams, Isobel Adams. You dream of family and permanence."

Izzy nodded, blinking back tears. He did know her.

"We could find that together," Chandler said in a voice as soft as his touch.

The front door opened. Two cowboys walked in, heading for the boot department.

Izzy put her hands on Chandler's firm chest and shooed him out from behind the counter. "Now isn't the time for serious talk. We need to decide what to do about the Santa letters."

Chandler shook his head again, slow like the pendulum in Earl's grandfather clock. "My dad recommended we go with the flow. Regardless of what he meant by that, I take it to mean the kissing flow, if I'm being honest, because I do like your kisses. And they seem like a requirement after the serious talk we just had." He leaned over, making a show of puckering up.

Boy, is he tempting.

The cowboys in the boot department laughed.

Common sense returned to Izzy like a plunge in Lolly Creek in spring. There was no kissing in the feed store. Certainly not any exchange of cowboy kisses.

She took a step back and kept her voice down. "Whoever we kiss this holiday season… Or for that matter in the coming months, will be seen as marriage material by our kids. The last thing I want is for Mae to be hurt if you get bored kissing me."

"Like that's going to happen." Chandler huffed, crossing his arms over his chest. "If you're agreeing to go with the flow, you can't want us to sneak around."

"No." Izzy backstepped. "That's no way to start a relationship."

"Neither is kissing *before* a first date." Chandler raised his brows, flashing that wicked smile as if to say, *point to me.*

The front door swung open once more.

"Chandler, I got your mother's meds." Frank walked into the feed store. "Are you ready to go?"

"Yes," Izzy replied for Chandler. "Yes, he is. We're done here."

Chandler gave her a hard look before reaching out to touch her chin with his fingers. "We're done. For now."

CHAPTER EIGHTEEN

WE'RE DONE. FOR NOW.

Chandler's voice echoed in Izzy's head all day while she worked at the feed store. He'd knocked her off her game. She'd very nearly sent a cowboy home with the wrong size boots (he caught her error). She'd had to ask another cowboy twice what he needed help finding in the tack department (he found a replacement bit himself). And Earl had to repeat himself three times before it sunk in that he was asking her something (if they had anymore white extension cords).

How could Chandler be so certain they had a chance at forever?

Because he knows me. He knows who I am, and what's important to me. He knows what I want out of life. And we want the same thing.

But wasn't that checking boxes? Every woman wanted that, along with a man who had a good job, a good sense of humor and no glaring bad habits.

Izzy talked herself in and out of love all day long, drank too much coffee and got very little done.

"Mama, are we going to Sam's ranch?" Mae asked

as she climbed into the back seat of Izzy's SUV after school that day. "I told Sam I'd help him make cookies for the hot chocolate table for tonight's round-about."

"We're not going to the ranch today, bug." Izzy carefully navigated the traffic out of the pickup line. "We have some clients we need to decorate for in town." John Stottle and… Someone else…

"Mama." Mae's disappointed voice, so seldom heard.

Izzy chewed her lip.

Once Mae learned that Mike was making a quick exit from her life, she'd latch on to Chandler as a replacement father figure.

And I don't even know if I love him. Or could love him. Or should love him.

It wasn't fair to Mae to lose two important men in her life. It was imperative that they stay away from Chandler and the impression that Mae was getting a new daddy for Christmas until Izzy knew how she felt about Chandler.

How do I feel about Chandler?

"Mama? Are you okay?"

Nope. Nope, I'm panicking.

But she needed to answer. "You know… I've… I've been thinking about puppies."

Della-Mae squealed. *"Puppies? Puppies?"*

"Yes. Yay," Izzy said with absolutely no enthusiasm whatsoever. "Puppies. A dog… A dog will always be there for you, no matter what." No matter what man let Mae down.

"And Sam? He's getting one, too? He has to get one, too." Mae was on a roll now, so excited, so hyped up. "Call Chandler, Mama. Call Chandler. He's picking up Sam. We can go to the feed store and decide on the puppies on the board."

Mae continued to rattle off ideas as Izzy drove them to the feed store because she had to get back to work and finish her shift before they transitioned to decorating some houses downtown. *If* they got to decorating houses in town. Puppies would throw everything off.

But Mae kept rambling and repeating, "Call Chandler, Mama. Sam needs a puppy, too."

And finally, Izzy did.

"THIS IS A bad idea," Chandler said to Izzy twenty minutes after she'd called him. "You complicated everything."

"I'm going with the flow, Chandler." Izzy sounded flustered and vulnerable as she stood behind the feed store sales counter. "It was either puppies or you. Mama Claus made a choice."

"I know what I would have picked," Chandler muttered. And it wasn't a puppy.

But he dutifully headed for the break room, thinking how odd this turn of events was.

He'd never seen Izzy have a meltdown. When she'd called, he'd been waiting in the school pickup line while kids slowly got in cars ahead of him and were even slower to buckle up. Chandler was tied up in knots inside and he wasn't honking his horn and inching up on the bumper of the truck ahead of him to reach Sam, who was talking to one of the school aides four cars ahead.

Oh, and those knots…

Chandler inched forward. They were there because Izzy…

That woman could second-guess a course of action when she roped the business end of a charging steer.

As he inched forward again, a call came in through the truck's Bluetooth link.

"Yeah," he'd shouted at the rearview mirror, which was where he'd always assumed the telephone microphone was. And after Izzy had identified herself and told him her idea, his initial reaction was to reject it.

A puppy was chaotic. And having Izzy around…

She was leaving a trail of chaos in her wake—her holiday decorations in Mom's house, the moved furniture in his house, the constant need to kiss her. Why did Chandler need more unpredictability, more…more…responsibility? Without any of the benefits of kisses?

He hadn't quite put it that way, but Izzy got the gist.

"Stop complaining or Santa will put you on the naughty list, Chandler. Pick up Sam and meet us at the feed store." And then she hung up.

And amazingly, Chandler smiled.

"Hi, Dad." Sam opened the back door of the

truck and threw his backpack in. "Can we get milk-shakes?"

"Hold that thought." Chandler really should have kept quiet, but he couldn't. "What do you think about getting a puppy today?"

Sam went so excited, he rolled down his window and yelled over and over, "I'm getting a puppy! I'm getting a puppy!"

And because the pickup line was so slow, Sam was practically hoarse when they finally reached the feed store.

"You get yellow, and I get brown." Sam giggled, falling prey to the joy of happy, loving puppies.

"But I like the black one." Mae had a black puppy in her lap.

Izzy stood on the other side of the puppy enclosure, hands shoved in the pockets of her gray Clementine Feed hoodie. "I like the black one, bug."

The black puppy was a male, and the male puppies were several hundred dollars less than the females. The kids and Chandler had chosen the Labradoodles from Earl's puppy board. The most expensive puppies, it seemed. They were practically the price of that princess bed Izzy had her eye on.

So much for dreams...

Chandler pointed toward the yellow Labradoodle. "But I think that one is—"

"Not going home with us," Izzy cut him off. The yellow ones were all females.

"Don't get mad at me," Chandler whispered. "This was your notion."

"I'm having second thoughts." There'd be vet bills. Dog food bills. Potty training. Leash training. The things destroyed that would need replacing. "It's all a bit overwhelming."

"More overwhelming than you and me?" Chandler laid his hand over the small of her back.

Izzy wanted to snuggle closer and let him settle her nerves with a touch, a kiss. But that would defeat the purpose of this puppy business. "Right now, you and the puppy are tied."

The kids laughed as a brown puppy lost his balance trying to wrestle a stuffed rabbit to the ground.

Chandler inched closer. "I was wondering if you could pencil me into your busy schedule this week."

Izzy stared at him incredulously. "Are you asking me out on a date? We're here to get puppies. And tomorrow I'll put letters in the mail from Santa, just as we discussed." Explaining to the kids how Santa couldn't deliver something like love.

But boy, Izzy did like the way Chandler smiled at her. Not to mention the warmth of his hand on her back. But she had to think of Mae. What if Chandler wasn't permanent? Mae's heart would be broken a second time.

"We'll need to make puppy playdates," Chandler said with a hint of that wicked smile. "The pups are siblings, after all. Wouldn't want to keep siblings apart."

"Or best friends," Izzy muttered, shaking her head. "Have you always been this incorrigible and I just didn't notice?"

"I think you bring it out in me."

And despite herself, or maybe because of it, Izzy laughed.

"GRANDMA MARY! Grandma Mary!" Sam ran ahead of Chandler through the main ranch house, carrying a brown puppy in his arms without the leash they'd entered with. "Come see our new dog!"

"Sam! Come back here." Chandler finished removing his boots and grabbed the discarded leash.

"This is unexpected." Dad turned from the stove where he was taking out two trays of lasagna. There was hardly any room to cook given the plethora of holiday decorations on the kitchen counter. "I thought you weren't getting a dog."

"Me, too." Chandler continued through the kitchen. "Izzy and I are going with the flow." Not exactly the flow he wanted but there was hope for that. He saw it in Izzy's eyes.

The living room was also crammed with decorations, making it seem small, even if it was empty of people.

"Isn't he adorable?" Mom said from down the hall. "Who is this?"

"This is Rusty." Sam gushed. "He likes chewing on my jacket sleeve."

"Hand over that little squiggle worm." Mom sounded happy. "Oh... Puppies like to chew on everything, don't they?"

"Even Grandma's pillows."

Chandler hurried into his parents' bedroom, not wanting little puppy teeth to sink into Mom.

"That's right, Sam." Mom had one hand on the football-sized brown puppy and the other on a small decorative pillow, which Rusty was gnawing on. "We'll have to make sure there aren't any Christmas decorations down low that Rusty can chew on."

"Sam, we agreed that Rusty needs to be on a leash," Chandler said gently. "For exactly the reason Grandma Mary mentioned. Don't want him to choke on pillow stuffing or cut his mouth if he takes a bite of a glass Christmas ornament."

"But Rusty doesn't like the leash." Sam climbed up on the bed and scooped the squirming puppy into his arms.

"He'll learn to like it if you give him treats." Mom stroked Rusty's curly fur. "Puppies are a big responsibility, just like babies."

Sam snorted. He hadn't been around any babies. "Rusty is smart. He'll be fine."

"He's still a baby." Chandler moved closer to chuck the puppy beneath its furry little chin, dodging his sharp little teeth. "We have to take care of him the way we do our other livestock. We don't let horses or cattle wander around unsupervised. And you did promise to take good care of him."

Sam gathered the energetic puppy close, giggling when Rusty licked his nose. "I'll be careful."

Chandler clipped the leash on Rusty. "And you'll keep his leash on? Even in the house?"

"Yes, Dad."

Chandler handed Sam a small bag of dog treats they'd purchased at the feed store. "Every time he does what you ask him to, give him a treat."

"Yes, Dad."

Rusty looked around the bed, and then lunged for the pillow once more.

Sam giggled.

"Go run around with him outside," Chandler instructed. "We want to tire him out."

"Okay." Sam slid off the bed and then carefully put Rusty on the floor. "Come on, pup. Come on, boy." He scampered out, followed by his new best friend.

Mom captured Chandler's hand. "What brought this on?"

Chandler explained about the letters Sam and Mae had written to Santa requesting he and Izzy find new spouses for Christmas. And how Izzy felt the puppies would be a suitable distraction because she didn't want to risk Mae getting attached.

"I love that little boy." Mom patted his hand and then leaned back on her pillows. "You could stand to learn something from him."

"Really? Like what?"

"Sam goes through life with such a big heart. He wants everyone to be happy."

"Here we go," Chandler teased. "Did you and Dad write a letter to Santa requesting I find a new wife, too?"

"No." Mom's expression turned serious, although her eyes sparkled with mirth. "But there's still time. Where's Izzy? If Mae got a puppy, I'd expect to see them here, too." She glanced behind him.

"She... She's not coming." Chandler's throat was suddenly thick. "I just don't know..."

"Oh, honey." Mom understood without him having to say more. "Izzy may not be ready to love you today, but that doesn't mean she won't realize she loves you tomorrow."

"Sure."

Mom hugged him, still too thin and fragile feeling. "Well, neither of you wanted a puppy. And look how quickly that turned around."

"BIFF IS THE best dog ever," Mae said to Izzy when she was being tucked in that night.

"He's a keeper," Izzy agreed.

The little black puppy was the runt of the litter and had collapsed from exhaustion before Mae's bath time. They'd put him to bed in Gator's old crate in the kitchen near a heating vent. But Izzy fully expected the pup to wake up later, disoriented and missing his litter mates.

"Now, go to sleep. We have a big day tomorrow. School and work."

"At the ranch?" Mae asked hopefully. "Biff could play with Rusty."

"No. Here in town. I played hooky from Christmas decorating today. Sleep now." Izzy kissed Mae good-night and made sure the small lamp was on by her bed before turning off the overhead light.

But she didn't leave the room, not immediately. She'd spent her savings for that princess bed buying a puppy. And she paused to mourn that fact.

Biff was adorable. Mae and Earl were ecstatic. What did it matter that Mae wouldn't have a dream princess bed?

The puppy whimpered tentatively, its cry carrying down the hall.

Sighing, Izzy hurried to the kitchen. "What's wrong, Biff?" She knelt at the crate, fingers reaching through the frame.

Biff licked her fingers, still whining.

She and the puppy hadn't bonded. Izzy had been too busy making sure Mae knew how to handle Biff safely and gathering all the puppy paraphernalia they needed. And then she'd been preoccupied mourning the loss of her dream.

It had been a frivolous dream. An impractical dream.

But just once, I want to be frivolous and impractical.

Chandler's wicked smile came to mind.

The puppy sat back, whining.

"All right, Biff." Izzy unlatched the kennel, resolved to do baby duty. Feeding, playing, potty, and then back to the crate. "Go easy on me, honey. It's been a while since I've taken care of a baby." Because she fully expected this to be just like nurturing a newborn.

Biff leaped out of the cage and into her lap and, without another sound, closed his eyes, apparently ready to fall back asleep.

And Izzy...

She fell instantly in love.

CHAPTER NINETEEN

"WHAT ARE YOU doing out here?" Chandler asked Mom, surprised to find her in the barn on Tuesday afternoon, standing at her horse's stall while holding Rusty's leash. It was good to see her wearing her usual ranch garb—white blouse, jeans, her cowboy boots and hat.

But Shirley and the surrey were due to arrive any minute. Dad had wanted his gift to be a surprise.

"Am I not allowed outside unsupervised anymore?" Mom stood at Taffy's stall, stroking the palomino's nose while Rusty sat at her feet staring up at the horse warily. "If you must know, I'm checking the property for Christmas decorations. There aren't any around inside here." She gave Chandler a sly look. "You know I always put decorations inside in the barn. You need to call Izzy and get her out here."

"That'll make Sam and Rusty happy." And Chandler.

A grinding sound cut through the air, like a large truck shifting gears. A few of the horses poked their heads over their stall doors.

"How about I walk you back to the house?" Chandler stepped forward. "*Rusty* looks like he could use a nap." He reached for the puppy's leash.

"This pup and I are bonding." Mom's fingers curled tighter around the leash. "I was considering going for a ride," she admitted wistfully. "Talking to my friends at the roundabout every night has reminded me what I'm missing."

"Uh-huh." The engine noise grew louder. "Nobody's ridden Taffy in months, Mom. I should ride her first."

"Kid gloves," Mom murmured, glancing down and catching Rusty's eye. "I'm not as fragile as they all make me."

"You'll be back to full strength soon enough," Chandler promised.

Outside, that loud engine sputtered and backfired. This wasn't going to be the surprise Dad imagined.

"Are we getting a feed delivery?" Mom moved carefully toward the barn door leading to the ranch yard, Rusty scrambling ahead, straining the leash. "I didn't think they delivered on Tuesdays. No matter. Rusty needs to get used to the sound of big rigs."

"Chandler, come quick! They're here!" Dad called from outside, clearly excited.

"What has that man done now?" But Mom chuckled. "Did he buy a new bucking bull?"

"Let's go see." Chandler held Mom's arm as they

walked out of the barn and into the bright winter afternoon sunlight.

A big rig drove toward the roundabout towing an open stock trailer.

"Your father did buy another bucking bull." Mom tipped her hat brim back.

"Nope."

Mom scoffed. "It has to be a bull, Chandler. Nothing else could be that tall."

Chandler picked up the pup while the trailer came closer, letting reality speak for itself.

"What to my wondering eyes should appear..." Mom spoke in a soft voice. "Did your father buy a draft horse for the rodeo clowns?"

"Mary!" Dad appeared, hurrying to her side. "I wanted this to be a surprise."

The big truck pulled slowly into the roundabout, revealing the surrey in the truck bed, yellow wheels and all, and an inquisitive Shirley taking a gander at them all.

Dad thrust out his arms and burst into song.

Chandler supposed it was the tune from *Oklahoma!* Dad had referenced the day they'd made their purchase. It sounded off-key and corny.

But Mom started to cry. Happy tears.

"DAD! DID YOU bring Rusty?" Sam scrambled into Chandler's truck Thursday after school.

The puppy whined from inside the cat carrier Chandler had used to transport him in, scratching at the door.

Putting the truck in Park, Chandler lifted the carrier from the front seat and put it in the back with Sam. "Don't let him out until we get to the feed store." They needed more chew toys and Chandler wanted to check in on Izzy. Were her ribs healing? Were she and Mae faring better at puppy care than he and Sam were?

Yes, he'd gotten to making excuses to see her. Rusty was getting along just fine.

A few minutes later, they pulled up in front of the feed store. There was a brief scramble to get Rusty's leash on and Sam safely to the ground with the pup in his arms. And then Sam made a mad dash inside, shouting, "Della-Mae! Della-Mae!"

Chandler hurried after them.

The two kids found each other behind the sales counter. They were giggling and squealing, ecstatically.

Izzy finished ringing up a sale for Sheriff Underwood. She was decked out to decorate someone's house. Her Christmas sweater was green with a cat batting at a string of lights on a Christmas tree. She wore a plain Santa hat. A tame holiday outfit compared with her previous wardrobe choices.

And darned if just looking at Izzy didn't fill his head with sleigh bells ringing.

Izzy's weary gaze found Chandler's. "How many times did you get up on puppy duty last night?"

"Too many times." Chandler came around the counter to see the kids with their puppies.

"It's worth it to see them with Rusty and Biff, though." She leaned against the counter, the pom of her Santa hat resting on her cheek.

"Ask me on Saturday," Chandler said. "Let's see how much REM sleep I have then."

Earl came from the break room to join them. "Toughen up, you two." He put his hands on his hips and smiled at the kids and puppies. "What a Christmas gift."

"Oh, this ain't our Christmas gift," Sam told him, glancing back at Chandler and Izzy. "We wrote letters to Santa."

Mae nodded, smiling up at Chandler like an angel. "We asked Santa to bring us something special."

"Santa always delivers the goods," Earl said gruffly.

"Oh." Izzy gripped the sales counter.

"Bet you aren't feeling so great about your decision now, are you?" Chandler couldn't resist asking.

"Ha, ha." Izzy sighed.

"Nancy's here for her shift." Earl waved at a teen with black hair who wore all black, even her Clementine Feed sweatshirt. "Kids, I'll treat those pups to a new toy. Why don't you go find one on the shelf."

Excited cheers filled the air. And then the kids ran around the sales counter and into the store, puppies trailing them. Nancy barely avoided being tripped by leashes.

"Let me get a coffee," Nancy told Izzy. "And then I'll be ready for my shift." She disappeared in the back.

Earl gave Chandler a searching look. "Are you helping Izzy decorate today? I heard tell she's running behind."

"Just a day," Izzy hastened to say. "Because of the puppies. I'll catch up on Saturday."

"What if someone cancels?" Earl leaned closer to her to whisper, "You need that money for Mae's Christmas gift."

"I'll be fine." But Izzy blushed.

"What are you working on today?" Chandler gestured toward her cat sweater with its tangle of lights. "Outdoor lights?"

"Yes. And no, I'm not worried about snarling string lights." But she wouldn't look him in the eye.

"Good. We'll tag along. Gotta tire out the puppies." And make sure Izzy took care of her bruised ribs.

Izzy shook her head.

The kids appeared from the pet aisle, each carrying a squeaker toy and chattering nonstop.

"Sam, you want to help Izzy decorate for Christmas?" he asked.

"Yeah, I do." Sam hopped around.

"Yeah, he does," Chandler echoed. "We'll get you back on track, Izzy."

"Chandler and Sam to the rescue!" Mae raised her chew toy in the air. "Yay!"

"Yay," Izzy muttered.

"HERE'S THE PLAN." Izzy began unpacking the tubs that contained Braxton McDavid's holiday lights, moving slowly and breathing shallowly. "Gables and porch, bushes and tree. Braxton said he had an inflatable snowman, but he can't remember where he left it in his garage." And Izzy hadn't been able to find it when she'd rummaged around.

Chandler had set up Braxton's ladder in front of the gables.

The kids and puppies were being watched by her elderly client. Braxton had a screened-in porch in his backyard so the puppies could meander safely.

If only Izzy could find that snowman, things would be great.

If only Chandler wasn't here, looking at her with a smile and making her nervous.

Except he wasn't looking at her now. He climbed the ladder—which was her job—and said, "Feed me the lights."

She glanced up at him. "Shouldn't we check to see if they work first?"

"I already did." He sat on the top of the ladder, staring down at her. "You were in the garage looking for Frosty."

"You're a step ahead of me." She fed him a strand, trying to be careful not to tangle them. "Is this what it's like to work for you?"

"Nope." Chandler made quick work of attaching the strand to the hooks that were already in place. "Mom wants you to come out to the ranch and decorate the inside of the horse barn. Caught her in there the other day."

Izzy nodded. "Your mom called me. She's on the schedule. But I'm—"

"Behind, yeah. I know." Chandler smiled at her. "If you get caught up, are you going to the Buckboard on Saturday night? I didn't get a dance with you the last time we were there."

Instead, he'd gotten a kiss.

Izzy felt her cheeks heat. "Are you asking me on a date?"

"Might be. Are you amenable to one?"

"Might be." The words were out before she thought about them. "You've got this. I'm going to go looking for Frosty again."

"Running away doesn't look good on you," Chandler quipped.

Izzy did it anyway.

She poked around Baxter's garage, lifting boxes of old books, moving an old stroller covered in cobwebs, shifting containers of antifreeze that were in front of a box that held an aboveground pool.

"Found Frosty!" Izzy called, peering over the pool box. "I could use some help dragging it out."

Chandler came to stand next to her. "Thank you for asking for help."

"My ribs appreciate you."

His arm curled around her waist. "I like standing next to you."

Chandler was so honest. He deserved honesty in return.

"I'm sorry I twisted your arm to get a puppy." Izzy turned to face him, except she stared at a shirt button over his heart. "I panicked and boxed you into a corner."

"Rusty is part of the family now." With a tender touch, Chandler lifted her chin until she had to look him in the eye. "With some work, you could be part of the family, too."

"Some work." Izzy chuckled. "Those are practically fighting words."

"No," he murmured.

"No?"

Chandler shook his head, leaning down to whisper in her ear, "When I say *some work*, I mean you and I need to work on that something between us to see what could be."

What could be...

That sounded like a partnership more so than a decision that rested on Izzy. The tension inside her, that knot in her stomach, it eased.

And then Chandler drew back, but only a smidge, because that's all he needed to fit his lips over hers.

The interior garage door opened.

Izzy and Chandler shifted apart.

The puppies tumbled forward, each leading a child holding a leash.

"Look, kids. We found Frosty," Izzy said, although she was staring up at Chandler with what she imagined were stars in her eyes.

They may have found Frosty, but so did the puppies. While they were inflating it, one of the pups chewed a hole in the white plastic, requiring an apology to Braxton and a patch kit.

CHAPTER TWENTY

"I LOVE SHIRLEY."

The large gray horse whinnied at the mention of her name.

Mom stood close to the Percheron with one hand on her headstall. With the other, she reached up and gave Shirley a loving pat on the neck. "But Frank, I'm really more comfortable with riding Taffy than driving a rig."

"What's going on?" Sam came to stand next to Chandler at the arena gate. He had a firm grip on Rusty's leash. "Sit, Rusty. Sit."

The little roly-poly sat, staring at Sam intently.

"Good boy." Sam dug a small dog treat from his blue jeans pocket and fed it to the pup. Rusty gulped it down without chewing. "Is Grandma taking to cart driving?"

"I'm an excellent buggy driver," Mom said from mid-arena, pride in every syllable. "Me and Shirley—"

The gray whinnied.

"—are getting along famously."

"It's me she's not getting along with." Dad moseyed over to where Chandler and Sam were standing. "All I tried to do was spoil her. And what do I get?"

"Nag, nag, nag," Mom answered. "I'm still new to driving a buggy and Christmas is just a few days away. What if I can't control her?"

"Can I try?" Sam asked, handing Dad the leash, and raced over to Mom and the rig. "Let me try, Grandma."

Deprived of his dog treat supplier, Rusty tried to reach Sam, using a racing start to jerk the leash right out of Dad's hand. The rascal charged after Sam, leash dragging behind him.

Shirley startled, tossing her head and sidestepping away from the approaching youngsters as her flight instinct kicked in.

Which would have been fine, if Mom had let go of her leather headstall.

Or if the puppy's trailing leash didn't vaguely resemble a snake, which caused Shirley to rear and those big hooves landed...

Where they shouldn't.

"IS MARY ALL RIGHT? I came as soon as I heard." Izzy burst into the hospital waiting room, spotted Chandler amid all the other cowboys and ran over to him. "Is anyone else hurt? You? Or...or Sam?"

Chandler sat slumped in a chair, knee bouncing, hat brim pulled down low. He looked... He looked the way he had that day in the principal's office. Demoralized, waiting to hear the worst.

Izzy came to a stop in front of him. "Is Sam okay? Are you?"

Chandler didn't look up. Didn't acknowledge Izzy in any way.

"We're fine," Frank said from a chair on the other side of the room. His face was pale and lined with worry. His wide white cowboy hat rested on his knee. "We're all wishing it had been us instead of her."

"What happened?" Izzy sank into the chair next to Chandler, worried for Mary but also worried for him. Something didn't feel right. "All Earl heard was that a horse bolted and knocked Mary down."

"It all happened so fast," Frank said in a faraway voice. "One minute we were teasing each other, the way we do. And the next…"

"Mom's in surgery." Zane was standing rigidly against a wall, as if the structure needed him to stay upright. "Doc said she needs pins to hold the wrist bones together."

"Oh, poor thing. I'm sure she was a trouper." Izzy couldn't imagine anything less from Mary.

Chandler grunted.

Wanting to comfort him, Izzy reached over and rested her hand on Chandler's bouncing knee. "Is there anything I can do?"

"You should go," Chandler said in a low, thick voice. A tone that sounded like…the day he'd first told her their kids should be in separate classrooms. "None of this would have happened if you hadn't started changing things. Dad wouldn't have gotten the idea to buy a horse and buggy. Sam would never have gotten a puppy."

Everyone in the room stilled. All those hurting cowboys. It was as if they all stopped breathing.

And Izzy… Izzy stopped breathing.

"Now, Chandler," Frank began.

"We all know it's the truth." Chandler jolted to his feet, staring down at Izzy with hurt in his eyes. "Izzy came in and changed everything."

"That's not fair," Zane said, bless him.

But Chandler was on a roll. "There's a cause for everything bad that happens. You can trace it back. And in this case, Mom would be fine right now if Izzy hadn't come to the ranch and changed everything."

Izzy's chest hurt. It hurt because her heart was breaking, and she was bent over and that always aggravated her bruised ribs. But the physical pain wasn't near as sharp as the emotional pain. And she knew why. Oh, she knew. And it hurt.

"Chandler, go take a walk." Frank was standing now, too. "Before you say something you'll regret."

"No." Izzy found her footing, coming to stand, finding her voice. "This was what I was afraid of." *I should go. I should go.* But Izzy couldn't seem to move because she felt so…broken. And betrayed. And it was all because of *him.* "I didn't ask to come into your life. I was in a safe space. I could handle what was on my plate. Alone. But then you… You all opened your hearts to me and Mae." Oh, no. Mae. Mae would be crushed. "And I knew deep down... I knew *something* didn't fit right. That you... That I...didn't belong." That those kisses and those feelings weren't to be trusted. "And maybe Chandler's right. Maybe some things shouldn't be changed or moved or tested or examined or..." *Loved.*

And that was it. She'd fallen in love with Chandler and the idea of a big extended family who loved each other through thick and thin. But from the very beginning she'd just been an outsider. Someone who was allowed to visit and experience that special place that was the Done Roamin' Ranch. But she didn't quite fit in, not all the way. She'd been so close to laying her heart at Chandler's feet except she knew. She knew with absolute certainty that this would happen.

She tried to draw a breath, but she'd clamped her lips and was fighting tears and that told everyone in that waiting room that she was going to cry.

"If Rusty isn't going to be a good ranch dog, Mae and I will take him." She sniffed again. A loud, watery sniff that had her stiffening. "But you better be quick about it so that you won't break his heart like..."

You broke mine.

THE HOSPITAL WAITING room was quiet after Izzy left.

The only sound Chandler heard was the echo of his harsh words in his head. The words fueled by fear because the foundation of the family he'd found in Clementine had been threatened.

You came in and changed everything.

There's a cause for everything bad that happens.

And when those words receded, Izzy's words took their place. Her frail, soft words that were like arrows shot through his heart.

This is what I was afraid of.

I didn't ask to come into your life.

Maybe some things shouldn't be changed or moved or tested or examined...

Her words faded away except for that last bit.

Maybe some things shouldn't be changed...

Like me. Like her.

Chandler's body felt heavy. He sank down into the chair Izzy had vacated. He stared at his hands without seeing them.

She'd held him when he'd recounted those days from his childhood.

She'd counseled him when he got defensive about Stephanie taking a new job. She said to listen. She'd said Stephanie was afraid.

He'd laughed when Izzy panicked the other day and practically demanded they get puppies because she... She was afraid, too. Afraid of change and risk and...love.

And today... Today when he'd panicked because seeing Mom go down, seeing that large hoof come down on top of her...

For a moment, Chandler had thought Shirley's hoof had landed on Mom's midsection.

And that fear… That cold, prickly fear had clung to him all the way into town, all during the exam and the wait and the arrival of Izzy.

The woman he'd fallen in love with.

"He looks like he's going to faint."

"Somebody get him some water."

"And a candy bar. I don't think he's eaten anything."

The words of his family surrounded him like a fog.

And Chandler couldn't say anything. Not a word.

Why would he?

He'd already said too much.

CHAPTER TWENTY-ONE

"You should all just go to the Buckboard without me," Izzy told her friends that night, hugging a throw pillow because Mac and Biff were spending the night with Earl. "I'm not good company."

Plus, her girlfriends all looked ready for Saturday night at the local honky-tonk while Izzy still wore her ugly Christmas sweater.

"I'm already making margaritas," Ronnie called from Izzy's kitchen, the proof of which was the mighty roar of Izzy's old blender.

"I brought a whole batch of chocolate chip cookies." Raising her voice to be heard above the blender, Allison opened the canister and set it on Izzy's coffee table. "Baked them today."

"I brought chips and salsa." Bess came out of the kitchen carrying two bowls. "Bought them today."

"And I bought guacamole." Jo appeared from down the hallway. "I hung up the Mrs. Claus dresses in your closet, along with Earl's Santa costume. Ma said to try them on in case she needs to make any adjustments." Ma being Lois, the object of Earl's unrequited love. "She said to tell you that she'll swing by with a wagon to pick you up on Christmas morning. I thought you were getting Mae a princess bed for Christmas."

Izzy explained about the puppy purchase.

"That's a shame." Allison selected a cookie from the tin. "Every girl needs a special place to dream."

The blender quieted.

"The princess bed was more for me than Mae," Izzy admitted. "And Mae already whispers secrets to Biff. He's such a sweet little puppy." Less rambunctious than Rusty, who had just as boisterous a personality as Sam.

Izzy's heart squeezed. It wasn't just Chandler she'd lost today. She'd grown fond of Sam, too.

"You need a place to dream, Izzy," Ronnie called from the kitchen.

"Oh... I'm past the dreaming stage," Izzy was quick to point out.

"You're never past the dreaming stage," Bess said.

"Agreed," Jo said.

Izzy felt all eyes upon her. Waiting for her to say something, no doubt. Izzy squeezed the throw pillow tighter to her chest. "If you all leave now, you'll still be there in time to line dance."

"If we leave now," Ronnie called from the kitchen, "we'll only sit in our booth and worry about you all night."

Sit in our booth.

"By Sunday church, the whole town will want to know why we aren't there tonight." A familiar wave of embarrassment washed over Izzy with a chill that quickly morphed into a hot, prickly skin tingle. She'd experienced the same feeling before— when Mom was sick, when Dad left, when Mike told her he wanted a divorce. "Isn't it funny how you think you're just you? And then you realize that you're interwoven into other lives."

"Our friendship circle." Allison nodded, taking a bite of chocolate chip cookie.

"The high school rodeo team." Bess nodded, scooping salsa with a chip.

"The roping circuit." Jo called from the kitchen, where presumably she was giving the guacamole a stir.

"The Done Roamin' Ranch." Ronnie nodded, setting a tray of margaritas in plastic glasses on the coffee table. "We're all tied to the Done Roamin' Ranch since that's where the men we love were raised."

"God bless those Harrisons." Jo returned from the kitchen with the bowl of guacamole. "And our fellas, the ones Frank and Mary raised right."

Izzy felt all eyes on her because this was a test, of sorts. If Izzy bad-mouthed Chandler, the others would support her, at least as far as admitting that Chandler had done Izzy wrong. But she didn't want to cause a rift.

"I'm not going to lie and tell you that Chandler's words didn't hurt." Izzy released the pillow, setting it in her lap and smoothing out the creases. In time, that's what she'd do with her emotions, too. Smooth over the scars Chandler had given her. "But everybody copes differently. And he... There was truth to what he said."

Ronnie scoffed, passing out drinks. "Didn't mean he had to say it."

"You'd rather he lie?" Izzy sipped her icy drink. "You'd rather he held it inside?"

"Are we making excuses for him now?" Allison demanded. "I came over here expecting to spend at least an hour bad-mouthing Chandler."

"But this is Izzy." Bess gave Izzy a sad smile. "Unlike me, she doesn't bear grudges against anybody."

"No." Jo raised her glass as if in toast. "Izzy is great at turning the other cheek."

"That bodes well for Chandler, I suppose," Ronnie said.

Izzy shook her head. "I close the door. I turn the page. I move on. But I don't think I ever completely get over it. I haven't tried to forge a relationship with my dad. Or with Mike. Evie Grace came in last week and I wasn't exactly charitable to her, Allison."

Allison chuckled. "Even I've given her a pass for cornering the market on peaches to try and sabotage my county fair baking."

"I hear what Izzy's saying." Ronnie set down her margarita glass. "This doesn't bode well for Chandler, does it?"

Izzy shrugged, dying a little inside. "His words showed me what's important to him, and that's not me."

"Idiot."

"Jerk."

"Fool."

"Troll."

Izzy stared at her drink. "He's scared. Scared of a future he can't predict. He's scared of losing Mary and the family dynamic that saved him. You can't fault someone for being scared. We've all got our fears and they all shape who we are. And Chandler's fear… That's probably part of what drew me to him. He's had family fold beneath him. And that's where we're the same. But he never learned to face his fears and make his way on his own."

"Like you did." Ronnie took hold of Izzy's hand. "Over and over. Our dear, sweet Izzy has picked herself up and moved on every time someone's broken her heart."

"Correction. I closed the door, *then* picked myself up and moved on." It was just that Izzy wasn't ready to close the door on those newly discovered feelings with Chandler.

But she had to. For Mae's sake, if not her own.

"CHANDLER… IS THAT YOU?"

Chandler jerked awake, nearly tipping the too-small hospital chair over in his haste to sit up. "Mom?" He blinked blurry eyes. "I'm here. What do you need?"

The hospital room came into focus. Beige walls. White bedsheets. Pale blue blanket.

And Mom. Tubes and wires every which way. Her injured left wrist bandaged and propped up on pillows. Metal screws rising up from the gauze, a reminder of how fragile she was becoming.

"You should go home," Mom said weakly. "I'll be fine here."

Chandler refused. He stood and came around the bed to hold her right hand. It was thin and cold. He gently cradled it between his larger ones, trying to transfer some warmth. "I'm the oldest. I took the night shift."

"Stubborn." Mom closed her eyes but not to sleep. "The oldest are always the most stubborn. And the most likely to take the blame when someone else gets hurt on their watch."

"True. But it was my fault. I should have held Rusty's leash instead of Dad." The little pup had an unexpected strength. "And I should have told Dad not to buy Shirley and the buggy. Makes no financial sense."

"Ah. You're in charge of the finances now, too." Mom's eyes were still closed. "And Izzy? I heard you blamed her for what happened to me."

"I'm not proud of that," Chandler said gruffly.

"You've always been too much in your head. Overthinking." Mom heaved a sigh. "Do you remember the early days? You were our only child for a few months. And then in came another. And another. And another, until we had a full house."

"Those were the days, weren't they?" Chandler could remember each new face. The guardedness that eventually gave way to careful smiles that eventually gave way to carefree laughter.

"You asked me how you could help." Mom squeezed his hand. "You watched over them. You noticed what upset them and you tried to put bumpers around them so that they'd never get upset again."

"Cause and effect." Chandler nodded.

"You were like a detective back then. Told all the boys they had to be honest and confess their transgressions. But you've forgotten one thing. I forgive everybody because nobody is perfect."

Chandler froze.

"I don't want you to take this wrong, honey. But just because someone is part of the chain of events that led up to an accident doesn't mean they're to blame. I don't blame you. Or Sam or Rusty or Shirley or your dad. And I certainly don't blame Izzy."

"I know. I let my emotions get the best of me because I thought..."

"I know. I heard you tell your father you thought Shirley had stomped on something vital." She smiled. "I'm getting older. And yes, at some point, I'm gonna take my last horseback ride. But I'm a gal who has to live her life on her own terms. I may get knocked down or set back, but deep down inside where it matters, I'm like all my boys. I get back up and keep moving forward."

"That's good to hear."

"Is it? Because it pertains to you. You made a mistake when you let your temper get the best of you. Whatever happens or doesn't happen with you and Izzy will be decided in the next few hours. The next few days."

"Oh, good. You're awake." A nurse wheeled in a cart with a computer on top. "Time to take your vitals."

"You think about what I said, Chandler."

"I will." But after the things he'd said to Izzy, he wouldn't blame her if she never forgave him.

"THERE YOU ARE." Ronnie panted, sounding like she'd been running. "Found him, Ginny."

Chandler was drinking coffee in the kitchen of the main ranch house on Sunday morning, testing and discarding different apologies for Izzy. Rusty slept in his lap. "You were looking for me?"

"Yes. Ginny has something to say to you."

There were sounds of boots and jackets being removed.

Finally, Ronnie propelled Ginny into the kitchen with her hands on the girl's shoulders. "We're here to make an apology."

"Sorry, Uncle Chandler," Ginny recited woodenly.

"Sorry for what?" Rusty stirred. Chandler rubbed the brown pup behind his ears.

Ginny bit her bottom lip and glanced over her shoulder at Ronnie.

With a put-upon sigh, Ronnie took a seat across from Chandler. "Ginny asked me to take her Christmas shopping after church. She wants to buy Wade something special for Christmas—a pair of new boots he's been wanting."

"The limited-edition ones?" Chandler whistled, which startled Rusty out of his doze. The pup sat up, blinking blue eyes over the edge of the table at Ronnie. "But those cost close to five hundred dollars."

"That's what I said." Ronnie clasped her hands on the table and glanced up at Ginny. "And then I asked her who she thought was going to pay for those boots."

"And she said…" Chandler prompted, studying Ginny's guilt-ridden face.

"I have money." Ginny's gaze dropped down to her toes. "I didn't realize I didn't have enough, though."

"Have you been saving?" Chandler asked, setting a squirming Rusty on the kitchen floor.

"Her allowance?" Ronnie gave a wry laugh. "No."

Again, Ginny looked tortured. "I started a home business. Like Mama Ronnie."

Ronnie's head bobbed. "Just like Mama Ronnie. She's been giving out relationship advice to kids at school. *For their single parents*, including Sam and Mae."

Chandler wasn't surprised, still… "That explains a lot."

"I don't think you understand, Chandler. Ginny told Sam and Mae to get into trouble to try and bring you two together. She's been recruiting underage clients ever since. She's been taking their allowance and lunch money."

"Not to mention she swiped a bunch of your buy one/get one free coffee, or in our case, hot chocolate coupons," Chandler teased. "Essentially, she's performing matchmaking without a license, stealing your clientele and your promotional items. Do I have that right?"

Ronnie made a growling noise.

"I'm sorry. Okay." Ginny sounded like she was sorry she'd been caught. In fact, she crossed her arms over her chest. "But I'm good at this. Look at Chandler and Miss Izzy. Look at Merick and Miss Dora. And I have tons of other works in progress."

"I thought you wanted to be a lawyer." Chandler reached down and pulled Rusty away from his sock before his sharp little teeth ripped a hole in it or sunk into his skin.

"Yes. A lawyer and a rodeo queen. But also an entrepreneur, like Mama Ronnie, Miss Jo and Miss Allison." Ginny folded her legs and sat down on the floor, reaching for Rusty. "I'm showing initiative. I'm pursuing my dreams. Isn't that what you and Dad always tell me I should do?"

Ronnie's head came down to rest on her hands. "I've created a monster."

"I don't think love is as easy as you're making it out to be, Ginny," Chandler said slowly. "Izzy and I smashed into the guardrails. And I don't think she'll listen to anything I say or do to try and win her back."

Ronnie raised her head. "Do you want to win her back? Do you deserve to? You accused her of being the cause of Mary's accident."

"I was wrong. And I've been sitting here this morning trying to come up with the words to make things right." He peered at Ronnie. "Unless you think I've ruined everything."

"Your window of opportunity is very small," Ronnie said cryptically. "Or should I say your door of opportunity is closing?" She shook her head. "Never mind. I have an idea but we have to act fast."

CHAPTER TWENTY-TWO

"MERRY CHRISTMAS!" Izzy bid the last feed store customer farewell and locked the door behind them.

It was Christmas Eve. She hadn't seen Chandler in two days. Not since he broke her heart.

Every time she heard the door open, Izzy glanced up with eager anticipation, only to chastise herself for hoping. Whatever she and Chandler had together was done and dusted.

"Earl, are you ready to close up?" Izzy had a turkey breast cooking in a slow cooker back home. It was a tradition that she and Mae hosted Earl for the holiday.

"Can't wait for our supper." He came out of the break room catching sight of Mae and Biff playing with a squeaker toy on the floor, who'd taken a cancellation of evening plans with her father well. "Best hurry, Mae." He grabbed hold of a small, flat box beneath the counter. "Or I'll get the biggest slice of pumpkin pie."

"We have to eat turkey and vegetables first." Mae stood, gripping both the dog toy and the leash tightly. Since she'd heard about Mary's mishap, she'd always taken a strong hold on Biff's leash. "Mama, are you sure we can't invite Chandler and Sam over for dinner?"

"I'm sure, bug." Izzy slipped on her coat and then helped Mae with hers.

"But Biff misses Rusty."

"I'm still sure, bug." Chandler was done with them. Izzy filled her lungs with air and her mind with the will to move on. "Earl, what have you got there?"

"Turkey platter. Destiny Rogers returned it today. Said it was too small for her bird but I thought it'd be just right for that turkey breast you always make."

"What a nice gift." Izzy herded her little family toward the door.

They are enough.

She didn't quite believe it. So, while they walked home with Earl and Mae chattering, Izzy kept telling herself reasons why she was fine.

My heart can't be broken. I didn't really fall in love with Chandler because I never told him those three words.

The nights aren't so bad. I've got the entire bed to myself.

Mae and I will retain control of the TV remote.

If Mae gets married someday, I'll walk her down the aisle.

"And tomorrow after *the real Santa* comes," Mae was telling Earl, "we'll dress up like Mrs. Claus and be part of the Santapalooza parade."

"I'll dress up as *Mr.* Claus," Earl clarified.

"Hey. What's that on our door?" Mae ran ahead, crossing the lawn just as the outdoor lights came on. The sudden flash spooked Biff, making him leap into the air, but he recovered, racing Mae to the front porch. "It's a letter, Mama."

Someone had stuck an envelope between the front door and the doorjamb.

"Looks like a Christmas card." Earl took it from Mae. "More square than rectangular. And it's thick." He passed it to Izzy.

Her name was written on the front in neat, block letters. Izzy handed Earl her keys, heart pounding. Was this from Chandler? She followed Earl and Mae into the house, which was filled with the smells of Christmas—turkey and pine. They all set their cowboy hats and jackets on a hook behind the door.

Mae unclipped Biff's leash before plopping on the floor and pulling off her pink cowboy boots.

"Who's it from? Not *him*, I hope." Earl took up residence in a chair before removing his boots.

"I haven't opened it yet." Izzy padded over to the couch in her stocking feet.

"It's from him. I can tell from the way you're staring at it." Earl wiggled his toes and leaned back in the chair. "Throw it in the trash. That's what I say."

"Without reading it?" Was it an apology? A request to try again?

"Open it, Mama." Mae came over to stand between Izzy's knees. "Read it to me."

"Just the good parts," Izzy hedged, hoping there would be good parts.

She tore open the envelope and withdrew the card inside.

"Puppies!" Mae leaned closer for a better look at the front.

There were indeed puppies on the front of the card. Their cute little faces poked out of a doghouse that had been decorated with lights and ornaments for Christmas. And the words above the visual read...

"I know I'm in the doghouse this Christmas..." Izzy opened the card. *"But I wanted to wish you all the best this holiday season."*

"That's it?" Earl scoffed, clasping his hands over his chest. "Wake me when the turkey's ready."

"There's more." Izzy read it silently first. "It says, *'I was wrong. Please forgive me. You've been making everyone else's dreams come true. I hope you don't mind that I tried to make yours a reality.'* It's from Chandler."

"What does that mean?" Mae's shoulders fell. She headed down the hall, calling for Biff to follow her. "I don't know what it means, do you, Biffy?"

"I don't know what it means, either," Izzy murmured, setting the card on the coffee table.

"Mama! Mama, come quick!"

At her daughter's shriek, Izzy came running.

"Look." Mae stood in the hallway, pointing inside her open bedroom door.

"What is it? A critter? Did something fall?" Izzy

swung into the doorway and came to a dead stop. "Oh."

There were Christmas lights hanging from the ceiling above Mae's bed, strung from the overhead light to her plain wooden headboard. Almost like half of a canopy bed. And Mae's bed… A pink unicorn bedspread replaced the sunflower quilt Izzy's grandmother had made. The pillows also had unicorns appliquéd on them.

"Mama, my room is so pretty." Mae walked slowly inside, looking around. "I have my Christmas tree and now a unicorn bed."

"What's all the ruckus?" Earl joined them. "Why, this is as pretty as a daydream, Mae."

"And it's mine." Mae flopped on the bed on her stomach, only to slide to the floor since the material was slippery. "Is it from Santa?"

"No, bug. It's from Chandler."

"And Sam," Mae said with certainty.

"Most likely." Izzy nodded, smelling turkey and thinking that she needed to get the rest of their meal started. But first, she wanted her slippers. Izzy opened her bedroom door and turned on the light. "What the heck?"

Mae ran past her. "He did it for your room, too, Mama."

Izzy's bedroom had a new pink and fuzzy bedspread emblazoned with the word *Dream* appliquéd in the middle in large letters. Lights outlined her bedroom windows. Lights ran along the top of the walls. And just like in Mae's room, lights streamed from the ceiling light in swooping lines that ended at her headboard.

Oh, Chandler.

He knew her so well. She had to forgive him.

"You should change the locks on your doors." And with that, Earl stomped back to the living room.

But Izzy and Mae?

Izzy imagined they had dreamy looks in their eyes the rest of the night.

CHRISTMAS MORNING DAWNED clear and bright with nary a blast of wind or frost on the ground.

Izzy and Mae wore long johns beneath their Mrs. Claus red dresses. They'd been given a pair of clear glass spectacles and a Santa hat to complete their wardrobe. They both wore cowboy boots and big grins, standing at the front window waiting for Earl to arrive.

Poor Biff was whining in his crate in the kitchen. He wasn't coming with them.

"There he is!" Mae jumped up and down in a circle very much the way Sam would have had he been here. "There's Santa Earl!" She ran to the front door, flung it open and began to sing "Here Comes Santa Claus."

"Ho-ho-ho. Merry Christmas, Mae!" Earl's suit had no padding. But he had a lovely white beard that hid his mouth and nose. "Merry Christmas, Izzy!"

They spent a few moments admiring each other's costumes.

The clip-clop of a horse had them turning to look down the street.

"There's another Mrs. Claus!" Mae hopped up and down again.

Sure enough, Mrs. Claus—or in this case, Lois Pierce—drove a horse and wooden wagon down their street. Next to her sat a Santa Claus, most likely her beau, Chet. His face was hidden behind a full white beard. The wagon had been outfitted with colorful Christmas lights, a small Christmas tree and red cushions for folks to sit on. Several Santas and Mrs. Clauses were in the passenger area, many with colorful Christmas blankets on their laps.

"That's Destiny Rogers sitting in there. And she's waving at me." Earl perked up. "Come along, Mae. If we're real nice to Destiny, she might invite us over for Christmas dinner."

"Hey," Izzy protested. "You always come to our house for Christmas dinner after the parade." Izzy had left a ham warming in the oven.

"Izzy, don't ruin this for me." Earl lowered his voice. "Look at the way Destiny is waving at me. That's a finger waggle. And finger waggles are a flirting tactic."

"I've never heard of finger waggles." Izzy followed Earl to the end of the wagon.

"You've never lived until someone finger waggles at you," Earl whispered, giving Destiny a jolly finger waggle in return. "Makes your heart flutter."

The sound of jingling bells at the end of the block had everyone turning.

A huge gray horse pranced toward them while pulling a fancy cart. There were bells on the horse's harness and a wreath around its neck.

"That's Sam," Mae cried. "That's Sam and… *Chandler Claus*." Mae grabbed Izzy's hand and tugged her away from the waiting wagon.

"I'm getting in this wagon." Earl ascended the small ladder in the back. "You girls should get in here, too."

"Gotta get moving," Lois added from the front.

Chandler pulled up to the curb behind the wagon. And then he…he…

Izzy couldn't believe it.

Chandler waggled his fingers at them. "Ho-ho-ho! Merry Christmas!"

Oh, my. Earl was right. Being on the receiving end of a finger waggle sent flutters through Izzy's chest.

Chandler was dressed in a Santa costume from head to toe, as was Sam, who had his hands beneath his chin and Santa beard and was waving the white fluffy whiskers like a flag. Frank and Mary made a perfect Mr. and Mrs. Claus on the bench behind him. Mary's arm was in a sling held close to her chest.

The big gray impatiently pawed the sidewalk

with a gigantic hoof, sending the harness bells tinkling.

"We're here to pick up a pair of Mrs. Santas," Chandler continued, warm brown eyes focused on Izzy.

"Come on, Mama." Mae tugged Izzy, trying to draw her closer to Chandler and Sam.

"Don't fall for it, Izzy," Earl called from the wagon. "Destiny says the retirement center has plenty of turkey and has invited us over to her place for Christmas dinner."

Chandler handed Sam the reins and leaped to the sidewalk.

Oh, my. That caused Izzy's heart to flutter, as well.

"Santa Chandler." Mae tugged his red pants leg. "Do you know what my Christmas wish was?"

"Yes, I do," Chandler said in a deep booming voice, turning his gaze to Mae. "You wanted your mama to find someone to love."

Mae nodded solemnly. "Someone good. Someone kind."

"Someone like my dad!" Sam yelled, eliciting chuckles from the elderly Clauses in both wagon and cart.

"Someone who wouldn't make her quiet and sad," Mae went on. "Someone to tell her she's pretty and smart and the best mama ever." And then she sniffed as if she was going to cry. "But that man wasn't under our Christmas tree this morning."

Chandler nodded, gaze turning back to Izzy. "That's because I was afraid, Mae."

Mae gasped. "You're too big to be afraid."

"Nope." Chandler reached for Izzy's hand. "Nobody is too big to be afraid. But I'm too big to let those fears put words in my mouth anymore. It took hurting you to make me see." His voice lowered, gentled. "I was wrong, Izzy. I said things I didn't mean. I'm sorry I hurt you. Sorry that I panicked."

"I panic, too, sometimes," Izzy admitted softly, having already forgiven him upon discovering his gift of dreams in her bedroom.

"But I learned something important that day, Izzy." He moved closer, taking her other hand in his. "I learned that I can't go back to living in a box. The world isn't a box. It rotates and changes and expands and contracts. The world... My world... It's wherever you are. I love you, Izzy."

Izzy's heart had lodged in her throat. Everyone heard those words. There were gasps and a smattering of applause from those in the wagon.

"He waggled at her, you know," Earl said knowingly.

Izzy smiled. "I love you, too, Chandler..." There was supposed to be a *but* in there. She'd closed the door on her feelings for him, after all.

"Can you find it in your heart to forgive me?" Chandler pressed a kiss on her forehead. "I was callous and a fool. And I promise to make every day we're together a joyous one."

"No one can promise that." But oh, how glad she was that Chandler wanted to try.

The big gray pawed the road once more, filling the street with the ripple of bells.

"Behave, Shirley," Chandler said.

The gray whinnied, making most of the folks around them laugh.

"I love you, Izzy," Chandler said again, loud and clear enough for everyone to hear. "And I'm just as bad of a negotiator as my father because I'm telling you that I have marriage in mind when I think of you. Marriage, love and a lifetime of happiness. With you. Only you."

"We're getting married?" Mae squealed, whirling to face Sam. "We're getting married!"

"Hurry up and kiss her, then," Lois called back to them. "I've got other pickups." She whistled and the wagon with Earl in it moved slowly forward.

"What do you say?" Chandler had his arms around Izzy now. "Are you up for a lifetime of family and dreams coming true?"

"I am." Izzy grabbed hold of his white faux fur trim. "But first, Lois is right. We've got to seal this deal and to do that—"

He kissed her.

EPILOGUE

"WE'RE JUST WAITING on Izzy," Ronnie told Chandler, smiling from behind the school office counter on Valentine's Day. "Have a seat."

"Got it." Chandler sat in the same seat he'd occupied in the office the day Reindeer Izzy had trotted into his life. And just like that fateful day, his knee bounced nervously. "Are you going to tell me what they've done this time?"

"And steal Principal Crowder's thunder?" Ronnie tsked. "Nope."

Chandler couldn't imagine why Sam and Mae had misbehaved. They'd been such angels since Christmas break.

Izzy blew in with the same intensity she'd blown into Chandler's life. She wore blue jeans and a Clementine Feed T-shirt beneath her red jacket. Her silver-blond hair brushed her shoulders. "I came as soon as I could. Ronnie, you said not to worry. No blood, right?"

"The kids are sitting in the library room. No blood," Ronnie assured them.

Principal Crowder opened his office door and gestured for Izzy and Chandler to come inside.

Chandler took a seat. Before he even settled back in the stiff chair, his knee was bobbing.

While the principal reviewed a sheet of paper, Izzy took a significant glance at Chandler's bouncing knee and then said softly, *"I love you."*

She laid her hand on his knee, her pretty engagement ring sparkling on her finger. Once they'd moved past the fears about change and the permanence of love, he'd proposed. That had been on New Year's Day. And she'd said yes. They'd rushed to commit but they weren't rushing to the altar. They'd agreed that too much change wouldn't be good for the kids. Stephanie had left town, taking that job in Texas. And Mike was almost completely out of the picture.

"I suppose you're wondering why I called you in today." Principal Crowder didn't sound happy as he returned the paper to the file.

"I was hoping you needed volunteers for something." Izzy chuckled. "Or perhaps the support of the Done Roamin' Ranch and Clementine Feed for the spring carnival?"

"We ran out of pizza today at lunchtime," the principal said instead of reassuring them.

"Mae loves pizza day," Izzy murmured.

"Sam, too." Chandler nodded, covering Izzy's hand with his own.

Principal Crowder frowned. "They loved pizza day so much that they staged a protest in the cafeteria when we ran out."

COWBOY SANTA

"They're seven," Izzy reminded him. "It can't have been much of a protest."

"Oh." Chandler thought of Ginny's side hustle, a business she was supposed to have closed down.

Izzy and the principal turned to Chandler for answers. Both saying, *"Oh?"*

"It's nothing. I just remembered something I forgot to do at the ranch."

"Your children are very impressionable," the principal said coolly. "As I understand it, the protest was a coordinated effort between Sam and Della-Mae." The principal rested his folded hands on the desk. "The cafeteria monitors didn't know what hit them, and only managed to reclaim control by promising everyone chocolate milk. Your children have been waiting for you in the library."

Chandler cleared his throat. "We're sorry. It won't happen again." He got to his feet and led Izzy out the door.

"I don't think the principal was finished," Izzy said from behind him.

"What else could he say that we haven't heard already?" Months ago. "Home lectures and reading messages sent on the online messaging system."

"We haven't managed to figure out the online messaging system," Izzy teased. "He might have recommended our children should be in separate classrooms?"

"Mrs. Stodimeyer didn't want them separated," Chandler reminded her. "And neither do we."

At the library door, he turned and drew Izzy close. "I don't like the principal's office."

Her arms wound around his neck. "Then, let's make sure we don't get called there again."

Chandler kissed Izzy. And in that kiss, he found the equilibrium and humor he needed to face their hooligans.

They entered the library. Chandler breathed in the smell of books.

Sam and Mae sat at a table in a corner, books open in front of them. They both looked very small.

"Hey, kids," Chandler said.

The librarian shushed him.

"Hey, kids," Izzy whispered, sliding into a child-sized seat across from Mae. She leaned forward, still whispering, "Would Santa approve of a pizza protest?"

Chandler stood behind her. "I wouldn't."

That earned him another dark look from the librarian.

"Mama," Mae whispered. "We've been talking in school about Cupid."

"And love," Sam added, also in a whisper.

"We're in love," Chandler reassured them in his outdoor voice.

The librarian shushed him again.

"You hurt the lunch ladies' feelings with that protest," Izzy whispered gently.

"We're sorry," they chorused back.

The librarian rolled her eyes and moved to another section of the library.

"Explain to me what Cupid has to do with pizza," Chandler said as softly as he could.

"Pizza? Pizza had nothing to do with Cupid," Sam said, as if this was common knowledge.

Chandler was speechless.

"Cupid is a baby, Mama," Mae whispered urgently, leaning forward as if this was an important concept that was hard to grasp.

Chandler's head hurt. He rubbed his temple.

"A baby, Mama," Mae whispered. "And that's what we want."

"A baby...ducky?" Izzy guessed, glancing up at Chandler with mischief in her blue eyes.

"A baby brother," Sam said at the same time that Mae said, "A baby sister."

The kids stared at each other. And then grinned and chorused, *"Twins!"*

The librarian shushed them from the other side of a bookrack.

And Chandler... He couldn't help himself. He laughed. He laughed so hard and so long that tears spilled over his cheeks. And those tears...

They had Izzy, Sam and Mae fawning all over him to make sure he was all right.

"I'm fine," he managed to say when his tears had dried, and he'd caught his breath. "I'm just surprised."

"Surprised?" Izzy shepherded them out of the library, waving apologetically at the librarian. "That our kids would make a ruckus at school instead of asking us if we planned on having more kids?"

"No. Not that." Chandler got on his knees and gathered Sam and Mae into his arms. And then he stared up at Izzy until she relented and crouched down to be included in a family hug. "I've been trying to start this conversation for weeks and every time I do, you change the subject, Izzy."

"That's not true." Izzy scoffed without looking him in the eye.

But the kids nodded. Smart ones, those two.

"We need to do a better job at communicating," Chandler told the kids. "There will be no more visits to the principal's office. And no more dodging important questions."

"Like when can I get a horse," Sam said.

"And me a kitten," Mae said.

"And me a baby," Chandler added.

A tear tracked down Izzy's cheek. "I changed the subject because... I thought you wanted to talk about *not* having any more kids."

Two wide-eyed young gazes swiveled around to focus on Chandler.

"See?" Chandler kept his calm. "This is what I'm saying. We need to talk freely about what we want in this family."

"Babies," the two kids chorused again.

"And a horse," Sam added.

"A kitten," Mae whispered.

"We need to talk about whatever is on our minds. That includes you." Chandler kissed Izzy's forehead. "And you two..." He kissed Sam's and

Mae's foreheads. "And most importantly what we need to talk about now is—"

"Babies!" they all chorused together, including Izzy.

Someone behind Chandler cleared their throat.

He turned. And stumbled to his feet. "Hey, sorry, Principal Crowder. We were just adjourning our family meeting. You won't have any more trouble from us. Will he, kids?"

"Oh, no," the kids agreed with faux innocence, standing.

Izzy chuckled and rose, too. "They're good kids, Principal Crowder, but the truth is we can't guarantee they'll always be angels. That's the way life is. That's the way love is and I love Mae and Sam, but there's no telling what they'll do from one day to the next."

Three months ago, the truth and unpredictability of that statement would have made Chandler nervous. Not now.

"There's no predicting what they'll do in the next hour." Chandler drew his family close. "And amen to that."

* * * * *

For more romances in
The Cowboy Academy miniseries from author
Melinda Curtis and Harlequin Heartwarming,
visit www.Harlequin.com today!